To Have and to Hold

To Have and to Hold

THREE AUTUMN LOVE STORIES

BETSY ST. AMANT,
KATIE GANSHERT,
BECKY WADE

ZONDERVAN

To Have and to Hold

This title is also available as a Zondervan e-book.
Visit www.zondervan.com.

Requests for information should be addressed to:
Zondervan, *Grand Rapids, Michigan 49546*

Library of Congress Cataloging-in-Publication
ISBN: 978-0-310-39593-5
Data is available upon request.

Interior design: James Phinney

Printed in the United States of America

16 17 18 19 20 21 22 / RRD / 20 19 18 17 16 15 14 13 12 11 10 9 8 7 6 5 4 3 2 1

Contents

Love Takes the Cake

BETSY ST. AMANT

To Jason and Tara Hardin—for living out a real life example of love. I love your story and your hearts!

It is a truth universally acknowledged that a woman in possession of pastries is in need of a hungry man.

He was back.

The bell on the door to The Dough Knot chimed a heads-up as the tall, semidark, and handsome not-quite stranger strolled inside, head down as he typed on his phone.

Charlotte Cantrell tried to disregard the flutter of butterflies in her stomach, but it was rather like ignoring a herd of stampeding elephants. You didn't linger in denial—you just got out of the way.

But Charlotte had nowhere to go.

Behind the display case full of pumpkin cheesecake muffins, orange-coated petit fours, and cinnamon pecan cookies, she pretended to clean the already spotless counter and tried to look nonchalant. Like it was every day a drop-dead gorgeous man with amazing hazel eyes walked into her bakery and placed an order.

It wasn't *every* day—it was actually only every Tuesday at 5:40. She could set her watch by him.

Charlotte automatically reached to box his standard to-go order—two of her delicious, secret-ingredient giant snickerdoodles—and hesitated. Would it be good customer service to let him know she remembered his order, or would it just come across as desperate?

She might be a single mom, but she certainly wasn't desperate.

She waited, taking the opportunity to study him while he was occupied with his phone. The sweep of dark hair over his forehead. The perfect cut of his button-down shirt.

Mr. Right, who came every Tuesday, without fail.

And bought cookies for another woman.

He looked up then, caught her in her hesitation, and offered a sheepish grin that made him all the more charming. "Sorry." He held up his phone. "I had to answer that. My friend's on his way to meet me here."

"It's no problem." She forced herself to act nonchalant. Or tried, anyway. Attractive, polite, *and* apologetic for something as small as texting while walking into a business?

So *that's* where Mr. Darcy went.

It was enough to make Charlotte swoon like one of Jane Austen's heroines, but then there'd be no one to work the register, and Ms. Mystery-Right wouldn't get her weekly treat. Besides, swooning had only left her with a broken heart in the past, and she had no desire to repeat history.

Mr. Almost-Right caught her gaze then and smiled broader, as if somehow he could read her thoughts. She blushed, afraid the heat of the attraction pulsing toward him over the counter might overbake the baked goods. "The usual?"

So much for pretending she didn't know.

She was a glutton for punishment. The man clearly had someone else in his life, someone he cared about enough to make a special trip to the bakery every single Tuesday. And yet Charlotte had deliberately sent her friend and part-time employee Julie on her afternoon break at five thirty so that she would be alone when Mr. Right showed up. What did she expect? That he would throw himself across the counter and proclaim his undying love?

It didn't matter. Julie was due back any time now. A new bride—Julie called her Bridezilla—was coming in to taste a wedding cake. Julie was going to work the counter while Charlotte dealt with the bride.

Charlotte had spoken with the woman on the phone the other day. She had managed to compliment *and* insult the bakery all at the same time, and yet somehow left Charlotte eager to please her.

Such evil was almost impressive.

"The usual, yes, please." He slid his phone into the back pocket of his jeans and pulled his wallet from the other side. No ring on his tanned left hand. A few weeks ago, she had wondered if maybe he was a single dad, and the sweets were for his daughter. She usually had a pretty accurate radar for picking out fellow single parents.

But all of his comments over the last month or so hadn't added up to that deduction. *Melissa said to tell you thanks. She said the cookies this week were even better than last. Melissa said she hasn't had a cookie this good since high school.*

Melissa was one lucky woman.

A wave of guilt pressed on Charlotte's shoulders, familiar and tangible. Had she been too flirty with this mystery man, considering she knew he wasn't available?

Charlotte had been on the other side of that equation. The rugged, football-playing smooth talker she'd dated her senior year in college hadn't been entirely honest about his relationship status—in other words, he'd outright lied to her face and was engaged to someone else. Charlotte ended up in the role of the "other woman," the home wrecker. And even if it had been unintentional, it was both painful and guilt-inducing, and she never intended to go that route again.

Once she found out the truth, that was the end of it, despite the positive sign on the pregnancy test. She would go it alone as a single mom, for better or worse. She was done with the handsome, charming types who *knew*, along with the rest of the female population, that they were handsome and charming.

As she told Zoe every time her daughter asked where her future stepfather was—they were waiting for God to send them a safe, predictable nerd.

Preferably one who bought baked goods for *her*, not for another woman.

Charlotte slipped the snickerdoodles into the bakery's signature turquoise and brown box, then removed her plastic glove and punched the buttons on the register. He was already handing her a five-dollar bill. At this rate, he might as well start a tab.

"Listen, there's something you should know." He darted

a glance over his shoulder at the picture window, then back at her, a sudden seriousness lighting his hazel eyes. "There's sort of this wedding, and . . ."

Wedding. Her stomach knotted. Of course. So Melissa was a fiancée. She dropped the money into the register and slid out his change, the quarters clanging loudly against the metal drawer. Why on earth did men not wear engagement rings the way women did? It wasn't fair to not be able to tell at a glance that a man was taken.

Still, it didn't matter. Not really. This man wasn't safe. Not judging by the things he did to her stomach. And while he might be a little predictable with the every-Tuesday-cookie thing, he wasn't a nerd. Not by far.

Charlotte needed "safe" for her and Zoe. This guy was a five-alarm fire.

"Wedding. Right." She fought for her most professional smile as she handed him his change and receipt, trying not to imagine what he'd look like in a tuxedo at the end of a long church aisle. "Congratulations."

Her mind raced through a blur of images, snippets of conversation pulled from their interactions over the past several weeks. How in the world had she known his favorite color was green, and that he loved desserts with extra nuts, and that he liked camping in Arkansas—yet didn't know he was getting married?

"No, no." He looked over his shoulder once more at the door, lowering his voice. "It's not for—"

"Here it is!" The door to The Dough Knot flung open as if rocked on its hinges by the force of the proclamation. A short, stick-thin brunette rushed inside, flaunting a white tank top with the word *Bride* spelled across the front in hot-pink rhinestones. On her heels trailed a guy in a ball cap and ripped jeans who mouthed the words *I'm sorry* as they entered.

This had to be Brittany, the Bridezilla who had the appointment for the cake tasting. She was early.

And even louder in person than she'd been on the phone.

Charlotte pasted on her most patient, professional smile—one she'd mastered over years of donating free pastries to school bake sales. She refused to complain about Brittany—or *to* Brittany, for that matter. Cake sampling equaled potential customers, and potential customers equaled money in the bank—not to mention exposure and word of mouth. The majority of The Dough Knot's custom wedding business came from guests who wanted a similar cake for their own upcoming nuptials.

And considering this past quarter's bottom line containing all of her spring wedding business, she couldn't afford *not* to keep Brittany happy. Not if she wanted to keep Zoe in private school, and keep them both in the safe, friendly apartment complex where they lived. Not if she wanted to keep baking.

And attempting to atone for her past.

"It's smaller than I pictured." Brittany planted her hands on her hips as she gave the bakery a quick look of disdain. Then she shrugged a tan shoulder. "But I guess we shouldn't judge the quality of the cake by the shop's décor."

Not fair—or accurate. Charlotte's shop was cute, with turquoise walls, trendy wall art, and gleaming mahogany tables, each boasting a teal and brown striped table runner. A chalkboard stand advertised the day's specials by the entrance. Just yesterday she had hung a beautiful crimson and orange autumn wreath on the door. Charlotte bit her lower lip, reeling in the sarcastic responses that crowded her mind. Too bad the customer was always right. Because so many things about Brittany were just plain wrong.

The man in the ball cap fist-bumped Mr. Not-So-Right over Brittany's head. "Sorry we're late." Wait, what? They knew each other? *Oh*. His friend he said was meeting him here. Then that meant . . .

Not his wedding.

Hope rallied, then immediately deflated. Melissa still existed, even if she wasn't quite ring-worthy yet. Charlotte needed to quit this train of thought, right now. She'd hold out for an accountant or a lawyer. With suspenders. And a bow tie.

Definitely not distressed-denim jeans and a dark gray button-down with the sleeves rolled halfway up.

"It's okay, you're not late." Mr. Right turned back to Charlotte. "I was just telling . . . um, Ms. . . . ?" His voice trailed off and he raised his eyebrows, waiting for her to fill in the blank, but the direct eye contact made her forget.

He didn't know her name.

Well, at the moment, she didn't either. She knew his favorite football team was the Saints and he knew she had an addiction to all things Jane Austen—but he didn't know her name. How had they never actually introduced themselves?

"Char—Charlotte." Great. This was college all over again—stuttering and moony-eyed over a hot guy who would inevitably break her heart if she handed it over. Chemistry wasn't everything. Hadn't she learned that the hard way? She was a grown-up, a *mom*, with her own business—and the debt to go with it—and had no time to waste on what-ifs that shouldn't be. She squared her shoulders. "Charlotte Cantrell."

"Charlotte. Right." His voice dipped low, and he held his hand out across the counter. "I'm Will Martin."

She shouldn't have taken off the glove she'd used when gathering his order. The contact of her palm against his sent a shiver down her spine and a burst of heat through her chest. "Nice to meet you."

"You might think otherwise in a minute." Will turned back to the bride and groom. "This is Brittany and Adam—the happy couple."

"Is that what we are?" Adam joked, and Brittany elbowed him in the gut.

"Very funny." Her glare proved it wasn't. "And we're not late. We're early."

Adam shrugged. "I told Will we'd be here at five thirty."

"Our appointment isn't until six o'clock." Brittany's eyes narrowed further, suspicion clouding her face. "Wait a minute. Why did you tell Will to meet us, anyway?"

Adam's mouth opened and closed like a fish. Brittany's eyes narrowed to slits. Charlotte watched back and forth like an observer at a tennis match. She should be going to grab the cake samples to intervene, but instead she held her breath and waited to see if maybe they'd just cancel the wedding altogether.

"This is *our* wedding, Adam." Brittany pressed her

manicured finger against his chest and then poked at her own. "Mine and yours. Not Will's. I know you guys were inseparable in college but believe it or not, you can actually do things without—"

"Actually, Brittany . . ." Will stepped between them, and draped an arm around their shoulders, his voice calm and soothing. The way you would address a wild stallion—or a tantrum-pitching three-year-old. Charlotte remembered those days of parenting all too well. "Adam just needs to give me the tux rental information he's got in his car. So he thought we'd meet here, since he knew I'd be coming to get Melissa's cookies this afternoon."

"Melissa?" Brittany pressed her lips together, one eyebrow quirked. There was so much more the bride obviously wanted to say, Charlotte could practically see the unspoken words dancing in her eyes. *Say it, say it. Solve the mystery of Melissa!* "You mean to tell me you're still—"

Adam coughed. Loud and hard.

"Whatever." Brittany flipped her hair back. "Never mind."

Disappointment rivaled relief. Oh well. She might never know about Melissa. And maybe that was for the better.

Brittany turned her steely gaze then to Charlotte, and Charlotte fought the urge to take a step backward. "We're ready now."

In other words, *hurry it up*.

Charlotte gritted her teeth and retrieved the samples from the kitchen without a single sarcastic comment. A huge, secret victory.

Brittany shoved a square of frosted cake into her mouth,

handed one to Adam as an afterthought, and then picked up another, studying it an inch away from her nose as if she could visually inspect every ingredient. "The vanilla is decent. I guess."

Standing behind Adam, out of sight, Will suddenly held up three fingers. Charlotte frowned, trying to decode his gesture while not making it obvious she was staring over the couple's heads as they debated the pros and cons of vanilla cake. What was he trying to say? She turned the tray so Brittany could access the next flavor in the lineup.

Will pointed intentionally at Brittany, then with an expectant grin, held up three fingers once more.

"I like this one." Adam mumbled around his smaller mouthful of cake. "It's not as boring as other vanilla cakes."

Charlotte beamed.

"Though by now, they kind of all taste the same."

Charlotte sighed.

Brittany picked up the next piece and shoved it into her mouth. Her eyes widened. "Oh, the strawberry is actually . . . good. Really good!" Like a starving woman, she shoveled in another two samples, this time of white chocolate and lemon. "Adam. This is awful. I can't decide."

Over their heads, Will held up two fingers.

Brittany wrung her hands in front of her. "I mean, seriously, Adam." The wringing turned to flapping her arms at her sides in a gesture of panic. "I have no idea what to pick." Her voice pitched and cracked.

Adam sidestepped as her flapping connected with his shoulder and nearly knocked his sample out of his hand. "Hey, careful there, babe."

Brittany's breathing became erratic. Charlotte darted a glance back and forth between the two of them. Should she call 911? Did this woman carry an inhaler? Why wasn't anyone else concerned?

Her gaze collided with Will's, who was still grinning and subtly holding up two fingers.

"The strawberry would be amazing with the champagne bar! But that chocolate was so moist!" Tears began slipping down Brittany's cheeks.

Charlotte stared at Brittany. In all her years of catering to brides, never had her cake brought one of them to tears. Hardly a testimonial she could add to her website.

Behind her, Will turned down another finger so only his pointer remained in the air. Then he mouthed the words. *Blast off.*

As if on cue, Brittany erupted. "What are we going to do?" She flung herself into Adam's arms. He stumbled back three steps before he caught his balance. Her fingers curled tight into the front of his T-shirt, gripping the material in both hands. "We can't have *three* wedding cakes!"

Adam nodded, patting her back as the dripping tears turned into shaking sobs. "You're right, babe. That's not really possible." He mouthed the next words to Will. *Or in the budget.*

Charlotte began edging her sampler tray away from the now hysterical bride. "So, um, I guess you probably don't want to sample the mint—"

Brittany's wails heightened in both volume and intensity.

Nope. No mint.

"Honey?" Adam gently pushed Brittany away from his

chest. Charlotte plucked a napkin from the dispenser and handed it to him over the counter. He began mopping her face, mascara smearing across the white paper. "I think I have a solution."

"Don't say vanilla. Don't you *dare* say vanilla." Her shoulders shook with silent cries as she snatched the napkin from him and continued rubbing at her eyes until she morphed into a raccoon.

"No, no. No vanilla." Adam pulled her back into a hug, rolling his eyes over her head at Will. "You're under a lot of stress. Wedding planning is rough."

Brittany nodded into his chest, her words muffled. "People just have no idea."

Charlotte understood the eye roll, now. How did this guy do it? Forget Bridezilla. This girl was Bridasaurus Rex. She could scare the garters off Bridezilla.

"May I make a suggestion?"

Three pairs of eyes drilled into hers. Two hopeful, one doubtful.

She cleared her throat. "We could layer flavors into one cake, if that helps make the decision less . . . daunting." She fought to keep a serious expression. "That way you wouldn't have to commit to just one."

Brittany looked up at Adam in confusion, as if unsure how to respond to the crazy cake lady with the horrible ideas.

Charlotte held up both hands in surrender. "Never mind. Just a suggestion."

"It's not a bad idea." Will spoke up, finally, a voice of reason from the madness.

"Are you kidding me? That just makes it even harder.

Which flavors do I layer? How many layers? Which ones will complement and which ones will just end up tasting like—" Brittany's voice cracked again.

Adam rocked her slowly side to side as he spoke. "Babe, I think you need to take a step back. Delegate a little."

"Delegate?" She looked up and sniffed. "You mean, tell other people what to do?"

He smiled. "That's your favorite thing, right?"

Will snorted, then covered it quickly with a cough. Charlotte shot him a look. That was it. Forget word of mouth and new business. She just wanted all of these crazy, nonsingle people to get out of her shop and leave her alone with the petit fours.

Julie wouldn't believe what she'd missed.

"You should delegate some of the planning responsibilities." Adam's words rambled faster now, almost mechanically, as if he'd memorized a script. Or maybe he just had a lot of experience talking his would-be bride off the ledge. "You should focus your efforts and attention on the things that matter most. Like your dress and your vows."

Brittany perked up considerably. "And the flowers."

"Exactly." Adam nodded. "And leave all the boring, overwhelming stuff like choosing the cake to someone else."

"But there's more than just the wedding cake to pick out." Brittany looked at Charlotte for the first time in ten minutes. "We'll need desserts for the engagement party and the wedding shower next month. And maybe the rehearsal dinner."

Wait a minute. That was a lot of business. Charlotte straightened. She might even be able to deal with a little

B-Rex if it meant dessert-catering a wedding *and* multiple parties. After all, she needed to start saving for Christmas presents soon, and she still owed the hospital from when they'd taken out Zoe's tonsils.

Brittany's hysterics rallied for round two. "But I can't just abandon—"

"Stop. It's not abandoning." Adam held up one hand. "Just think of it as getting to tell people what to do *three* times."

Brittany's mouth opened, then shut, as if even she realized she couldn't argue with that. "Okay. But who would do it? Who would pick all this out for us?"

Adam turned toward Will.

Charlotte didn't know a lot about hunting, but she saw, right now, right here in her bakery, a ten-point buck caught in the crosshairs. Will's eyes widened. He stepped backward, arms raised in surrender, shaking his head. "No way. Don't even think about it."

"Oh, come on. You'd be perfect. You're already in this place, like, what, once a week?" Adam gestured wildly around the bakery. "You know. For Melissa."

It was Will's turn to glare and Brittany's turn to sweeten it up. "Yeah, Will, and we all know you like to eat. You'd make great choices."

There again with the double insult-compliment in one. The girl should audition for the role of a Disney villain.

Will's hands went to his stomach—his totally flat stomach, that no doubt boasted a six-pack of abs under that shirt. "Me? Why me?"

"Because you have good taste in food, *and* you're the best

man." Adam clapped his hand on Will's shoulder and whispered, "And besides, choosing a wedding cake won't make you certifiably crazy."

Brittany's head snapped back to Adam. "What'd you say?"

He backpedaled quickly. Again, probably not his first rodeo. "I said, Will wouldn't be lazy. In getting all this planned out. You know Will." Adam patted Will's shoulder again. "He used to be in the military. The dude thrives on a schedule. He'll get all this taken care of in no time."

"Right. No time. As in, *not at all*." Will ran a hand over his five o'clock stubble. "No way, guys."

Adam's voice lowered an octave, and the humor fled his tone. "You know Melissa would think you should do it."

Will glared at Adam. "Fine. As your best man . . . I'll do it."

Brittany squealed. Adam slapped him a high five, and Will sighed like a man heading toward a frosted guillotine.

Charlotte plastered on a smile as she tried to dissect the emotions coursing through her body. Relief. Trepidation. New business—that was a good thing. And Brideasaurus Rex was now out of the picture—also a very good thing. Besides, she'd get to work with Will from here forward—

Yeah, that. Maybe not such a good thing.

She drew a tight breath. Regardless of how she felt, facts were facts. She'd been handed a lucrative baking contract on a silver platter . . .

Along with the opportunity to prove to herself that she had what it took to resist the wiles of handsome, charming—and unavailable—men.

"I'm sorry you had to see that." Will waited until the bakery door swung shut behind Adam and his crazy fiancée before he apologized to Charlotte, who now leaned against the counter as if it were the sole thing keeping her on her feet.

Not surprising. In the six months since Adam proposed, he had seen Brittany lay out enough emotion for ten brides. Just watching her was completely exhausting. "I warned you a minute ago that you might regret meeting me."

Of course, that was when he thought he was simply apologizing in advance for Brittany's erratic behavior. Now he'd been shanghaied into this wedding cake task for his best friend's wedding. A wedding he barely had time to even attend, much less perform a starring role in.

But he and Adam went way back, and if he'd learned one thing from his time in the army, it was that duty ruled. He owed it to his friend to be at his side during his wedding.

After that, the dude was on his own.

Will shuddered at the idea of being stuck with someone like Brittany, day in and day out. No thanks. He'd been with his share of selfish, vain girls over the years, living the illusive frat-boy dream, and he was done with that life. Melissa had seen to that. He sobered immediately at the thought of her.

Charlotte smiled, as sweetly as always, her cheeks a rosy pink. In fact, they were always pink, as if permanently flushed from the warmth of the bakery. The sight of it melted a bit of his stress. "No worries." She shrugged. "It's good business."

Business. Right. He should remember that's all it was, too, though something about Charlotte's electric blue eyes and chestnut-brown hair made him want more snicker-doodles. As in, every day, til death do us part.

He shook his head as the phrase took hold in his mind. He'd apparently been around Adam and Brittany's wedding planning way too long. He was *not* the marrying type. They hadn't called him Free Willy all through college for nothing.

It was still true. Just now for an entirely different reason.

He winced. "I didn't mean for that to happen."

She shrugged. "I deal with difficult brides all the time, it's nothing new."

Oh. He meant his strong reaction to Charlotte, but yeah, that too. He struggled to clear his head. The scent of cinnamon and sugar was getting to him, making him soft. He didn't have time for anyone, even someone as sweet as Charlotte. He had more duties than just Adam's wedding to attend to, and he wouldn't make the mistake of putting Melissa last—ever again.

In fact, he should probably get moving. She'd be expecting her cookies.

"I'd better go." He took the bakery box from the counter and then held up his left wrist bearing his favorite waterproof watch. "But I'll be back."

"Right. Next Tuesday, at 5:40?" Charlotte stopped, her pink cheeks now a fiery crimson.

She knew his schedule. Habit from the military—he liked patterns and routine—but he never thought she'd notice. "No, actually, I meant sooner. To discuss the cakes and whatever else Brittany wants for all these wedding parties." He never understood the point of showers, anyway. Didn't people just bring gifts to the actual ceremony?

Melissa had never made it to hers. He tightened his grip on the box.

"Oh, of course." Charlotte, still crimson-faced, nodded furiously. "Right. Sooner, then. Tomorrow, maybe?"

Tomorrow. He'd promised Melissa he'd take her out, but maybe he could come by afterward. It had to get done, like it or not. Brittany would kill him otherwise—and after surviving ten years of service including several year-long deployments, he really didn't want to go out because of a five-foot-two woman with a grudge.

Still, the prospect of working with Charlotte made the whole dessert-planning responsibility seem like much less of a chore.

"Tomorrow sounds good." Too good, unfortunately. He didn't have time for this. Didn't have the right to enjoy it.

But he did a little bit, anyway.

"So tell me. How did buying snickerdoodles turn you into a wedding planner?" Melissa shook her head—silky dark hair swinging below her chin—and laughed, that easy, musical laughter that used to come so easily. The laugh reminiscent of a few years ago, before life got so complicated. Before everything changed because of one rainy night and one bad decision on his part.

Will reached forward and tucked the blanket tighter around Melissa's feet, covering her toes that peeked out from under the edge of the fringed quilt. Sitting with her here, both of them on the couch, surrounded by pillows and snacks, almost made him forget she was paralyzed.

Almost.

The wheelchair by the edge of the sofa was a stark reminder, as was the lower placement of the light switches on the wall and the ramp he'd built to the front door.

"Not the wedding." Knock on wood. Just let Adam get *that* idea next. He definitely didn't need his best friend getting any crazy matchmaking schemes. "Only the wedding cake." And the other prewedding events, which apparently involved even more desserts, but he wouldn't think of all that yet. Charlotte could help figure that out . . .

"You know the cake is like the secondary star of the show, right? Next to the dress." Melissa nibbled another bite of her cookie, then pulled it away and studied it. "Are you trying to make me fat, by the way? It's not like I can go jog this puppy off my hips."

She grinned, her bright green eyes twinkling, but Will was reminded once again that her handicap still bothered him a lot more than it bothered her.

But that's because she didn't have the guilt of it weighing on her shoulders, a constant shadow by day and heavy ache by night. He shifted on the couch, simultaneously glad she could joke about it but wishing she wouldn't. It was awkward. It hurt.

He couldn't fix it.

Growing up, he'd fixed all of Melissa's problems. That's what a big brother should do. Broken doll? Superglue. Friend mad at her? Make prank phone calls. Boyfriend trouble? Fistfight in the parking lot. It was always easy.

But this . . .

He tried to shake it off. "Whatever. You weigh, what? A hundred and ten pounds? Your weekly snickerdoodles aren't going to hurt." His sister was tiny. He'd always been able to throw her over his shoulder whenever he wanted.

Well, until the last two years, anyway.

"Will. Come on, now. Stop it." Melissa's voice, so much like their late mother's, softly pulled him back from the brink. "I think this wedding will be good for you. You need to do . . . stuff. Things. *Anything*, really." She reached over and squeezed his hand, just like she did that time they went to the state fair when she was five and she was afraid she'd get lost. Like she did during that scary movie he'd talked her into seeing in the theater six Halloweens ago. Like she did at their mother's funeral.

Like she'd done when he stood by her hospital bed after the accident.

"You're turning into a hermit." She wrinkled her nose at him. "And it's not flattering."

"Hey now, enough with the insults." But inside, he was just grateful she still had a sense of humor. She could call him anything she wanted and he'd embroider it on a pillow. What Melissa wanted, Melissa got. It was his job to see that happen.

Which was precisely why he didn't have time for this wedding, or anything else that didn't involve paying the bills and making sure Melissa had everything she needed.

"Maybe not a hermit. But you're heading toward anti-social at best. It's not healthy." She settled back against her nest of pillows. "You don't even work anymore. Besides part-time personal training."

"I just do that to kill time until I decide what's next." Will had cut back to reserves after Melissa's accident, so he could be around when she needed him. Thankfully, he'd been wise with his finances over the years and had been blessed with some good moves in the stock market. He could afford to take a breath for right now.

"It's time for next, Will." Her eyes dared him to argue, and he wouldn't. But inside, he was yelling protests. It wasn't her decision to make. He wasn't ready.

"You've given up all your hobbies besides working out too."

"No, I haven't." Man, when did cookie time turn into lecture time? "I still watch movies with you. And watch you make those crafty thingies you sell online. And I run." He straightened, shoving his hair back, then smoothing it flat again. He couldn't get too agitated. This was Melissa. She'd see right through it, anyway.

"Like I said, besides working out or wasting time being lazy with me." She tilted her head. "When was the last time you went hunting? Or cooked?"

"Spaghetti—for you—two nights ago. Was it that forgettable?"

Melissa snorted. "I mean *really* cooked. Your famous gumbo recipe, for example. Or that barbeque quiche you made for Mother's Day a few years ago. Or that awesome fried mac and cheese you used to make on my birthday."

It was pretty awesome. He even put bacon in it—and ground venison. But he couldn't cook anymore. It reminded him of his life before the accident, before everything changed forever. Reminded him of Mom.

Of how he'd failed them both.

"I don't have time right now for any of that." Straight-up lie. He had nothing but time.

Thankfully, Melissa got the hint and didn't push it any further. "Well, who knows? Maybe you'll meet someone at Adam's wedding." She wiggled her eyebrows up and down in anticipation, and Will's stomach tightened. He'd rather go back to the previous lecture than start this particular new one.

"You know that's not going to happen." An image of Charlotte in her apron flashed through his mind, and he shook his head to clear it. No. It wouldn't happen. Couldn't.

Melissa snorted. "You might be a hermit, but you're still good-looking. It'll happen eventually."

He smiled to pacify her, but no. He couldn't take any more time away from his sister. And what woman would understand his responsibility toward her? A girlfriend, or wife, was just a complicated mess waiting to happen. His duty was here.

Chapter Three

Always the baker, never the bride.

She ought to needlepoint that and hang it on the wall.

"Mommy?"

Her five-year-old daughter's tiny voice barely registered above the electronic beeping of her handheld game. Zoe accompanied her to The Dough Knot every Saturday morning and alternated between "helping" mix batter, playing games, and reading books under the high stainless-steel counter in the kitchen.

Right now, though, she sat at one of the tables in the vacant dining area, driving Charlotte semicrazy with her endless random questions. The elderly couple who had just left with their weekend brownies had found it adorable.

Charlotte half wished she could ask them to babysit.

"Yes, Zoe?" She tried to keep the impatience out of her tone. Usually, Charlotte loved their weekends together, but this particular Saturday was different.

She turned from putting the last few rose petals on the layered strawberry cake she had baked that morning, already boxed up for delivery. If she had a dime for every fake flower petal she had ever created out of icing or fondant, she could probably fund her own wedding.

Not that there was a groom in sight.

Zoe's voice finally registered through her drifting thoughts. "Mommy, can I have a cookie?"

"Have you already had one today?" She couldn't remember in the Saturday rush if she'd given one to Zoe with her ham sandwich for lunch.

"No."

"Look me in the eyes, Zoe." Charlotte looked up from her piping bag long enough to lock gazes with her daughter across the room. Used to the drill, Zoe stared back, wide-eyed, open, honest. Sincere.

Eyes didn't lie.

"Okay, you may have just one."

"Chocolate chip?"

Charlotte smiled. "What else? It's your favorite."

Zoe scrambled out of her seat and hurried to claim her prize. Charlotte snagged a chocolate-chip cookie from the top rack and handed it over the counter to her.

"Julie! This cake's ready for the van." Charlotte tucked the corners of the lid inside the turquoise folds of the box, trying not to think about her to-do list. Normally, she loved lists. She was almost addicted to the rush that came with productivity and accomplishment, the thrill that came with checking off a completed item. She'd even taught Zoe the principle, and was constantly finding pink sticky notes that read *Potty* and *Play with dolls* stuck around their apartment.

But next on her list was meeting with one Will Martin, and—well, that was going to complicate her afternoon, not streamline it.

"Mommy?" Zoe said, more persistent this time as her heels kicked against the chair legs. "I'm bored."

Of course she was. Charlotte wrestled the last corner fold into the box. "Your books are in the kitchen, sweetie."

"Which ones?" Zoe twisted a blonde braid around one finger and narrowed her eyes.

Charlotte wracked her brain to remember which ones she had grabbed on the way out the door, but she couldn't concentrate. Could barely remember her own name, much less story titles. "Um. *If You Give a Moose a Muffin*, I think."

Zoe made a face. "I've read that one three times."

"The two dozen cupcakes for the Lopez birthday party are out of the oven and cooling." Julie came from the kitchen, cupcake batter smeared across the front of her apron, and tucked a stray strand of red hair behind her ear. "These cakes go to the Sinclair wedding, right?"

"Yes, and those too. It's a three layer." Charlotte pointed to the other two boxes awaiting delivery on the counter behind them. "Keys should be on the ring by the back door."

"Mommy? What other books are there?"

Charlotte closed her eyes. "Zoe. I don't know, honey. *Goodnight Moon*?"

"That's a baby book."

"Two steps ahead of you, Boss." Julie jingled the keys

in her hand. "Why aren't *you* taking these, by the way? Normally you like to be the Cake Naz—I mean, you like to set up layered cakes yourself."

Charlotte wrinkled her nose at her friend. "I've told you not to call me Boss." Julie was teasing, of course, about the Cake Nazi. She just liked things to be under control. Simple—no messes. And she couldn't guarantee perfection if she wasn't there to oversee it for herself.

But today . . .

"Remember? I have a three o'clock consultation." She tried to keep her voice even, but despite the effort, her voice rose half an octave. Why was she so nervous? Will Martin didn't have the potential to be anything more than a temporary client. She'd met his pretty-boy type before, plenty of times, and had no intention of going down that road again. What she needed was stability. Commitment. A man of honor and loyalty, who kept his promises.

Unfortunately, most of those men didn't come in Will-size packages—at least not in Charlotte's experience. She needed a small, contained bonfire. Smoldering sparks in a fire pit. Will was more like a Colorado wildfire—and she'd been burned enough.

This time, she refused to let Zoe get caught in the smoke.

Julie frowned in confusion. "Wait. Is this the consultation for that Bridezilla who is making her best man choose the cake?"

"Yes." Charlotte cleared her throat.

Julie put her hands on her hips, keys jangling. "Then why don't you let me go through the initial run-through with him, while you take the cakes?"

"Because." Flustered, Charlotte tried in vain to think of an excuse that would sound like anything other than what it was. "Just . . . because. Please?"

"You got it, Boss." Julie tossed the keys in the air with one hand and caught them deftly in the other. "But when I get back, I expect a better explanation than that."

"I want to go!" Zoe slid down from her chair and danced first on one foot, then the other. "Can I help make the delivery?"

Julie shrugged. "Sure, kiddo. If it's okay with your mom."

"That's fine. Her car seat is already in the back." Charlotte breathed a little easier as Zoe grabbed her for a good-bye hug. Now Zoe would have something to do and wouldn't interrupt the consultation.

On second thought, maybe having Zoe nearby wouldn't have hurt.

Julie took the cake layers out to the van, then returned and motioned to Zoe. "Let's go, kiddo—"

The bakery door swung open, interrupting her sentence. Will strolled inside, a handful of dry burgundy leaves skittering onto the tiled floor in his wake.

"Sorry about that." He caught the door with one hand and tried to kick them back out, looking up with a bright, apologetic smile that could have sold toothpaste to millions.

"Ah, never mind. No better explanation necessary." Julie winked at Charlotte. "We'll just be on our way . . . Boss."

Then they were gone, leaving Charlotte alone with Will and the kaleidoscope of leaves on the floor.

For some reason, that particular mess didn't bother her one bit.

She braced her arms against the counter between them, briefly wondering if his girlfriend Melissa was typically the mess-intolerant type too. Maybe she and Melissa had things in common. Maybe she'd meet her during one of the wedding events for Adam and Brittany, and they could be friends.

Surely then she could put a stop to this uncomfortable and unnecessary magnetism toward Will.

Charlotte took a deep breath and wished for the thousandth time that she had known six years ago what she knew now.

Well, five years plus nine months, anyway.

Will leaned against the counter opposite her, bracing on his forearms, and gestured to the swinging door in Julie's wake. "Is she always that perky?"

Charlotte started to answer, then met his eyes and hesitated. From this closer vantage point, she could see weary wrinkles lining his eyes, attesting to a false front. He'd apparently had a rough day, or something heavy weighed on his mind.

She knew the feeling. She rarely got a break from her own burdens. In fact, if it wasn't for the light Zoe brought to her life and the fact that she got to bake for a living, she'd buckle right underneath them. God had been good to her, despite her mistakes, and had blessed her in spite of herself.

Her defensive guard slipped a little under this wave of compassion toward Will, and she fought to rebuild the retaining wall, avoiding eye contact as she brushed at some imaginary crumbs on the counter. "Sometimes. Julie's a redhead, so you never know what you're going to get."

"She can't be as bad as Brittany."

Charlotte snorted. "No one's as bad as—" She winced. This was a client she was railing to—and the best man, no less. Not exactly professional. "Sorry."

"Don't worry. Your secret is safe." Will winked, and the stress lines around his eyes edged away as a real smile replaced the forced. "I mean, the truth hurts, right?"

"It definitely can." A huge understatement. Painful or not, *knowing* the bad was infinitely better than being deceived. She shrugged away the memories. "I guess some people don't realize how they come across."

Will's fingers drummed a rhythm on the countertop. "Just between us, I think Brittany knows how she is, and just chooses to be that way anyway. Mostly because everyone lets her."

"You don't think there's a chance she's misunderstood?" Charlotte knew not to jump to conclusions, not after she'd naively dated an engaged man for months. Everyone on the school campus had assumed she knew exactly what she was doing, and she hadn't had a clue. She'd let herself be swept away, let herself be sweet-talked against everything she'd ever stood for.

No one believed her, especially after she turned up pregnant. And she wore the Scarlet Letter all the way to graduation day. Zoe's father refused to be a part of any of it. Never showed a moment's interest, never paid a dime in child support.

It was just as well. Charlotte wanted nothing to do with him, ever. At least she'd been able to move back to her hometown, start The Dough Knot, and make a decent life for her and Zoe.

"There's always a chance, I suppose." Will shrugged, as if it didn't really matter.

Charlotte's breath tightened in her chest. His flippancy over such a deep topic annoyed her more than it should.

"I just don't believe people change—not easily, anyway, or completely." Will's eyes flickered with some undefined emotion. "My mom used to always tell us that if someone tries to show you who they really are, then let them."

Charlotte felt her neck flush with indignation as she pushed away from the counter. Away from Will's judgment. "But what about those people who are really good at appearances?"

She fell headlong into the flashback, feeling exactly the way she had in college, defending herself all over again. No one believed she was innocent—especially not her ex's fiancée, who had accused her of being a home wrecker in front of a stadium full of students.

Charlotte crossed her arms over her apron and ignored the rose petal icing that smeared across her elbow. "What about those people who make you believe they're one way or one thing, when they're really not?"

Will frowned, confusion replacing the tired creases in his forehead. "What about them?"

Reality sank in, and as her anger diffused, Charlotte let her arms slowly unfold. What had she just done?

"Never mind." Embarrassed, exhausted tears pricked at her eyelids, and she brushed at the front of her apron until she regained a semblance of control. "Um . . . maybe we should just discuss the cake order."

Or maybe he should just leave. Maybe she should forget

baking for this entire wedding. But no—she needed this. For Zoe. For their security. Who knew when the next big order would come in?

Will stared at her until she had no choice but to make eye contact. "Charlotte."

She raised her eyebrows, still not trusting her voice, and blinked a few times to clear her eyes.

He leaned forward over the counter, something soft and inviting sparking in his hazel eyes. "Were we having the same conversation just now?"

No. She opened her mouth, then shut it, debating how much to divulge. She'd clearly been fighting some battle with her past and projecting it onto this man—this taken, unavailable man. Her palms grew damp. What was she thinking? She couldn't confide in him or get emotionally involved. Was she so scared of history repeating itself that she was destined to self-fulfill the prophecy?

There was only one thing to say.

"Are you leaning toward the lemon, white chocolate, or strawberry cake?"

Will knew after the first bite that the secret ingredient in Charlotte's amazing snickerdoodles was cream cheese. He knew that if an egg was spoiled, it would float in water instead of sink. And he knew rolling limes with the palm of your hand made them easier to juice.

Will knew food.

But Charlotte Cantrell was one recipe he couldn't analyze.

From his position at the counter barstool, he watched her through the kitchen doorway as she quickly fixed another tray of cake samples. She had switched from passionately debating some inscrutable point, to nearly crying over the same topic, then changed subjects so swiftly he half wondered if he'd made the whole thing up.

The hardest part to figure out, though, was that it wasn't anything like crazy-Brittany-I-need-attention. No, he'd gotten good at reading people during his years in the service, and he'd bet his last dollar that Charlotte was operating out of a painful past.

"Here you go." She set the tray of cake bites on the counter before him, each one nestled on top of some girlie, lacy looking white paper. "You didn't eat any the other day when Brittany was here, so I figured it'd be best if we just started over."

Started over . . . with the cakes?

Or with him and her?

Will took a bite of the little yellow square before he attempted to answer his own question and get them both in trouble. "That's really good." He tried the next one—white chocolate, or something along those lines. It melted in his mouth. "Okay, I'm starting to see Brittany's dilemma."

"Are you going to cry?" A tiny smirk twisted Charlotte's lips, and he nearly sprayed crumbs with his laughter.

"No tears. I promise." He swallowed, still chuckling. "I mean, it's not *that* good . . ."

Silent laughter lit her eyes, and she swatted him across the counter with a pink oven mitt. "Give it time. You haven't tried the marshmallow caramel apple cake." She turned the tray and he obliged.

Heaven and a campfire and a late summer fruit tree collided on his taste buds. "Wow. That's amazing."

Charlotte practically glowed under the warmth of his praise. It was a little unsettling how much she enjoyed it—and how much he enjoyed giving it to her.

Then her light dimmed. "It's not traditional, though, for a wedding cake." A troubled frown pinched Charlotte's brow as she studied the sampler between them. He wanted to smooth the crease with his finger, make her laugh again. Erase her worry.

And figure out exactly what the heck had set her off earlier.

Most of all, he just wanted her light to turn back on. "What if we did the marshmallow caramel apple for one of the prewedding events?"

She tilted her head. "That could work." The light began to shine, just a little, as her hopes rose. "Let's see. Brittany mentioned an engagement party on . . . what date?" She pulled a daily desk calendar from a stack near the register and began flipping through the pages.

"It's soon. Like, next week." Will pulled out his phone and read the dates and times for the upcoming parties. "Adam texted me the schedule last night. Yeah, there's the engagement party, next Friday night. And a couple's shower two weeks later, at six p.m. on Saturday."

One he'd have no date for. Melissa would never let him hear the end of that one.

"And she wanted dessert for the rehearsal dinner too?"

Will adjusted his position on the barstool. "Adam mentioned cupcakes for that one. To mix it up."

"Okay, perfect. What if we did the caramel apple cake as cupcakes that night? I could use my autumn harvest colors for the frosting."

The light was back. Mission accomplished.

She was on a roll now. "And for the engagement party, what about cinnamon pecan petit fours? With caramel orange icing?"

His stomach growled in resounding agreement. "And for the couple's shower?"

She tapped her polka-dotted pencil against her chin. "A different batch of cupcakes?"

"What about snickerdoodles?"

Her smile wavered, just slightly, but enough that he noticed. The mention of the cookies had disappointed her. She corrected, but it was too late. "Sure. That'd be . . . good."

She said *good* the way a person would have naturally said *sewer*. Or *toxic waste*. "It was just an idea."

He could have kicked himself, but he still had no idea what he'd done wrong. Or why disappointing her was one of the most unsettling things he'd ever experienced in his life.

He pressed his fingers against his temples. This bakery was like some kind of time warp. It did things to him, made him forget the past and wish for a different future and expect things in the present.

So, so dangerous.

"Did I say something wrong?" He had to know. The

longer he sat there, the more trapped he felt, caught in a perfectly wonderful, terrible, addicting kind of parallel universe. He'd never cared what people thought before. He lived his life, did his duty, took care of those he was responsible for, and that was it. If someone didn't like it or how he went about doing it, that was their problem. He knew his role in life and performed it well. He never intentionally hurt anyone, but he'd learned not to waste time on opinions.

And somehow, suddenly, offending Charlotte or hurting her feelings seemed akin to a sin he couldn't bounce back from.

She shook her head, not speaking, which only confirmed that yes, he'd said something horribly wrong.

"Charlotte?"

She averted her eyes, rearranging the remaining samples on the tray between them. A fierce and irrational desire came over him—to knock the cakes out of the way, slide over the counter, cradle that adorable face of hers in both hands, and insist she confess right away. After he kissed her, of course.

The more rational part of him was staying busy just trying to convince the first part not to act.

"You didn't say anything wrong." She rolled in her lower lip, an innocent action that increased his initial desire tenfold. "I just . . . I just forgot."

Forgot what?

Unfortunately, judging by the seconds ticking away on the cupcake-shaped clock on the wall, he might never know.

A hushed silence pulsed over the counter. Then came

her voice, small and timid and two octaves hopeful. "I could make a snickerdoodle cookie cake."

The proposition sounded like a peace offering. But what was she even apologizing for?

"That sounds delicious. And unique." His voice sounded tired, even to his own ears.

"Will Brittany like it?"

Who cared anymore? But yes, she would. He nodded in affirmation.

She kept shuffling the samples around the tray. "And you . . . you'll like it?"

He met her gaze, suspecting that something immensely important was riding on that question, but for the life of him, he was unable to decipher exactly what. All of the people skills, survival skills, and analytical skills he'd developed over the course of his career were absolutely useless in the undertow of Charlotte's sea-blue eyes. "I'd like it a lot."

Was that *his* voice, so husky? He sounded like he had strep throat.

He rocked back off the barstool so forcefully that it clattered to the floor. He had to get out of this bakery. Before those cake samples went flying and he did something really stupid and totally wonderful.

Like kiss Charlotte Cantrell and forget all his obligations and promises to his sister.

Chapter Four

It'd been a week since Will had flown off The Dough Knot's barstool so fast that he hadn't even picked a wedding cake flavor. Charlotte wasn't sure if she should call him, wait for him to contact her, or just go ahead and pick a flavor by herself. He hadn't even come in for his customary Tuesday cookie purchase. What had gone so wrong that he propelled himself out of the bakery with little more than "Gotta go, see you later"?

She had replayed their conversation over and over in her head, but couldn't see where she'd offended him. She had embarrassed herself, for sure, by connecting with him . . . *really* connecting . . . only to remember he was taken the moment he said the magic word, *snickerdoodle.*

When would she ever learn?

On the one hand, she was glad he'd left so fast, glad something—whatever it was—had broken the spell. That felt a lot safer than all their laughing and joking and bonding.

Safer than the way she'd felt her heart bloom under his praise for her baking. Safer than noticing how his eyes lit with extra fire when he looked at her.

Fire. See? Time to quit playing with it, before she let her heart go up in smoke.

After she'd tortured herself with all the possible reasons for him to leave so quickly, in the end she had done nothing. Nothing but stall in making a decision while checking her watch, playing Candyland with Zoe, and hosting a pretend baking contest for her daughter's plethora of stuffed animals.

And now, in a few minutes, the decision would most likely be made for her.

Charlotte maneuvered the two giant trays of cinnamon pecan petit fours out of the back of her van, grateful Julie was with her this evening for the delivery. Thankfully, the engagement party started after the bakery closed for the day, so one of them didn't have to stay to man the counter. After last week's confusing and emotional interaction with Will, Charlotte was grateful for her friend's company and the distraction she offered.

And thankful for the extra set of arms.

"Anything else, Boss?" Julie teased as Charlotte set the second covered tray of petit fours into Julie's arms and shut the door to the van. She pretended to stagger under the weight. "I could juggle or spin some plates for you real quick."

"Very funny." Charlotte took the second tray back, and motioned for Julie to walk first up the walkway to the house—no, on second glance, make that *mansion*—that was hosting the party.

"What a house," Julie mumbled as they made their way

up the bricked path to the monstrous red door. "They better tip well."

"Julie!" Charlotte tried to infuse a touch of shock and offense into her tone, but couldn't quite pull it off since she'd just been hoping for the same thing. If she had to see Will and deal with the awkwardness between them, it had better be worth it.

Her stomach twisted into a nervous knot. Maybe when she saw Will, she'd realize her silly crush had been just that, and had passed. Merely a temporary physical attraction to a handsome man who frequented her shop.

Julie shifted her tray to her shoulder and rang the doorbell. Charlotte tried to look at her watch, but couldn't risk tilting her own tray. When they pulled up in the van, the clock had read twenty til time for the engagement party to begin. They had deliberately come early to put the petit fours out before the official start, but apparently, the party was already in full swing. Music, heavy with bass, thumped from inside the house, and loud laughter rang from the backyard.

The door swung open, and a middle-aged woman in a white blouse directed them to the kitchen. Charlotte focused on the end goal as they traipsed through multiple rooms, all decorated with black and white balloons and ornate signs congratulating the happy couple. Hopefully they could just leave the disposable heavy trays in the kitchen and head out before she even saw Will.

"Brittany asked if you ladies would please arrange the desserts on the silver holders." The woman gestured to several sterling tiered stands on the table.

No such luck.

They set down their trays and began arranging the petit fours, which seemed to multiply by the second, onto the decorative stands. The woman bustled away.

"Was she a servant or someone's mom?" Julie whispered.

Charlotte tucked another petit four into place. "I was wondering the same."

Julie giggled. "I can't even imagine all this chaos and expense once I get married. If my wedding or prewedding events cost more than my first house, please promise to slap me."

"I promise." At this rate, Charlotte didn't have to worry about securing the same guarantee. Always a baker, never a bride. For now, that seemed the safer route, for both her and Zoe.

She glanced at Julie's progress unloading the petit fours. "Try to hurry. I've got to pick up Zoe from her after-school babysitter." That was *part* of why she was rushing, anyway. Not a total lie. She cast an anxious glance toward the picture window displaying the yard, but couldn't see well enough to know if Will was anywhere in sight.

"Are they here yet?" Brittany's strident voice preceded her entrance into the kitchen by mere seconds. Not nearly long enough to brace for the onslaught.

"Finally. Better late than never, I guess." Brittany swirled the contents of her champagne glass and raised it in acknowledgment.

Beside her, Julie stiffened at the insult, and Charlotte quickly handed her another petit four to place on the stand before her friend could voice the thoughts rolling through both their heads. "Ignore her. She's tipsy," she whispered.

"That's still not an excuse to be rude."

Charlotte snorted. "You should have seen her sober."

"What are you two whispering about?" Brittany's voice slurred, and she pointed with her glass, nearly spilling the contents on the kitchen floor. "Hey, if those square thingies don't taste good, do I blame you? Or Will?"

Great question. Not that she particularly cared, though Brittany seemed legitimately confused about the potential dilemma. Right now, Charlotte just wanted to finish arranging the stupid things and get back to the van before she saw him. Wanted to pick up Zoe, go home, make popcorn, and watch some mindless show on the Disney Channel while snuggling her little girl and reminding herself of all the reasons why they were better off this way.

She opened her mouth, then closed it, unsure how to answer Brittany, or if she even should.

Didn't matter.

Brittany tilted her head back and bellowed toward the backyard. "WILL!"

No. No, no, no. Charlotte drew a sharp intake of breath. Julie shot her a questioning look.

Brittany pouted, her glossy red lips exaggerated. "He can't hear me."

Julie smirked, muttering under her breath as she secured another petit four on the stand. "Can't everyone? Like, on every planet in the solar system?"

Charlotte bit back a laugh and nudged her friend in warning, but Brittany appeared to not have heard. Before she could decide how to change the subject, Brittany grabbed her wrist and began to tug. "Come outside. We'll ask him."

"No, really. That's not necessary." Charlotte struggled to free her wrist as politely as possible, but Brittany was on a mission. She really didn't want to cause a scene at the party, so all she could do was shoot Julie a pleading glance as Brittany propelled them out the backdoor.

"I'll just finish up in here!" Julie called before the door swung shut behind them.

Great. Always the model employee.

Charlotte caught a glance of her friend in the picture window, giving her a wide grin and a thumbs-up. Why hadn't she filled Julie in on Will before the party? Then maybe she could have had a little backup. Now Julie was probably thinking this was a great matchmaking opportunity.

Not that Charlotte would have ever expected *this* to happen. She squinted as a sudden gust of wind raked her hair off her shoulders and shook the tree branches overhead. Maybe she could just blow away.

"Hey, Will!" Brittany's voice screeched across a wide expanse of manicured lawn, lit with various-sized tiki torches. Groups of twenty-somethings, sipping from polished glasses and wearing everything from jeans to cocktail dresses, stopped and stared as Brittany dragged Charlotte around a flower bed and a gurgling birdbath.

She stopped short near a table laden with wrapped gifts. "Oh, look. Bed Bath & Beyond." She let go to check the name tag dangling from the silver package. "I hope it's that blender I registered for."

Charlotte sidestepped away from the crazy bride, rubbing her wrist. Who'd have thought a baker would need to incorporate hazard pay into her billing? Now, if she could just sneak back into the house, maybe Brittany would keep ogling gifts and forget the whole thing.

"I'm so sorry." Adam appeared at Charlotte's side, holding a plate full of cheese, crackers, and mini sausages and grinned even as he shook his head. "Brittany gets a little . . . aggressive when she's had alcohol."

Then why in the world would you give it to her? Charlotte forced a smile as Brittany began picking up packages and shaking them. "No problem. She must have forgotten what she'd wanted. I'll just head back—"

"Oh, right. Will. She had been calling for Will." Adam turned and cupped his hand beside his mouth as he shouted across the torchlit yard. "Hey, Will!"

"No, really, it's fine." Her panicked heart drifted toward her toes as she realized she was fighting a losing battle. She felt heat run up her neck and across her ears. Could this get any worse?

Charlotte reluctantly followed Adam's gaze and finally saw Will standing near the back fence, surrounded literally on all sides by giggling blondes—well, and one brunette. One had her arm linked through his, head tilted back, laughing as Will gestured dramatically with his can of Coke. The other flipped her hair back flirtatiously and leaned in, putting her hand on his arm and saying something softly that made Will laugh.

All of them were tall, leggy, and gorgeous—and definitely did not look as if they baked or taste tested very many sweets.

Not that Charlotte had a reason to be jealous. Will wasn't hers. He was Melissa's. And speaking of—was one of them Melissa?

She had to know. For no logical reason—or at least, no reason she was willing to admit to herself—she had to find out. She turned to Adam and offered what she hoped came across as a casual smile. "I was hoping Melissa would get to try one of the petit fours. Where is she?"

"Oh, she's not here." Adam shoved a cracker topped with cheese in his mouth and kept talking. "She doesn't ever come to this kind of stuff with Will."

Really? Was she so secure in their relationship that she didn't mind the way he acted with other women? Or did she not know how he acted when she wasn't here?

A voice whispered inside her head: *None of your business.*

But every fiber of her being screamed otherwise. She hated for any woman to get caught up in the lies, the triangle, the heartache that she'd been trapped in for so long. Her eyes narrowed as she took in the sight of the brunette leaning in close to Will's shoulder and feeding him something off her plate.

She had dodged a bullet with Will, that was for sure. He was exactly like her ex—the same kind of guy she swore never to get involved with again. She wouldn't put herself or Zoe through that kind of torture. And apparently, she'd proven that she couldn't trust her instincts—Will had seemed really nice at the bakery, very gentlemanly and mature.

But maybe that level of nice was just another method of flirting.

Her breath tightened at the close call. She'd almost done it again.

She strode away from Adam without another word and back toward the house, half hoping Will hadn't seen her and half hoping he had. If Melissa ever came in The Dough Knot with him . . . well, she'd have a moral dilemma to deal with then. It wasn't her business, not directly, but seriously, how could all of Will's friends—Brittany and Adam, especially—treat Melissa this way? Why hadn't anyone ever told her the kind of man Will really was?

Why hadn't anyone ever told Charlotte about her ex?

She rushed back into the kitchen, paused, and took a deep breath. She couldn't afford to let the anger from the past get the best of her.

But she could sure as heck make certain never to repeat it.

This was why Will hated parties. A bunch of loud people who only grew louder after they'd been drinking, and perfectly made-up women who seemed to think of him as either a child to be doted on or a fish to be caught.

Exhibit A—the girl who kept trying to feed him off her plate. It was weird, and he didn't know how to stop it without causing a scene. And Brittany had already caused plenty of those all by herself. He didn't need to up the tally. What had she been doing earlier, dragging some party guest through the yard and hollering, before abandoning her near the gift table?

He caught a glimpse of the woman's back as she headed toward the house, anger stiffening her spine. She tossed back her hair, and Will swallowed the lump of cracker lodged in his throat. Charlotte?

His heart soared. He hadn't realized she'd already

brought the petit fours. He wanted to see her. Badly. Wanted to apologize for the way he'd acted at The Dough Knot, wanted to confess his fear and coward's way of handling it.

Wanted to get away from these Stepford blondes who were fighting over him in that subtle, catty way only women could.

His initial plan—to leave the obligatory party early after charming Adam, Brittany, and the other guests into forgiving his lack of sociability—had backfired. He'd intended to be the life of the party just long enough to make a quick escape. But now he had a herd of women sticking close enough to him that he was suffocating on the mix of perfume and hair spray, and he didn't know how to bail.

If he'd still been in his college frat-boy days, this would have been a dream. Bragging rights to take back to the frat house, full of exaggerated stories and plenty of kissing and telling.

But those days were long over, and he didn't miss them a single bit. Now he didn't want a conquest. He didn't want a story. He just wanted to leave.

And he really wanted to try one of Charlotte's petit fours.

He disentangled his arm from the red, inch-long nails of the brunette gripping it, and smiled to soften the rejection for her. Maybe he could catch Charlotte if he hurried, try to smooth over last week's bakery bailout, and load up a plate of goodies for Melissa. He couldn't let himself get *too* close to Charlotte—that was still unwise.

But taking a week away from the bakery to get her out of his head obviously hadn't worked, given the spike in his heart rate when he spotted her a minute ago. If he couldn't be around Charlotte without wanting more, and if he couldn't be away from her without nearly obsessing over her—what option remained?

She had sneaked inside his head, and was getting dangerously close to his heart. The heart he'd put on hold indefinitely. But now he wasn't sure he could get it back even if he wanted to.

He took a few steps toward the house. The curly-haired blonde to his left pulled him back.

"Where are you going?" She batted lashes so heavily coated with mascara he wondered how she could manage to blink.

"Inside." Without a second glance, he tugged free and resumed his trek through the yard. Did women actually think this level of clinginess and control worked? Then again, in his former life, it probably would have. He shook his head in disgust over his own past. It had taken Melissa's accident to awaken him.

And that just made him feel all the more guilty. If he'd been a better man, maybe that accident would never have happened.

His steps faltered. Maybe he didn't need a petit four. Maybe he didn't need to find Charlotte, after all.

Maybe he just needed to keep hiding. Right out there in the open, in that circle of beautiful, shallow females who only confirmed he was doing the right thing and missing absolutely nothing of substance by avoiding a relationship.

Then he glimpsed Charlotte through the window, stacking giant silver trays. He opened the door.

She looked up, windblown and clearly aggravated, judging by the tight lines around her mouth and the pinch between her eyebrows. Then he remembered—Brittany. Charlotte had been the woman he'd seen Brittany toting around outside. He'd been so glad to see her, he'd forgotten about Brittany being . . . well, Brittany. No wonder Charlotte looked as if she could smash someone in the face with a petit four.

Which looked delicious. He stepped inside, closer to the dessert table, and smiled at Charlotte and her friend. But Charlotte's tense expression didn't relax. Uh-oh. Maybe it wasn't just about Brittany.

Her redheaded coworker's eyes widened. She looked back and forth between Charlotte and Will and then snatched the trays from Charlotte's hands. "I'll load the van." And just like that, she was gone.

He glimpsed the anger in Charlotte's eyes and was tempted to call the redhead back as mediator. Instead, he took a bite of an orange-topped petit four. "Wow, these are amazing. Good call."

He wasn't exaggerating. It was the one of the best desserts he'd ever tasted. He'd had never thought to try the orange caramel flavor with cinnamon and pecans, but it worked. And was that nutmeg?

Charlotte was inspiring him to want to cook again. He hadn't thought twice about ingredients in years, but everything he tasted of hers made him want to examine it to find the best part. Find *her* best part.

She softened, as if on autopilot, before quickly stiffening again. "Thanks. Now if you'll excuse me, I've got to go." She started to push past him toward the front of the house.

"Charlotte." He stepped in front of her, and her eyebrows shot up.

"I said, excuse me."

He'd heard her. Still didn't like it. "What's the hurry?"

"I've got to be somewhere." She checked her wrist, then must have realized she hadn't put her watch on. She tapped her back pocket and pulled out her cell phone. "I'm running late."

Something else was up. She wouldn't make eye contact. Was this because of his quick departure and week-long absence from The Dough Knot? He cleared his throat. "Listen, about last week . . ."

She didn't give him a chance to explain—not that he'd totally figured out the right words to say, anyway. Avoiding his eyes, she shrugged, gaze glued to the floor. "Forget it."

"No, I clearly hurt your feelings. I want to make it right."

"It's not a big deal."

She was trying to move past him again, and if he didn't relent soon, he'd just be a jerk. Still, he wanted her to hear him out.

But what excuse did he have that he could actually voice? "I left in a hurry, and it was rude. I'm sorry." The facts, if nothing else.

"You have nothing to apologize for." She cut him a sharp glance, one that made him wish she'd go back to averting her gaze. "You owe me nothing."

Ouch. "I thought we were friends." He wanted to be more than that. Didn't he? He didn't know anymore. He only knew that the thought of Charlotte holding anything against him made him want to fix it. He already missed the friendly banter they'd created over his weeks of Tuesday visits to The Dough Knot. The thought of losing that made his head throb. "Aren't we friends?"

She lifted her chin. "You're my client."

That one cut even deeper. He silently stepped aside. She slipped past him without a backward glance.

He knew, because he watched her leave.

Chapter Five

"Why are all men the same?" Charlotte struggled to keep her voice down as she rinsed out a mixing bowl in the industrial kitchen sink.

It was Tuesday afternoon, but Zoe was in the dining room, eating a chocolate-chip bagel and baking pretend cupcakes. She'd been out of school for the day for teacher conferences, so Charlotte had set her up at one of the tables with a rainy-day toy baking set she'd stashed for just such an occasion.

"Is that a rhetorical question?" Julie paused to swipe a lick of cheesecake batter from a spatula before tossing it in the other side of the sink. "Or are you actually expecting an answer?"

"I don't know." Charlotte dried the bowl and set it on the counter. She needed to zest the lemons for the next batch of lemon bars. Needed to put the leftover cake pops from the Hannigans' birthday party in the front display case. Needed to sort through inventory for their upcoming order. She was pretty sure they were running low on bakery boxes.

But all she could think about was whether or not Will would show up at 5:40 and what on earth she would say if he did.

"Rhetorically, I agree." Julie ran hot water over the dirty dishes, then shut it off. "But technically, it's not really true. You just had a bad experience."

"Bad *experiences*." Charlotte emphasized the plural.

"Every guy isn't the same as Zoe's dad."

"I know." Maybe. But Julie didn't know the whole story. Didn't know that Charlotte had been the other woman. Didn't know about Will and the mistake she'd almost made—*again*.

Unless Charlotte was terribly mistaken, Julie didn't have any major mistakes in her life that she was still trying to atone for. She wasn't a single mom struggling to overcome a bad reputation—one so mottled she still wasn't entirely sure which stories were lies anymore.

She grabbed the grater and pulled a lemon from the bottom drawer of the refrigerator. Zoe's sing-song voice carried from the front of the shop as she made up a poem about her toy cupcake. *My cupcake is big, my cupcake is yummy, my cupcake will go straight to my tummy.*

Zoe deserved better than this. Better than a mom who still carried a Scarlet Letter of shame. Better than a mother who was still somehow drawn to the Wrong Guy.

My cupcake is glad, it never has a frownie, my cupcake is marrying the crumbly Mr. Brownie.

Better than a dad who allowed his fiancée to talk him out of his daughter's life.

Her grater worked faster over the lemon. Would she and Zoe ever be able to settle down with someone predictable? Safe? Committed?

"Careful there, Boss." Julie's voice rang a warning as she started digging through their pile of bakery reject cookies. "Don't want to add knuckles to the ingredient list in those lemon bars."

Some days, Charlotte felt like a reject cookie herself. Good enough for someone to be attracted to initially, but not worth selling out for. "It's just . . . you know Will?"

"From the Bridezilla wedding? Of course." Julie popped one of the too-crispy-to-sell cookies in her mouth and mumbled around it. "Your very own Mr. Darcy."

"Hardly. Mr. Darcy isn't available. But you wouldn't have known it from the way he flirted at that engagement party." Just remembering that crowd of women gathered around him twisted her stomach. But not from jealousy—just out of respect for Melissa. That was all.

"Wow, really?" Julie reached for another reject, eyes wide as she absorbed the news. "You wouldn't have known it from the way he interacts with you here at the bakery."

Charlotte's hand stilled on the next lemon. "What do you mean?"

"You haven't noticed the way Will looks at you?" Julie asked incredulously. "I thought it was obvious. That's why I always tried to leave you two alone. I was playing cupid."

Cupid aiming at the wrong heart.

Charlotte began to zest again, her thoughts racing. Was Julie right? She'd automatically assumed she'd been leading Will on in her attraction to him. Apparently, that was what she did, if the accusations of her ex and his fiancée had any merit. Was it possible Will had been coming on to *her* instead?

But Julie didn't say flirting. She'd said "the way he looks at you." Which to Charlotte, went a lot deeper than mere witty conversation or banter.

Eyes didn't lie.

Either way, she didn't want to be that woman. No, wait. She *wasn't* that woman. Why did she keep forgetting that she hadn't known about her ex's fiancée? She definitely hadn't been living a lifestyle she was proud of at the time, but she would have never cheated on someone she loved—or helped someone else cheat. Still, the accusations from years ago lingered. She was . . . stained.

Charlotte had to avoid any man the least bit like Zoe's charming, attractive, flirty father. It was too risky, too complicated. Too dangerous.

She dropped her grater and grabbed a reject cookie for herself. "Cupid needs to quit fooling around and bring me suspenders and a bow tie."

"What does that mean?"

"Suspenders and a bow tie. You know, a nice, predictable, stable nerd."

Julie stopped chewing and stared at Charlotte as if she'd completely lost her mind.

"Doesn't matter," Charlotte said. She tossed the remainder of the cookie into the trash can. "Doesn't matter at all."

It wasn't quite 5:40 yet.

Will hesitated outside the front door of The Dough Knot, lingering just out of sight of the picture window that boasted the bakery's name in gold script. A little girl sat at a table inside, head down as she scribbled on top of a—was that a toy cupcake?—with a pink marker. Other than that, the bakery appeared empty. Charlotte must have been in the kitchen, or on the other side of the counter that he couldn't quite see from this angle.

He paced back and forth on the sidewalk, hands in his pockets, braced against a sudden gust of September wind. The temperature was starting to change, some days dipping lower and hinting at the coming autumn, other days burning hot and clinging tight to summer. Like the world couldn't make up its mind if it was going to transition or not.

He knew the feeling.

If he went inside The Dough Knot and told Charlotte everything that his heart wanted to say, he'd be free falling through transition himself.

But if he didn't . . . well, how could he keep this up? He'd have to buy cookies for Melissa elsewhere, and that was the least of his problems. He saw Charlotte's face every night before he closed his eyes and woke with her the first thing on his mind.

Yesterday at the gym, he was trying to teach old Mr. Conrad how to lift weights without throwing his back out.

Adam had been there, following him around and bending his ear about Charlotte.

"Go for it, man," Adam said. "You know we've been trying to set you up with someone for months now. Don't you want the bliss me and Brittany have?" He winked.

Conrad, a feisty old geezer who had to be ninety if he was a day, seemed to have an opinion on everything—including Will's love life. "Sounds like this girl's a keeper," he huffed between bicep curls. "You better make your move or somebody else will." He grinned, showing a mouthful of perfectly white, straight dentures. "Or if you don't, give me her number."

"He's right," Adam said as he spotted Will on the weight bench. "How come you're dragging your feet? You could do a lot worse than Charlotte, dude."

No kidding. Charlotte easily beat every one of those superficial women who had been at the party the other night, without even trying. Maybe that was *why* she beat them. She didn't try. She didn't have to. She was real. Had substance. Was sweet—and beautiful, without having to flaunt it. She was just . . . Charlotte.

And that was more than enough.

But it wasn't about simply not being single anymore. If that was the case, he'd be content being Free Willy for life. His priorities shifted the day that SUV crashed into Melissa's car, and it wasn't his decision to shift them away from her now. Over and over again he tried to explain that to Adam, who didn't get it. After denying Mr. Conrad Charlotte's digits and after a pointless argument with Adam, his friend had finally resorted to assuring Will that in a few weeks, all of their wedding stuff would be over and Will's life could go back to normal.

But normal meant only seeing Charlotte every Tuesday at 5:40, and he was pretty certain that wasn't going to be good enough anymore.

He checked his watch: 5:32.

Maybe it was time for a few changes after all.

He opened the door to The Dough Knot.

The little girl looked up, pink marker in hand, and smiled—Charlotte's smile. Was it? Yes. It had to be. She had the same dimple in her cheek too. But how—

"Welcome to The Dough Knot." She said it so properly, he couldn't help but grin. She clearly had a lot of practice.

"Thank you." He couldn't stop staring at her. Charlotte had a daughter? He didn't see that coming.

"Want a bite?" She held out the cupcake she'd been working on so diligently.

He hesitated, then took a step forward and accepted the offering. "It looks delicious."

She capped her marker with a flourish. "It is."

Confident little thing. Good for Charlotte. He pretended to take a bite of the icing and made a show of mumbling his appreciation. "Best cupcake in the store."

The little girl's shoulders straightened and she twisted her braid around one finger. "One day it will be. When the shop is mine, of course."

She couldn't be more than what . . . five years old? Six, tops? And she was already planning on taking over the world. He grinned wider. "When it's yours, will you give me a discount on cupcakes?"

She rolled in her bottom lip, thinking hard. Then she nodded solemnly. "But only if you buy two. Then you can get a third one free."

He leaned his head back and laughed.

Charlotte appeared through the door behind the counter leading from the kitchen. "Can I help—oh." She looked at her watch, which made him look at his.

5:40.

They locked eyes. Charlotte tucked her hair behind her ears then crossed her arms over her flour-streaked apron. "The usual?"

"Yes." But that wasn't all. Not today. He strode toward the counter. "Your daughter is just like you."

A flicker of pride danced through her eyes before the wall went back up. "It's just me and Zoe, so she doesn't have many other influences, I guess."

"I didn't realize you were a single mom."

She grabbed a bakery box and began loading in the snickerdoodles. "Well, less than two weeks ago, you didn't know my name, either."

Somehow, she was right. How they'd managed to connect so quickly before ever even introducing themselves was beyond him. But that didn't matter anymore. "You've done a great job."

She glanced at Zoe, then at him, before concentrating back on the cookie order. "Thank you." She cleared her throat. "Will that be all?"

Forget this distant, professional thing. He leaned across

the counter, crowding her space a little in order to speak privately. "There's something else I need."

Her breath hitched, and her neck flushed. "Oh, right. You never picked a cake flavor for the wedding. I really need to get that on the books."

Cake flavor—oh, for crying out loud. He wracked his brain for a flavor, any flavor besides vanilla, which would just make it obvious he didn't care anymore. Brittany and Adam were just going to smash the stuff in each other's faces and drive away married, anyway. Wasn't that all that mattered? "The chocolate one."

"Plain chocolate or the white chocolate?" She pulled a notebook from near the register and clicked a pen.

He shrugged. "Sure."

She shot him a glare. "Will."

"Either is fine."

She huffed. "Did you even think about this decision?"

No, but he'd thought plenty about a different one. "Go out with me."

Charlotte's face drained of color.

That hadn't come out as planned. He'd intended to be more intentional, more romantic. More like those characters in those Austen books she was always talking about. He cleared his throat. "Please?"

"Mom! Say yes!"

Oh, man. He'd forgotten they had an audience.

"He's super handsome. And he liked my cupcakes." Zoe grinned, her arms draped over the back of her chair.

"Zoe." Charlotte closed her eyes and forced herself to breathe. "I think Julie needs you in the kitchen."

"Really? She never needs help." Zoe slowly climbed down from her chair, her expression a mixture of confusion and happiness. "Are you sure?"

"Positive." She ushered Zoe around the counter and through the swinging door. "Wash your hands first. Julie! Um, let Zoe help, okay?"

"Help me with wha—" Julie caught the swinging kitchen door, took one look at Will, and her mouth dropped open. "Oh. Right. With *that*." She grabbed Zoe's hand and tugged. "Come on, kiddo. Want to lick the spoons?"

The door swung shut against Zoe's exuberant agreement.

Will rested his elbows on the counter between them, hoping she wouldn't hear even at this distance how fast his heart was beating. "Seems I have one vote in my favor." And a foot in his mouth, but maybe she wouldn't notice that either.

"I can't believe you." Charlotte's tone now possessed a steady sternness that threatened to rock Will back a step. Two-thirds Mama bear and one-third elementary school principal.

He blew out a short breath. "Look, I'm really sorry I asked in front of Zoe." He lifted both hands in defense. "I wasn't thinking. I know you probably have rules about that."

Charlotte let out a strangled laugh. "Rules about—are you kidding me?" She reached up and briefly pinched the bridge of her nose as if gathering her composure. "Let me ask you a question. What would Melissa say about this?" She gestured between them.

He hesitated. That was the question of the hour in his

own heart, but if Melissa meant what she'd been preaching at him for weeks now . . .

He calculated his answer carefully. "I think Melissa would be proud of me."

Charlotte's eyes widened. "*Proud* of you? Of all the nerve . . ."

"You're right. It took nerve to ask you out." So much so, that in fact, he was starting to wonder why he had. The longer this went on, the more his pride was curling into the fetal position. "You know, a simple no would have sufficed."

"There's nothing simple about a practically engaged man asking me out on a date. Again!" Her face flamed so hot he could have baked a cookie on her cheekbones. With anger? Or embarrassment? He could relate to both at the moment himself.

Then her words registered. *Again*—what *again*? He'd never asked her out before this moment. Never even hinted at it. "What do you mean, practically engaged?" He hadn't dated anyone in years, much less proposed.

"I'm not stupid, Will."

"What are you talking about, Charlotte?"

She pointed to her bare ring finger, as if playing charades would help him comprehend. "You. And Melissa."

She shook her head, palms landing with a slap against the countertop. "You know, I fell for this kind of thing years ago, but I won't do it again." Her cheeks grew redder and her voice louder the longer she ranted. "Melissa deserves a lot better than this. I don't even know her, but no woman deserves to be tricked and manipulated and treated like—"

"Melissa is my sister."

She stopped midlecture. Arms braced against the counter. Cheeks glowing with indignation. Mouth open. She swallowed. "Sister?"

"Yes. Sister. What did you think—" Oh. *Oh*. He snorted. "You thought . . ."

She dropped her head to rest on her elbows, hiding her face. "I can't believe I assumed she was your girlfriend."

He tried to remember all of his references to Melissa during his interactions with Charlotte. He couldn't grasp details to give merit to the confusion, but clearly he'd never specified who his sister was.

But that still left one question. "Now that you know I'm not a total sleazebag and hitting on you while I have a girlfriend . . . will you let me take you to dinner?"

Charlotte snorted back a laugh, her head still buried. "I can't even look at you right now. I'm going to burst into flames I'm so embarrassed."

He wanted to see that. He gently prodded her bent arm. "Waiting on an answer here." Third time was the charm. "Charlotte? Will you go on a date with me?"

Zoe suddenly barreled back through the kitchen door. "Mom! Say yes. Please!"

Julie popped her head around the frame. "We really need better soundproofing back here."

Charlotte lifted her head, cheeks red, eyes closed. Hope built in Will's chest. She was caving. Slowly.

"Mom, if you say yes, I won't eat sweets for an entire day." Zoe's wide-eyed, solemn promise couldn't have been more perfect if Will had planned it. He held his breath.

Charlotte looked at her daughter, then at Will. Then at Julie, who gave a thumbs-up, then back at Will, and released a sigh. "Make it two days."

"Two?" Indignation filled the little girl's voice.

Will raised his eyebrows at her. Mouthed the word *please*. She frowned, twisted her braid, and then nodded. "Okay. It's a deal, Mommy."

Charlotte met Will's eyes and offered a timid smile. "It's a deal."

Chapter Six

"I can't believe you thought I was dating my sister."

"Will!" Charlotte kicked him under the table, stifling a laugh. Talk about poor timing for their waiter. He delivered a fresh basket of chips and fled the scene.

When he was gone, she leaned forward across the white tablecloth and lowered her voice. At this point in the evening, they'd probably annoyed their table-neighbors enough with all their laughter. "I didn't think you were dating your sister. I didn't *know* she was your sister. Big difference there."

Once again, those hazel eyes kept drawing her in. All of her doubts and fears about this date had dissipated halfway into their appetizer of queso and tortilla chips.

Earlier Zoe had caught her double-checking her reflection in the mirror. "Don't worry, Mommy," she said. "You look like a princess."

Now she was beginning to feel like one.

And it was about time she'd found someone remotely prince-like.

Will leaned back in his chair, one arm slung along the back. "Eh, details." He winked.

She shook her head. "You're incorrigible."

He snagged a chip from the basket and popped it in his mouth. "I was once. Not anymore."

"Because of the military?"

He shrugged. "Partly. You get used to being corrected pretty quickly in basic training." He picked up another chip, but didn't eat it. Just turned it end over end in his hand, as if he'd gotten lost in thought. Or in the past.

She could relate to that. She sensed he wanted to say more, but couldn't. Wouldn't? Maybe it was her turn. After all, he'd taken the first step in asking her out. Now that Melissa wasn't an issue between them—obviously—Charlotte had no reason not to see what could develop.

That didn't make her feel any less terrified, but at least it offered possibilities.

"Do you regret leaving the military?" The words slipped out before she could fully weigh them. If that was the reason for his hesitations in their conversation, then her bringing it up could backfire. She held her breath.

"No, I'm happy in the reserves." The chip turned faster in his hands. "There were some family issues that needed to be taken care of a few years ago, and well—I didn't have much choice."

Family issues. She was a single mom. Say no more.

"I'm still trying to figure out what to do next. I don't

want to be a trainer all my life, though the time in the gym has been productive."

She definitely concurred with that, but didn't have the nerve to say so. "Okay, so no full-time military, and no permanent training plans in the cards for you. What else do you like to do?"

He studied the chip in his hand as if it held the secret to some long-buried question. "I used to cook a lot, actually."

"Really?" She raised her eyebrows. "Are you thinking about giving me competition?"

He shot her a glance. "Cook. Not bake."

"Lucky for you."

He grinned at her tease. "Maybe it's lucky for *you*."

She was already feeling pretty lucky just sitting here across from him. And now she really wanted him to cook for her sometime.

Will finally dropped the chip, giving her his full attention once more and making her stomach cartwheel with the intensity of it. "So, what about you? Any regrets?"

Speaking of single motherhood. She bit her lower lip, wishing she had a chip to spin now. She didn't want to lie—and he'd already met Zoe. But still . . .

"That word—regret—it seems so harsh." She lifted one shoulder. "I don't regret Zoe. Not for one single second. I just sometimes regret the way all of that came about."

He nodded. "Bad breakup?"

"Ha. That's an understatement. More like shocking." She hesitated. "When I told him I was pregnant, he didn't want to be part of Zoe's life. At all." The words poured out, faster and faster, as if some inner dam had burst. She hadn't vented this story in a long time. "Apparently it cramped his fiancée's style. I haven't seen him since he wrote me a pretty pathetic check and told me to hit the road."

"That's unbelievable. Zoe is . . . just . . . she's . . ." Will hesitated, as if searching for the right words.

She waited, fully understanding his dilemma—Zoe blew her mind daily with her sweetness, her charm, her talents. She was so blessed.

"She's just so awesome."

Exactly. She *was* awesome. "Thank you." It was completely her dad's loss. Zoe deserved more than a donor—she deserved a full-time father figure to dote on her.

All the more reason for Charlotte to choose carefully.

She picked a chip out of the basket and began breaking it into several pieces on her plate. "I never bothered trying to sue. Couldn't afford a lawyer at the time, and decided I'd rather make my own way than drag him unwanted into Zoe's life."

And God had provided for her—for *them*—one step at a time the entire way. She still didn't deserve such grace.

"Wait a minute." Will frowned, scooting his water glass out of the way so he could lean forward. He braced his arms against the table and lowered his voice. "Did you say *fiancée* a minute ago?"

She'd wondered if he'd caught that part. She nodded, trying unsuccessfully to throttle back the fear. "My boyfriend—Zoe's dad—was engaged to another woman while we were together." Even now, the shame of that truth rubbed a raw spot.

"And you didn't know." It wasn't a question. The

matter-of-fact way he uttered it warmed a long-frozen spot in Charlotte's heart.

"Right. I didn't know."

The usual rush of memories—vivid reminders of that cold football game, that horrible showdown in the stadium in front of the entire school, the pounding of her broken heart now beating for two—didn't come. Instead, there was calm. Peace. As if she'd finally taken a step away from her past and into her future.

Will cleared a spot as the waiter brought their plates of enchiladas. When the waiter had refilled their water glasses and left, Will turned back to her with eyes she could only describe as kind. "You've been through a lot."

She spread her napkin in her lap. "Not as much as some."

Will took that in, nodding. "Not as much as some. But I'm sorry you—and Zoe—had to go through that kind of pain."

"I should have known better." She picked up her knife and began to cut into the mass of beef and cheese on her plate. "He didn't pass the eye test."

"The eye test?"

"The eyes don't lie. It's what I tell Zoe all the time." She forked a piece of the cheesy tortilla. "He never could look me directly in the eyes."

"What a coward."

She could come up with a dozen other accurate, suitable names, but she was tired of talking about her ex. "That's enough about me." She blew on her next bite to cool it off, grateful that the mountain in her past was already starting to fade behind them. "Tell me more about Melissa. Are you guys pretty close?"

"Nah. I just bring her two giant cookies every week because I hate her guts." Will said it with such a straight face she almost snorted her food.

And just like that, they were back to laughing, annoying their table-neighbors, sharing bites of their dinner—and making Charlotte wonder why they hadn't done this a long, long time ago.

He hadn't told her about Melissa. About the paralysis, about his regrets, about the night his selfish mistake almost destroyed one of the people he loved most in the world. He'd had the perfect window to disclose it all, but he couldn't make himself put a damper on such a great evening.

As he pulled his truck into the parking lot next to Charlotte's apartment, he hoped that decision wouldn't bite him later. He swung into an empty space. Julie's car was parked in the spot next to them—or he could only assume it was Julie's, judging by the pink fuzzy dice hanging from the rearview mirror, The Dough Knot decal on the back windshield, and a bumper sticker that read My Cupcakes Could Beat Up Your Honor Student.

"You and Julie are good friends?" He shifted the truck into park, not in a hurry to get out and end their night.

"A lot more than that. We're almost like business partners. She's part time at the bakery and helps me out with Zoe when I need it." Charlotte tucked her hair behind her ears, eyes bright even in the dimness of the truck cab. She always lit up when talking about something—or someone—important to her. Her theory was right—eyes don't lie. "She's my best friend."

"That's great you get to work together." He gestured toward the apartment. "So, did she give you a curfew?" He hoped midnight. Though he doubted Charlotte would turn into a pumpkin or however that fairy tale went. And the whole "left her shoe" behind thing was a genius way to get a guaranteed call back from the prince. Too bad he and Charlotte were in his truck tonight, or he might try to play the same card.

Because right now, he couldn't imagine waiting until next Tuesday at 5:40 to see Charlotte again.

"She didn't say." Charlotte glanced at the clock on his dashboard. "It's not quite ten o'clock yet."

"Then there's plenty of time to ask you a question." He leaned toward her, unable to resist the magnetic pull she had on him since the first moment he stepped into The Dough Knot and saw her in that cute little apron.

"What question?" Her hand brushed his on the truck seat, and their fingers threaded together as if they'd had a lifetime of practice.

"A very important one." His eyes lowered to her lips, pink and glossy, and a hint of color flushed her cheeks to match.

"Important how?" She lifted her chin a notch, eyes expectant. Waiting.

He leaned an inch closer, his voice deepening. His heart started a stampede in his chest. "Important to me."

Her dark lashes fluttered shut.

He shouldn't do this. It was their first date. But it felt as if he'd known her his entire life. As if all those weeks of small talk at the bakery had counted as dates leading up to this moment. He had no intention of wasting this moment or attempting to recreate it later. For the first time in a long time, he wanted to live right now. With Charlotte.

He pressed his lips against hers.

She kissed him back, her grip on his hand tightening. He used it to pull her closer on the bench seat, then cupped his hand around her neck and deepened their kiss. Her free hand clutched the front of his shirt, wrinkling the green button-down he'd spent fifteen minutes ironing earlier that evening.

He didn't mind.

She broke away first, turning to press her cheek against his and catch her breath. "That wasn't a question."

It had most definitely been a statement. He grinned, rubbing his cheek against hers before pulling away to look her in the eyes. "I was just going to ask if I could kiss you."

She studied him a second. "No you weren't. You had a real question, and you got sidetracked."

She'd nailed that one. His eyes couldn't lie, either, apparently. He grinned back, wanting to kiss her again. He leaned forward to do just that, but she pressed her palm flat against his chest and held him off. "Wait a second. What's the real question?"

He stole a quick peck on her cheek anyway. "Brittany and Adam's couple's shower is coming up. And I want you to come."

"I have to, silly. I'm delivering the cookie cake, remember?"

She was even more adorable when confused. He reached

up to tuck her hair behind her ear before she could do it first. "I know. I mean, I want you to come with me. As my date."

It would completely throw Adam for a loop after their conversation the other day at the gym, but he'd explain ahead of time what had changed, if need be. His friend would be happy for him.

Hopefully, Melissa would be too.

His exuberance dimmed slightly. Melissa. He had put the guilt out of his head all this time, wrapped up in the joy of this . . . this *thing* developing with Charlotte.

Would Melissa ever have this kind of relationship with someone? Ever feel this connection? Her fiancé had bailed on her. Her accident had been Will's fault. It didn't seem fair, or right, that he was free to do as he pleased while she remained so limited.

He tried to shove the doubts away, but they wouldn't quite budge. Maybe he was moving too fast. Maybe he should slow down and not get involved—

Charlotte slid closer to him, craned her neck, and planted a soft kiss on his cheek. "I'd love to come with you."

He shoved the doubts away and returned her kiss.

Chapter Seven

How could one man possibly be so talented? Will obviously possessed a variety of survival skills from his time in the service. He knew how to iron, could parallel park on a dime, and sang along to the radio better than the majority of the artists playing. On top of that, boy, could he kiss.

And she hadn't even tasted his bacon mac and cheese yet.

Charlotte shot Will a sidelong glance as he helped her unload the snickerdoodle cookie cake onto the dessert table at the party, this time hosted by one of Adam's family members. Sometimes that niggling voice in her head tried to convince her that the man standing beside her was too good to be true. Why would a really attractive, sweet, gentlemanly type of guy be interested in her? Somehow, she'd only ever attracted the party guys, the liars, the permanent frat boys with a case of Peter Pan syndrome—afraid to grow up.

So far, Will Martin seemed like the real deal.

And it terrified her.

The other night after their date—and extended kissing session in the parking lot—she'd confided her uncertainties to Julie, who encouraged her to just sit back and enjoy the fairy tale.

She couldn't help but finish the unspoken cliché: enjoy the fairy tale . . . *while it lasted.*

She tried to shake off the negativity and sense of foreboding. Things were finally going well in the love department. She had to quit being so negative and take Julie's advice—enjoy the moment and quit expecting it to blow up in her face at any second.

She set a dessert knife beside the cake. Julie was off duty tonight, babysitting Zoe for her again, so Will offered to help her with whatever she needed. She tried not to think about how awkward it felt arriving at the party as part of a hired service, and then staying as a guest. But Will had invited her, and he was the best man, so surely no one minded.

She glanced down at her black dress pants and long-sleeved coral top. Hopefully this wasn't another semiformal party where the other women would be in cocktail dresses. Not that she had one to wear even if it had been. Rarely—no, never—did the occasion arise for her to need one anymore.

"Looks like you're all set here." Will stood behind her and rubbed her shoulders. "If you move that cake one more time, I'm going to think you have a twitch."

"You're right. I'll try to stop." She winced at how nervous she sounded. She automatically reached out to tweak something else on the table, then stopped herself and turned to face Will instead.

"I'm glad you came." He smiled down at her. "Everything looks great. And that cake is going to be the hit of the party."

"I'll say." Adam came into the kitchen, snagged a cherry tomato from the veggie tray at the next table, and popped it in his mouth. "Brittany's already worried about not fitting in her wedding dress after all of The Dough Knot's treats."

Charlotte winced. That was all she needed—Bridezilla to have another reason to attack. She eyed the veggie tray. Maybe she could put the cookie cake in the background and move the veggies—

"Don't even think about it." Will tucked her hand through the crook of his arm and tugged her away from the table. He bent to whisper in her ear. "Quit worrying so much. You did your job—now just be my date."

His warm voice in her ear sent shivers down her spine. She relaxed against his arm. "Sounds good."

They joined the rest of the guests in the sunroom at the back of the house, which had been decorated in red, black, and white. Bold—like Brittany. If Julie was here, they'd be discussing what color themes they'd use in their own weddings one day. Charlotte had never allowed herself to think that far ahead. It seemed so out of reach. But here, now, holding on to Will's arm . . . maybe purple. Purple and silver.

She sat on the edge of an empty loveseat. Will sank into the space next to her, and seconds later, a thin blonde in a red sheath dress squeezed in next to him. "Will Martin? I wondered if that was you." She shook her head, red lips parting. "It's been years."

Charlotte glanced around, suddenly realizing there was

a lot more red in the room than just the decorations. Every guest, even the guys, were wearing black, red, or some form of both. Brittany had paired red slacks with a black sparkly top. Adam wore a black polo, and the three women lining the couch opposite the sunroom wore a variety of black and red dresses.

Will hadn't told her. Probably hadn't realized, but his dark-wash jeans and black button-down must have been a lucky accident. She looked down. The clash of her bright coral top against the sea of red stood out like a lighthouse in a storm. Already she felt out of place, the hired help crashing the party, and now this.

Will hadn't noticed her discomfort. The blonde—who Charlotte now realized was an old friend from college—was still chatting him up. Another girl knelt on the floor by the loveseat and joined the conversation.

She shifted on the loveseat, wishing the small talk was over. Wishing she could snag a piece of cookie cake and disappear somewhere with Will. Wishing she wasn't so out of practice at these kind of events. She was used to being in the background, serving, not front and center, dating the popular guy.

A crowd was beginning to form around Will.

The flashback started, grainy around the edges, then gaining clarity. Zoe's father, football helmet tucked under his arm. Laughing with the college cheerleaders while she stood awkwardly behind him. Zoe's father, with his password-protected cell phone and constant texting.

No. She shook herself free of it.

A tall, dark-haired girl wearing a red and black

long-sleeved shirt plopped down on the ottoman that had been pulled up next to the couch. She smiled at Charlotte.

Charlotte's hopes lifted. Maybe she could find an ally in this sea of strangers.

"Hi. I'm Charlotte."

"Nice to meet you. Mia." They shook hands.

Mia sipped from her cup of red punch. "So . . . are you a friend of the bride or groom?"

Charlotte gestured to Will, still talking beside her. Warmth radiated from his arm pressed against hers. "I'm with the best man."

It felt good to say—maybe a little too good. One of those dangerous good feelings, the kind that nudged the subconscious and shouted *Warning, warning, you're putting too much into this!* But she ignored it. She wanted to belong, and right now, her claim to Will was the only thing keeping her anchored in the room.

"Will Martin?" Mia brightened. "I haven't seen him since college! Where's he been?"

"I—I don't know, really. He did some time in the army." She didn't really want to disclose how little she knew of Will's past. "He's a personal trainer now."

"I'll say." Mia winked over the rim of her punch cup. "Sign me up for that workout regimen."

Charlotte opened her mouth to reply, but Mia didn't give her a chance. She leaned in closer over the arm of the loveseat, lowering her voice. "So how'd you do it?"

Charlotte blinked. "Do what?"

"You know. Catch Free Willy." She gestured with her cup.

"Free—who?"

"Free Willy." Mia rolled her eyes. "We dubbed him that in college. He was the permanent bachelor type, you know. Never going to get married?"

Charlotte's tense shoulders relaxed. That made sense, after the comments Will had made recently about not getting out much and how this wedding was the first big social thing he'd done in forever. "That much of a hermit even then, huh?"

Mia almost sprayed her punch. She choked, laughing and pounding herself on the chest. "Will Martin? A hermit? Oh, that's a good one."

Okay, now that *didn't* make sense. A sinking sensation filled Charlotte's stomach—like being trapped in a roller-coaster car perched high at the very top, about to speed down the hill, with no way out.

Mia must have caught her confusion, because she calmed down and set her cup on the end table. "How long have you known Will?"

"A few months." Charlotte didn't bother to clarify that their first date had only been about a week ago.

"Ah." Mia's know-it-all smile held two parts pity and one part condescension. "Well, let's just say he didn't earn his nickname for lack of female options."

And the roller coaster roared down the hill.

Charlotte had often been accused of baking with her emotions. And right now, The Dough Knot's counters were littered with bottles of cayenne pepper, Louisiana hot sauce, and candied red hots.

She'd suffered through the end of the couple's shower last night, forcing smiles and participating in just enough conversation with Will to avoid causing a scene. It wasn't difficult, distracted as he was by most of the female party guests. To his credit, Will had made several attempts to draw Charlotte into the conversations, but after Mia's nearly endless accounting of the ghosts of girlfriends past, her heart wasn't in it.

Charlotte had always thought Zoe's father had been the consummate life-of-the-party frat boy. But apparently Will could have taught him a thing or two.

She sprinkled a liberal helping of cayenne pepper into her batter for chocolate chili cupcakes. The bakery was closed this Sunday afternoon. Zoe was in the front of the shop with the doors locked, coloring and whistling off-key while Charlotte took her aggression out in new recipes. Baking cleared her mind, gave her perspective, an outlet.

She glanced at the far counter holding two pans of Mexican hot chocolate brownies and a dozen spiced cookies.

So far, it wasn't working.

Her cell phone buzzed in her apron pocket. She pulled it out, saw Will's number, and dropped it back in. He tried twice more, and she forced herself to keep stirring. As much as she wanted to give him the opportunity to explain his way out of this, she knew what she'd seen. What she'd heard. What her instincts shouted.

She couldn't trust him. Zoe's dad had thrown excuse after excuse at her in the past, and she'd believed him time and time again. She'd been down this painful road before, and she couldn't allow herself—or Zoe—the chance to get more attached to Will than they already were. It wasn't fair.

She swallowed hard. None of it was fair. She'd tried to explain that to him last night when he'd dropped her off after the party, but he didn't get it. How could he? He hadn't walked in her shoes. He didn't feel the pang of old scars. He didn't bear the weight of regret and shame that she carried daily.

He didn't have a five-year-old looking to him for protection and guidance.

He'd lied to her, just like Zoe's dad. Presented himself to be one way, but proved the opposite once he got in social settings. Words were cheap—actions were expensive.

Her phone continued to buzz unanswered. Then the wall phone rang. She glanced at the caller ID. Not Will's number. She frowned. The Dough Knot wasn't officially open on Sundays—who would call her here? "Hello?"

A female voice. Not Will. "Hi there. Is this Charlotte?"

"Yes, this is Charlotte with The Dough Knot. I'm sorry, we're not open." She started to hang up.

"I was hoping to talk."

Huh?

"This is Melissa. Will's sister."

Charlotte sank against the counter. "Hi."

"I'm glad I caught you!" Melissa's upbeat voice brought instant ease. Charlotte relaxed slightly. "I called the bakery hoping the answering machine would give me your cell number or something." She paused. "I didn't want to ask Will for it because he doesn't know I'm calling."

Aha. "He must have told you about last night."

"He's frustrated. He doesn't get it. Thought things were going well with you guys." Melissa exhaled heavily. "Listen, Charlotte, I don't usually get involved in these types of things, but Will is my big brother—my only brother—and I thought maybe you should understand something about him."

Charlotte rolled her eyes and braced herself for the sisterly, biased defense.

"He's an idiot."

Charlotte snorted, then laughed.

"I'm serious, girl. He has no idea what he's doing anymore. He's been out of the dating game a long time, and with that big ol' compassionate heart of his, well—he doesn't know how to turn people away. Sometimes it gives the wrong impression."

"A long time, huh?" Charlotte wished she could see Melissa's eyes right now. But why would his sister lie to her?

"You have no idea. *Years*. He's put his life on hold for me, and—it's gotten ridiculous, to be honest. I've told him to get back out there a hundred times, but he never listened." Melissa hesitated. "Until you came along."

The admission thawed a piece of Charlotte's heart she'd tried hard to freeze. She clutched the phone a little tighter.

"That's why I'm calling. I hate to get in the middle and make this worse, but I had to try. Will is special, and you must be pretty special, too, if you could tug him free of this cycle he's been trapped in for years."

Charlotte closed her eyes against the dozens of thoughts vying for attention. "I—I don't know what to say."

"Just say you'll give him a chance. I don't know exactly what happened last night, but I know Will would never hurt anyone on purpose. He's grown up a lot in the last several years—I didn't really give him a choice in that matter."

"What do you mean?"

"Will hasn't told you?"

Her cell phone chirped, this time announcing an incoming text. Will.

Are you ok?

She hesitated, then shouldered the phone and wrote back. *Baking.*

I'm coming over.

She wanted to see him. But no. She had to protect her heart. Had to process all that Melissa just told her. She bit her lip, then typed back. *I'm really busy.*

Too late.

She jerked her head up, nearly dropping the phone as Zoe's voice hollered from the dining room. "Mom! Will's here!"

No. She closed her eyes. "Melissa, I'm sorry. Will just got here. I need to go."

"That's fine." Melissa's voice sped up, just like Will's did when he got in a hurry. "Just hear him out, okay? He's an idiot, for sure, but he's a great guy. I can vouch for that."

Charlotte blew out her breath. "I'll try."

"Thanks, Charlotte."

"Thanks for calling." She hung up, her heartbeat roaring in her ears.

Charlotte gave Zoe permission to unlock the front door—even though she was pretty sure she'd already done it. As she headed to the front, the bell chimed, confirming her suspicions.

Zoe held up a page from her coloring book of a giant cupcake, decorated in every color of the rainbow. Will exclaimed over it and waited while Zoe tore the page free and handed it to him. He folded it carefully and tucked it in his jeans pocket.

Charlotte waited behind the counter, hands shoved in her apron pockets, fiddling with her phone and wishing she had just answered. It'd be much easier to have this conversation over the phone than in person.

"Hey." Will made his way behind the counter. "We need to talk."

"You're right. In the kitchen." She led the way, wishing her heart wasn't so soft. Wishing he didn't smell so good. The door swung shut behind them, and she took a ragged breath. She didn't know what to believe. What to risk.

She wanted him to leave.

Wanted him to hug her.

"Are you still mad?" Will crossed his arms over his chest and studied her.

She shrugged, fiddling with a striped oven mitt. "I don't know what to think."

"I think you overreacted."

Her defenses flared. "Are you kidding me?"

He spread his hands wide. "I didn't do or say anything inappropriate at the party. And yet you were jealous."

"Jealous?" Hardly. More like just trying to survive and be wise. All of Melissa's precursors fled away in the light of his accusation. "I highly doubt that."

"I tried to bring you into the conversations. You checked out."

"I checked out because everyone there kept telling me all about Free Willy." She narrowed her gaze at him. "Did you know you're a legend?"

He closed his eyes briefly. "Free Willy. Are you serious? Someone told you that?"

"Yes." She blinked back tears of aggravation, slapping the oven mitt on the counter. "I already felt left out and out of place because of my stupid shirt and—"

He frowned. "Your shirt?"

She brushed it off. "Forget it. I just meant I didn't belong, and hearing all about your frat-boy, glory-day stories from those women . . . it was too much." No wonder he was confused. Even now, it sounded superficial, empty, shallow. Exactly like overreacting.

But in her heart, it was so much more than that. Her defensiveness morphed into frustration. With Zoe's father, for being such a jerk. With Will, for making her care so much so fast.

With herself.

"You know what I think?"

"Oh please, enlighten me." She didn't even try to keep the sarcasm from her tone.

"I think you're scared."

She blinked at him, and he came closer, walking toward her until he backed her against the counter.

"I think you're afraid to trust anyone again, and you're so used to searching for reasons not to, that you've started making them up."

"What? That's—that's crazy."

"Is it?" He had her pinned against the counter now, one

arm braced on either side. "I have a past, one I'm not proud of. That's a given."

Don't we all? a voice inside her head whispered. *You're a fine one to hold a grudge against someone because of their past.* Guilt nudged her stomach.

"But do you really believe I'm still Free Willy, Charlotte?"

She refused to look in his eyes, staring instead at the Adam's apple bobbing in his throat. A muscle in his jaw clenched. Was he nervous? Nervous because he was lying?

She risked a quick glance at his face, then away. No, not nervous. Anxious. Because this mattered to him.

She mattered to him.

She closed her eyes. Her head throbbed with all the indecision and uncertainty. "I don't know."

"You do know." His breath warmed her neck as he drew even closer. "Look in my eyes, Charlotte. Eyes don't lie. What are they telling you?"

She didn't want to look. Didn't want to know. Didn't want to risk it. What about Zoe? What about her own heart? She couldn't afford to let it break again. Couldn't afford to be made a fool again.

"Look at my eyes, Charlotte." He waited, not budging, making her decide.

She swallowed hard. Memories of her time with Will flittered through her mind. Their nonstop laughing at the restaurant. The way his eyes twinkled when he bought snickerdoodles. His warm kisses. Zoe's smile when he walked into the bakery.

She met his eyes. Saw how they brimmed openly with sincerity. With honesty.

With—love?

This wasn't Free Willy anymore. This was a man who had been changed and remade and who was taking his own risk by stepping out toward her. And all he asked is that she step out and meet him halfway.

He wasn't exactly safe. Or entirely predictable. But he'd looked into her eyes and she had seen the truth there. He had nothing to hide—and everything to give.

"I believe you." The whispered words had barely left her lips before he covered them with his own. He kissed her deeply, erasing any further doubts.

Then he pulled away. "Are you sure? Last chance to change your mind." He grinned, as if he knew there wasn't a chance at all.

"I'm sure." They kissed again, slower this time, until Charlotte's insides melted like the hot chocolate in her brownie batter.

She turned her head slightly, pressing her cheek against his. "I'm sorry I doubted you."

"Everyone heals in their own way, in their own timing." Will rested his forehead against hers before dropping a kiss against her nose. "Though I have to say, I'm glad it didn't take you any longer."

She swatted him with her oven mitt, then pulled him back for another kiss. "I thought I wanted safe."

"And I'm not?"

She smoothed the front of his shirt. "Safe is a bow tie. And suspenders."

Will tilted his head as he considered her. "So, safe to you is an elderly banker?"

"No!" She swatted him again and laughed. "That's what I always joke with Julie about. Bow tie and suspenders is my metaphor for some safe, predictable nerd. The opposite of a ladies' man." She hesitated. "Someone who won't leave."

"I get it. But safe can be way overrated." He gestured around them at the bakery. "You probably see it all the time. You know when married couples cut their cake and feed each other at the reception?"

Charlotte blinked at him. "I have no idea where you're going with this."

"Safe is feeding each other wedding cake, nice and polite and without a mess and passing napkins afterward."

He had a point. It sounded . . . a little boring, to be honest. Picture-perfect. Not entirely real.

He grinned down at her. "Wouldn't you rather have someone who smears icing on your face—" His finger gently trailed the length of her cheek. "And then gently kisses it off?"

She drew a ragged breath at his proximity. That actually sounded amazing. Maybe she'd had it wrong all this time. Maybe God hadn't sent her what she wanted because it hadn't been what she and Zoe needed at all.

"See? Safety is vastly overrated." He grinned and pulled her in for a tight hug. "Then again, for the record, I could probably rock a bow tie if I had to."

"But that's the best part." She smiled up at him, trusting fully for the first time in a long time—maybe ever. "You don't have to."

Chapter Eight

"*That might have been the most awkward toast in the history* of toasts." Will leaned close to whisper in Charlotte's ear.

She giggled, nudging him with her elbow. "Shh. They'll hear you."

They'd suffered through several wedding speeches so far at Adam and Brittany's rehearsal dinner, each one worse than the last. And he'd kept her laughing through all of them.

"I mean, come on. Pass the butter. That toast was *dry*."

Charlotte snorted, and elbowed him harder in the ribs, the sudden motion clanking her used silverware against her discarded plate. The man at the table opposite them shot an amused glance over his shoulder, and Charlotte immediately blushed.

They needed to quit acting juvenile. But Will couldn't help it. He loved the sound of her laughter. And before their big talk last Sunday in the bakery, he wasn't sure if he'd ever get to provoke it again. He wanted to hear it while he could, and never take it for granted.

The mother of the bride took the platform for her turn, and Will tried to tune her out so he wouldn't be tempted to tease again.

He pressed a kiss against Charlotte's hair instead, glad she had been able to accompany him tonight, and happier still that Julie was able to babysit Zoe and give her the chance to come. They really should do something special for her friend as a thank-you. She'd even helped deliver the desserts earlier, before whisking Zoe back to their apartment for a promised game of Chutes and Ladders. Maybe he'd pick up a gift card, or ask Melissa to make one of those crafty signs for her that she occasionally sold online.

Charlotte's marshmallow caramel apple cupcakes, each perched in a slow-rotating miniature Ferris Wheel, had earned an entire table over on the side of the banquet room. She'd thrown in some of her favorite double-chip brownies for the chocolate lovers as a last-minute addition—a side effect of her good mood the last few days.

A few last-minute wedding gifts filled another table. Will shook his head. At this rate, Adam and Brittany would be set with appliances, gift cards, and kitchen towels until their twenty-fifth wedding anniversary. Did newly married couples really need that much stuff?

Eloping was starting to look pretty good.

He slid his arm around the back of Charlotte's chair. Make that *really* good.

Brittany's mother finished her speech, blinking back tears as she expressed her joy over the upcoming ceremony.

That was sweet. Sounded like something his mom might have said at Melissa's rehearsal—had either of them been able to make it. He sobered, hating how the past seemed to constantly rear its head during moments like this—moments he should be able to just enjoy.

He shoved away the familiar guilt and clapped along with the others as Brittany's mom left the platform with instructions for everyone to hit the dessert table. He stood, pulling Charlotte's chair back for her, just as his cell phone vibrated in his pocket.

He motioned for Charlotte to get in line ahead of him, then checked the caller ID. Melissa. That was strange—she knew he was at the rehearsal tonight. Maybe she hadn't meant to call. But no, now that he looked at his screen, she'd already tried calling three other times while it had been set on silent.

His heart stammered. He quickly stepped in line behind Charlotte and jabbed the accept button, plugging one ear with his free hand as the volume in the room increased with laughter and exclamations over the desserts. "Melissa? I can barely hear you."

"Will." Her voice, weaker than usual, registered faintly through the phone speaker. "I need help. I fell."

Charlotte had no idea what had happened. She just knew there was no way Will could be driving the speed limit.

She watched the muscle in his jaw clench and unclench, watched his white-knuckled grip on the steering wheel, watched the agitated way he kept checking his rearview mirror as if daring a policeman to try and slow him down. "Is—is she okay?"

All she knew was they'd been standing in line to get a cupcake, when he'd grabbed her arm, said, "Melissa's in trouble, we've got to go," and ushered her out of the banquet room. It was the first time since she'd known him that he hadn't opened the truck door for her.

He had barely given her time to climb in before he gunned it across the parking lot.

He either hadn't heard her question or was ignoring her. She decided—for once—not to assume the worst, and repeated it. "Will? Is she okay?"

"I don't know." He bit the words off sharper than he probably meant to, but he didn't apologize.

"What happened?"

"Don't know that either."

Not a very productive phone call, then. Charlotte swallowed back her defensiveness and took a deep breath to attempt to calm her own nerves, reacting to his. He was obviously under a lot of stress and worried about his sister. She could forgive the lapse of manners.

And forget the questions. Guess she'd find out on the scene—wherever that was.

His truck screeched into the driveway of a small but cozy-looking yellow house. A wooden ramp climbed one side of the porch, concrete stairs laced in ivy on the other. A tiny picket fence lined the majority of the yard. He skidded to a stop and had his door open before the keys were even out of the ignition.

Charlotte hurried to catch up as he rushed toward the front door to what she presumed was Melissa's house.

"Mel!" he bellowed, rattling the knob. "Mel! It's me. Can you open the door?"

Charlotte's heart rate kicked up a notch. What was going on? Had Melissa hurt herself? Had an accident? If so, why had she called Will and not 911? She didn't understand.

"MEL!"

"It's locked." Her voice, tiny and exhausted, finally sounded from inside. She said something else Charlotte couldn't catch, and she raised her eyebrows at Will. He shook his head, having missed it too. He looked ready to kick the door down.

"Do you have a key?"

"Yeah, somewhere." He searched through his key ring, fingers shaking. "I never have to use it. She's always home and has it unlocked when I come." Judging by the trembling of his hands, he seemed full of enough adrenaline that Charlotte wondered if maybe he *should* kick in the door, just to release it.

He fumbled the keys twice, then dropped them. Charlotte took them from his unsteady hands. "Which one?"

"The red plated."

She quickly inserted it into the lock and he wrenched the door open. "Mel! Where are you?"

"Kitchen."

Charlotte followed him around the corner, through a cheerful living area decorated in aqua and coral. Melissa had good taste. She stopped short before she plowed into Will's back.

"Oh, Mel." This time, his voice sounded broken, more than angry or panicked. Then he rushed to her side, providing Charlotte her first view of Melissa, sprawled on the wooden floor. Petite, dark-haired, freckle-faced Melissa.

And the wheelchair on its side halfway across the kitchen.

"What happened?" Will's hands hovered over her body, as if he wanted to help but wasn't sure where to start.

"Don't even ask." She sounded more agitated than hurt. Clearly, the apple didn't fall far from the Martin tree.

Melissa met Charlotte's eyes and found a smile. "We meet at last. Didn't expect it to be like this."

"Me either. Can I help?" Charlotte stood near the kitchen door, afraid to get in the way.

"No, we've done this before, unfortunately." Melissa winced as she attempted to move. "Just straighten my leg out for me, Will."

He obliged, carefully. "Nothing broken?"

"How would I know?"

"Very funny."

"I'm fine, Will. Was trapped, is all. I'm just glad my cell was in my pocket."

Slowly he straightened her other leg. "Where's the ambulance?"

Melissa motioned for Charlotte to bring her wheelchair closer. "I didn't call them."

"You *what*?"

Uh-oh. That didn't sound good. Charlotte slipped into the kitchen and pushed the wheelchair toward them, remembering to lock the wheels before she parked it.

Will's big-brother mode was nearing dangerous levels. "Melissa. You told me you called them already."

"A little white lie. I knew you'd overreact." She brushed her hair back from her face, wincing a little as Will lifted her into her chair. "I don't need them, I'm fine. It just scared me when I fell. I didn't mean to ruin your night."

"Ruin my—are you kidding me?" Will stood upright, raking his hands through his hair. "This is madness. I *knew* you shouldn't live alone."

Charlotte backed slowly across the kitchen as the facts began to snap into place. His close relationship with his sister. His doting on her, the weekly cookies, the sense of responsibility. His putting his life on hold for years. Melissa was handicapped, and for some reason, he'd taken that burden upon himself.

Melissa's phone call made sense now. The last thing Melissa said before Will had interrupted them the other day in the bakery was, *Will hasn't told you?*

No, he hadn't.

The question was—why?

"Will, listen to yourself. What are my options? A group home? I'm fully capable of taking care of myself. You've renovated this entire house to be wheelchair friendly." She grinned. "Just apparently not that particular spot."

Will wasn't laughing. "It's not funny. You could have been hurt."

"But I wasn't." The humor drained from Melissa's face, and she threw her hands up. "What do you want? For me to live like you—terrified of every possible what-if?"

Will opened his mouth, then shot a glance at Charlotte

as if remembering she was standing there. "Let's talk in the living room, please."

Charlotte couldn't decide if she was grateful for the reprieve or offended that she wasn't included.

Melissa mouthed *I'm sorry* at Charlotte and rolled herself toward the door. "Answer my question, Will."

Their voices muffled as they relocated to the living room. Out of sight—but not out of earshot. Charlotte couldn't help it. She pressed against the side of the door frame and listened.

"If being terrified of what-ifs keeps us all alive and safe, then yes. That's just fine with me."

Silence filled the living room. And then Will brought down the hammer. "I can't handle any more of these phone calls, Mel. I'm moving in."

"You're *what*?" Melissa spoke the same words, in the same tone, that Charlotte mouthed silently to herself from the kitchen.

"I'm moving in. This wouldn't have happened if I'd been here. Nothing would have ever happened if I'd been there!"

"Will, don't overreact."

"I'm not. I should have done this a year ago."

"Things are different now. You can't move in with me." Melissa's voice lowered, but not enough. "You have a life—a life you deserve to have. You have a girlfriend!"

"Not anymore."

Charlotte's heart skipped a beat, then thudded back to life with all the finality of a door slamming. Slamming on her future. Her hopes.

And in that moment, she knew the answer to her own question.

He hadn't told her about Melissa because deep down, he hadn't expected to be around long enough for it to matter.

Chapter Nine

He didn't mean it.

The words flew out of his mouth, hard and flippant and so foreign he didn't recognize his own voice in them. He ducked his head, covering his face with his hands as the pressure of the last several years settled hard. Like Atlas, holding the weight of the world. What had he become? He was standing in his sister's living room—the living room he'd renovated for her, the living room she'd worked hard to decorate and make her own afterward, to make normal, to make cheerful—*yelling* at her.

All while verbally disowning the only other female who had ever brought joy to his life.

"Will." Melissa's voice, calm and even, brought him back from the ledge as it'd done a hundred times before. Maybe a thousand. "Will, sit down."

He obliged, mostly because of his guilt, partly because

he knew she hated people looking down on her—literally or figuratively.

She wheeled closer to him on the couch. "You can't fix me."

"I know. I *know*." Why did she have to keep reminding him of the obvious?

"So stop trying, big brother. You know I love you, but you have to quit trying." She reached across her lap and grabbed his hands. "You have an amazing woman in that kitchen right now, and if you don't get your head out of your you-know-where, you're going to lose her."

"I don't want to lose her."

"Then let me go. You can't hold her hand if you're still holding mine." She pointedly looked down at their clasped hands resting on his knees.

He squeezed tighter. "You're my sister."

"And I have my own life. I'm fine, Will. I'm happy. And I'd be even happier if you'd settle down already and quit being Free Willy. Save all of us a little drama."

He shook his head, hating that stupid nickname that kept coming back to haunt him. But when it came down to it . . .

"Mel, I'd rather be Free Willy for the rest of my life than you be alone another minute."

"*Pssh.*" She shook her hair back from her face, taking on an intentionally haughty expression. "I *know* I've still got it. Some man is going to be lucky to marry me."

There was the sister he knew and loved. Will allowed himself a smile. "He'll need a manual, that's for sure. I should start writing that now, actually. Save him the trouble."

Melissa laughed. "See? He's coming. We both know it. I might not get married as soon as I'd planned once, but you know what, Will?" She tugged at their joined hands until he met her eyes. "If my ex couldn't handle the 'for worse' before we even got married, then he sure as heck doesn't deserve my 'for better.' I'll wait for the guy who can."

He'd never thought of it that way—that being jilted by her fiancé after the accident could have been a blessing in disguise. Melissa always chose to view the hard things in life that way. He could learn a lot from her.

But it still wasn't right that he didn't have to pay the same price Melissa did. He gripped her hands tighter. "It was my fault." His voice hitched. Had he ever owned that to his sister before? He'd admitted it a thousand times in his own head, but out loud? He wasn't sure.

"What was your fault?"

"The wreck. Your accident." Unshed tears slashed at his throat. "It's all my fault."

Confusion filled Melissa's face. "Will. That's crazy. You weren't even there."

"Exactly. I was supposed to have picked you up." His words tumbled over themselves. "If I had been there, you wouldn't have gotten a ride with Taylor."

He remembered that night all too well. He had promised to pick Melissa up from the New Year's Eve party at her work. She didn't want to drive herself and park and walk in the rain while dressed up, and her fiancé had been out of town on business. So Will had agreed to come get her before midnight.

But he'd been at his own party, living it up with friends

he didn't even talk to anymore, friends whose names he couldn't even remember. Flirting. Pitting girls against each other to compete for him. Being a womanizing jerk. And he'd forgotten his promise. It was well after midnight that he remembered, saw all the missed calls on his cell, and tried to call her back. He couldn't reach her—but the police finally reached *him*, and that particular call changed his life forever.

"I was the one who refused to wait for you and asked Taylor for a ride home. I knew how he felt about me. I should have known he'd start a fight about me being engaged." Melissa shook her head. "You know all this, Will. Yeah, maybe you should have picked me up, but I shouldn't have asked Taylor to drive me. And Taylor shouldn't have gotten so agitated while driving. And the person who hit us shouldn't have been speeding. There were a lot of mistakes that night." She squeezed his hands. "But it wasn't your fault. It was an accident. You have to let it go."

It couldn't be that easy. That simple just to . . . let it go. What would he even do without the weight of guilt anymore? It had been his constant companion for years.

He tried the idea on for size. It wasn't his fault. Melissa's accident wasn't his fault.

It wasn't his fault.

The burden shifted a little. He closed his eyes. It wasn't his fault. He didn't have to stay under it anymore. He was free.

He took a deep breath.

Free to live his life.

He slowly released Melissa's hands.

Free to let Melissa live hers.

He turned his palms up to the air.

Free to love Charlotte.

Charlotte. His eyes flew open. Melissa must have been on the same page, because she immediately rolled her chair back so he could stand up. "Charlotte? It's safe to come out now!"

No answer. No footsteps. No shuffling.

In fact, it had been quiet in there for some time. Too quiet.

Melissa's grin faded. They looked toward the front door at the same time. Open a crack.

Will's heart thudded painfully against his chest as he leapt to his feet. "Do you think she heard—"

Melissa nodded. "Yep."

Will closed his eyes, sinking back onto the couch. It was too late. He'd blown it. "I'm an idiot."

Melissa patted his arm. "Don't worry. I already told her that."

The last thing Charlotte wanted to do was deliver the cake to Adam and Brittany's wedding. She wanted to stab it with a knife. Maybe don sweatpants, grab a fork, and eat every bite of it, all by herself.

And yet, underneath the anger threatening to boil over at Will's rejection, she understood it. Understood the helplessness and fear that drove someone to make such a decision. Hadn't she almost made the same one about him? She understood it and hurt for him.

And that just made her even madder.

Charlotte parked the van and stared at the vintage barn that had become the city's most popular wedding venue, where Adam and Brittany would be saying their vows in just a few short hours. Julie climbed out of the passenger side. "Ready, Boss?"

Not even a little.

She got out of the van.

Julie pulled the rolling cart out of the back. Hopefully they'd be able to get everything inside the reception area of the barn without pushing over too many bumps. At least the ground looked relatively level between the van and the door.

Charlotte helped load the boxes with the white chocolate wedding cake onto the cart, then checked to make sure she had the assembly tiers and piping bags for touch-ups.

This had potential to go down in history as the fastest wedding cake assembly *ever*. She had intentionally left Zoe with a different babysitter this afternoon, so Julie could help Charlotte get in and out of the venue in warp speed. Julie had come and picked her up a block from Melissa's house last night. Her friend had commiserated properly, but one thing she'd said kept rolling around in Charlotte's head.

People say things they don't mean when they're scared.

Maybe that was true. But at the same time, she wasn't ready to talk to Will, evidenced by her ignoring his dozen phone calls and half dozen texts after she'd left Melissa's. Of course he had been scared and stressed. Nothing about his behavior last night at Melissa's lined up with the Will she knew. He'd been on edge, agitated—and obviously fighting some kind of demon that had nothing to do with her. But her cracked heart couldn't take the risk again.

Because what if he *had* meant it? What if she was truly that disposable? He hadn't made any effort outside of a few phone calls and text messages. If he wanted to fight for her, wouldn't he have come over? Shown up, the way he did that day in the bakery? Maybe he'd just been calling to tell her the break-up news officially.

And that was one phone call she could do without.

She pushed the cart through the grass toward the barn, head down, eyes averted as Julie trotted beside her, opening the front door, holding back the red balloons tied to the entrance, and shuffling chairs out of her way. The barn had been decorated with stacked hay bales, mason jars tied with red ribbons, and tiny sparkling Christmas lights draped beam to beam. The vast space was set up for both wedding and reception, but the wedding party was nowhere to be seen. No doubt they were busy behind the scenes—taking pictures, touching up makeup, and panicking over last-minute details.

Funny how she knew so much about something she'd never experienced.

Charlotte located the cake table, decorated with lace and flowers and sprinkled with black and red beads, and began unpacking the cake stand. As soon as this thing was set up, she'd be back in the van, hightailing it back home. To Zoe. To their predictable life.

Which might be a little boring, but at least it didn't hurt.

"I'll go find Brittany and tell her we're here." Julie hurried out the side door across the barn, pausing to straighten the white runner she'd wrinkled on her way. The wooden door banged shut behind her.

Charlotte kept focused on the task at hand, trying to ignore the musty smell of hay that somehow managed to seem romantic. She just wanted to be done with this cake. Wanted to go home and forget the last couple weeks had ever happened. She'd been content before Will had started frequenting The Dough Knot. Content before he'd upset her life and her heart with his charm and laughter and hazel eyes. Eyes that could look right into her and see the truth, tell the truth.

He had meant what he'd said in the bakery, when he passed her eye test.

Her heart ached and her hands shook as she began setting the pillars into the stand. Why couldn't he *keep* meaning it?

She'd never be able to make another snickerdoodle again.

She fastened the next pillar, looking on her cart for the last one. This was why she'd wanted safe. This up and down, back and forth—it was too much. She needed someone she could depend on. Needed stability.

Which this cake stand was also going to need if she couldn't find the last pillar. Had she or Julie forgotten to pack it?

"Don't forget this one."

An outstretched hand—a male hand—offered the missing pillar.

Will.

She took a step back, refusing to look at him. She plucked the pillar from his hand and finished stabilizing the last tier. If only it were so simple to stabilize her heart. "What are you doing here?"

She could hear the smile in his voice. "I'm in the wedding, remember?"

Oh, she remembered. That's why she was trying to leave so quickly.

She ignored him as she began setting the layers in place. A corner of the icing smeared, and an edible pearl bounced across the table. Great. Now she'd have to fix that with her touch-up frosting before she could leave.

But she couldn't concentrate with him standing that close. "I'm really busy here, Will." He was making her nervous, and she hadn't even seen him in his tux yet. She fumbled for her piping bag.

"Look at me, Charlotte."

No. She wouldn't. Couldn't. With shaking hands, she began piping the icing. And smeared another edge.

"I know you heard what I said about us at Melissa's house. I was out of line."

"No. You were just being honest." Charlotte bit her tongue to keep back the tears as she ducked her head and painstakingly repaired the icing damage. "You said we were done, and ta-da. You were right. We're done." She tried to put a hardened edge into her voice that hadn't yet made it to her heart.

She could feel him staring at her. Staring hard as she carefully cut a sliver of cake off the back that hadn't baked evenly, then re-iced the gap and tossed the rejected piece into the box on her cart.

Rejected.

Tears pricked despite her efforts, and she blinked rapidly. If she could just hang in there another few minutes . . .

His footsteps shuffled nearer, nearer, until she could see the shiny leather of his black shoes in her downcast vision. He hadn't touched her, yet the warmth of his presence seared her. "I *was* being honest last night, Charlotte—finally, totally honest for the first time in forever—but not like you think. The honesty part came later. You missed it."

"How convenient." She straightened, refusing to listen to his lies anymore. Had he just come over here to defend himself and offer excuses?

She finished the icing repair, capped the piping bag, and shoved it into the box on her cart. Done. Cake assembled. She could leave. At this point, she didn't even care if she got paid. She just wanted out. Wanted to go back to safe and secure, even if that meant being alone.

It had to be better than this.

"I beg you. Hear me out." Will reached for her arm, but she dodged his grasp, still avoiding looking at him dead-on, and began pushing her cart away from the cake table.

"Charlotte?"

She turned around slowly.

There he stood, feet braced apart, hands tucked in his pockets, shoving back the corners of his coat to reveal a black bow tie and suspenders. "I love you."

He closed the short distance between them and pulled her into his arms. "I love you, Charlotte. I have since the moment you turned around in that apron and sold me my first snickerdoodle. It's always been you."

She allowed him to hold her, allowed her arms to hold

him back. Allowed the tears streaming down her cheeks to pour like rain. But she couldn't allow her heart to trust.

"You reminded me what it was to want to live again," he said. "You inspire me, Charlotte. You make me want to be a better man."

She closed her eyes as his words streamed over her. "I felt the same way, Will. You convinced me to trust again. You proved that men weren't what I thought they were. But then you bailed. At the first sign of conflict, you disowned me."

He shook his head. "I'm an idiot, Charlotte."

She opened her eyes. "Yeah, I've heard that rumor."

"Melissa told me she talked to you."

She nodded.

"Charlotte, please believe me. I reacted last night out of fear and frustration. I was wrong."

She wanted that to be true. So badly. Her fingers dug into his biceps, holding on for dear life. Afraid any minute she'd have to let go forever.

"What I hadn't realized until last night is that I've been living my own version of safe. Seeing Melissa on the floor like that, helpless—it brought it all back. Her accident, me thinking all these years it was my fault . . ." His voice trailed off. "I snapped. But Melissa's taught me something that I'm finally starting to let sink in."

She felt her heart caving. Softening. Like butter in a mixing bowl. She wanted her hard edge back, but she was losing it. "What's that?"

"She's learned to find the good in the bad. All these years I've stayed focused on the bad, afraid to look for good. Afraid I didn't deserve to find it." A muscle twitched in his jaw. "I'm a better man now than I was before her accident. I should be living up to that, rather than hiding from it."

She searched his eyes. He was telling the truth. "You realized all of that last night?"

"I told you, you left way too early." He ran a finger down her cheek. Even with the lingering remnants of anger and hurt, his touch still sent shivers down her spine. "Did you walk home? I called you ten times."

"Julie picked me up." She squinted up at him. "And it was actually a dozen."

"Not that you were counting." He pulled her close, his expression serious once more.

"Do you forgive me, Charlotte?"

She hesitated, wanting to be sure. Wanting to know she was safe. She tugged at one of his suspenders.

"I'm not safe." He whispered the words, low, close to her lips. "But you know what? You're not, either. We'll probably hurt each other again. There are never any real guarantees."

That truth sank in hard and deep. She tightened her grip on the suspender strap. He was right. But how could she keep risking her heart over and over?

His voice deepened an octave as his grip around her waist tightened. "One thing I can guarantee. I love you."

She looked at him. "You were wrong about one thing."

He eased back, concern spreading across his face. "What's that?"

"You most definitely *can't* rock a bow tie."

"Hey now—"

She cut off his indignant protest with a kiss, one that

lifted her to her tiptoes and quickened his heartbeat beneath her hand.

She pulled back for a breath. "And by the way . . ."

He raised his eyebrows.

"I love you too."

She reached over, snagged the icing-covered cake remains from the cart, and smashed them straight into his face.

Then she kissed him.

He tasted like buttercream.

Acknowledgments

Much gratitude to my editor, Becky Philpott—I love you more than cupcakes!

To the entire editorial and marketing team at HarperCollins—you guys rock!

And to my agent, Tamela Hancock Murray with the Steve Laube Agency—thank you for your consistent support and cheerleading.

To Anne, for being a friend, a first reader, and a voice of reason and truth. I am so grateful for your friendship.

To Jacki, for always being willing to fly with me into the unknown. You're a warrior!

And to Audrey—my Little Miss, who's always up for dessert. I love you! Let's eat cake!

Discussion Questions

1. Charlotte was a single mom convinced God would send her a certain kind of man because of her fears and regrets from the past. Yet when Will came into her life, he was anything but what she expected. Have you ever had God bless you with a desire of your heart that went beyond what you felt you deserved?
2. Charlotte was living her dream of running her own bakery, while Will was still trying to figure out what to do next after his step down from active military. What would you do career-wise, if you could be guaranteed not to fail?
3. Will felt responsible for his sister's accident that made her paralyzed, and he carried that weight to the point of it stifling his own life. Have you ever taken on a burden you weren't meant to carry? How did you get past it?
4. Charlotte struggled at one of the wedding showers, having come both as the caterer and as Will's date. Have you ever

been in a social situation that was awkward because of mixed roles or for feeling like you didn't belong?

5. Because of her past, Charlotte struggled with jealousy when it came to Will, even though he'd done nothing to give her reason to. Have you ever allowed your insecurities to almost ruin a good thing in your life out of fear or misunderstanding? How did you handle it afterward?
6. Like Will, Charlotte also struggled with regret and bearing the burden of false guilt, and had to learn how to go to God and be set free from those misconceptions. What misconceptions or false truths are you tempted to believe about yourself?

About the Author

Betsy St. Amant lives in Louisiana with her young daughter and has a heart for sharing the amazing news of God's grace through her novels. A freelance journalist, Betsy is a member of American Christian Fiction Writers. When she's not reading, writing, or singing along to a Disney soundtrack with her daughter, Betsy enjoys inspirational speaking and teaching on the craft of writing.

VISIT HER WEBSITE AT WWW.BETSYSTAMANT.COM

FACEBOOK: BETSYST.AMANT

TWITTER: @BETSYSTAMANT

The Perfect Arrangement

KATIE GANSHERT

For Mom.

You listened raptly to my little-girl stories. It gave me courage to write the bigger ones.

Chapter One

"Get off the sidelines, Amelia."

I'd heard this approximately 624 times in the past twelve years. Once a week, from the lips of my best friend, Rachel. We were an unlikely pair—Rachel and I. About as opposite as two people could be. If not for sharing a small dorm room on the tenth floor of Witte Hall in Madison, Wisconsin, our freshman year, I'm confident our paths never would have crossed. Or if they had, we wouldn't have given each other a second look. I'm also confident I wouldn't have lasted a single semester at such a big college without her. But we did share a room, and our unlikely friendship tethered me to Madison when homesickness yanked mercilessly at my heartstrings.

According to Rachel, I lived timid.

"It's time to get in the game already," she liked to say. *"Enough watching. Start experiencing!"*

As I took a left-hand turn onto Mulberry Avenue, I

couldn't help but wonder what Rachel would say about this. Nothing good, I'm sure. In my defense, when the man you thought you'd marry—the only man you'd ever dated—weds another woman in a town not more than thirty minutes away, it's only natural to spy. I had planned to drive by the church as inconspicuously as possible to see what I could see, then drive back to my quirky hometown of Mayfair, Wisconsin, where nobody would be the wiser. I should have known by then that life—at least for me—rarely went as planned.

My sweat-slicked palms grew sweatier as the steeple arose over a row of maple trees, their green leaves giving way to the faintest hints of yellow and orange. White, puffy clouds rolled across blue sky, forcing the sun into a game of peek-a-boo. I slowed to a stop at a streetlight, praying nobody would recognize me.

Thanks to Rachel's friendship and my decision to stay in Madison, I ended up meeting Matt in my second semester Poli Sci class freshman year. We dated for four years, which meant his family knew me. And then there was the matter of my stepsisters—both bridesmaids—to consider. If either caught me spying, I'd never hear the end of it. They would assume I still loved Matt, which wasn't true. Our relationship had ended years ago. My broken heart had long since mended. I was simply curious.

The light turned green. I pulled the bill of my hat down low and eased onto the gas. The steeple loomed taller. Parked cars lined the street on both sides—an overflow due to the too-small church parking lot. The maples broke apart at the same time as the clouds, and there it was—the church, bathed in sunlight. Several bridesmaids stood outside on the front lawn, my stepsisters among them. My cantering heart accelerated into a gallop. I slid down in the seat and observed what I could as discreetly as possible.

They wore strapless tea-length dresses in light mocha. Not tight-fitting satin, but a flowing chiffon. Each one carried bouquets of yellow, white, and peach. I tipped my sunglasses up and squinted out the open window. Cabbage roses, mums, billy balls, and ranunculus. Not too fallish, but not too summery either. A perfect September bouquet that matched the dresses wonderfully. I craned my neck to soak up some more details, but my foray into spying was going . . . going . . . gone.

Perhaps once more around the block wouldn't be too conspicuous. The street in front of the church wasn't bustling with traffic, but it wasn't empty of it either, and I *was* wearing a hat and sunglasses. My tan Honda Accord was pretty standard fare when it came to cars. And I hadn't even seen the bride or the groom. I peeled my attention away from the shrinking wedding party in my rearview mirror when everything in me seized. My heart, my muscles, my grip on the steering wheel. I inhaled a sharp, loud, gasping breath and slammed my foot onto the brake. I wasn't quick enough.

My Honda rear-ended the car in front of me.

For a second, or maybe two, I didn't move. I sat behind the wheel, staring wide-eyed at the back end of a maroon Subaru Outback with a sticker on the rear window that said Team Oxford Comma. It wasn't until the driver stepped out that panic set in. Full-throttle, mortifying panic. The kind that made me want to curl into a ball underneath the steering wheel and never come out again. Or hit the gas and take off—my first and hopefully only hit-and-run. One thing was certain. I couldn't get out of my car. Not with the wedding party a block away. But the driver stood at the place our two cars met, shielding his eyes from the sun and surveying the damage, leaving me no choice but to join him.

I snagged my purse from the passenger seat and slipped outside. "I am so, so sorry!"

The man I approached had a head full of thick, dark hair, nicely gelled, and wore well-fitting tan dress pants with a matching suit coat draped over his arm, a white dress shirt, and a gold tie. I could only assume he was a wedding guest. Thankfully not one of Matt's college friends. I didn't recognize him at all.

He squinted against the sun. "Are you okay?"

"Yes, I'm fine." Besides the heart palpitations anyway. "Are you?"

"I've survived worse." He smiled when he said it, but any and all humor was lost on me at the moment. Perhaps someday I would laugh at this. A long, long time from now, when it didn't feel like the world's most embarrassing thing ever to happen.

"I can't believe I ran into you like that," I said. "I'm so sorry."

"It's okay. Really. There was no damage done, see?" He patted his body to show himself intact.

"Yes, there was. I put a dent in your bumper." I tucked a strand of hair behind my ear, thankful the hat covered my copper-colored locks from view. They were too recognizable. "I wasn't paying attention. It was completely my fault. I'm really, truly sorry."

He smiled again, like my level of remorse amused him.

I shot a nervous glance over my shoulder. One of my stepsisters peered through the afternoon brightness in my direction. My panic peaked. I dug inside my purse, pulled out a business card, and shoved it into the man's hand. "This has my e-mail and phone number. Please get in touch with me, and I'll—I'll get you my insurance information."

He looked down at the card, then back at me with his head slightly atilt.

I'd already started backpedaling. "I'm very sorry. I'm in a bit of a hurry." I glanced again over my shoulder. One stepsister was now nudging the other stepsister, pointing in my direction. "It's an emergency, actually."

His head tilt grew more pronounced.

"Please get in touch with me. I promise to plead one hundred percent guilty. Really, I'm so sorry." Before the man could object, I dove inside my car, reversed, shifted into drive, and drove away. As fast as the speed limit would carry me.

From: gallagher24@gmail.com

To: amelia@forget-me-not.com

Date: Sun, Sep 13, 2015 8:06 p.m.

Subject: Brief Encounter

Dear Ms. Woods,

Is that too formal? It feels formal. But I'm not sure what the proper protocol is when addressing someone I met in such circumstances. My name is Nate. I'm the gentleman you bumped into this past Saturday outside Good Shepherd Episcopal Church—the one on Mulberry Avenue? I don't know why I'm feeling the need to be so specific. Unless you make a habit of running into cars often, you probably remember the incident just fine without any prodding.

You were in a bit of a hurry. I must admit, it felt a little bit like meeting Cinderella at the end of the ball, only instead of leaving behind a glass slipper, you left me with a flowery business card. The name on the card given to me said Amelia Woods, so I'm assuming you are the right person. If not, I apologize for the confusion.

You asked that I contact you regarding insurance information. I wanted to let you know that it's not necessary. The bumper isn't so much dented as minutely scratched. Nothing a little spit and polish won't fix. There's no need to worry, and I say this only because you seemed very worried during our brief encounter on Saturday. I hope your emergency wasn't too serious and that everything worked itself out.

All the best,
Nate Gallagher

"There are far, far better things ahead
than any we leave behind."
—C. S. Lewis

From: amelia@forget-me-not.com
To: gallagher24@gmail.com
Date: Mon, Sep 14, 2015 6:23 a.m.
Subject: Re: Brief Encounter

Dear Nate,

I am incredibly embarrassed and really very sorry. I promise I'm not usually so scattered and frantic, nor do I make a habit of fleeing the scene of an accident. It didn't hit me until later that what I did was most likely illegal. Saturday was . . . I don't even know what to call it. An unusual sort of day. It's probably best if I leave it at that.

Thank you for being so kind and gracious, but I insist on filing a claim. Despite being in a hurry, I did see the dent. I don't think spit and polish will fix it. Please send me your full name and insurance information, and I will call. It would make me feel better.

My apologies,
Amelia

PS: The subject line of your e-mail made me think of that old black-and-white movie with Celia Johnson. Have you seen it? So many people think it's a romantic movie. I happen to think it's depressing.

Inhaling the tantalizing scent of pumpkin muffins one last time, I waved good-bye to Eloise over my shoulder and exited her bakery. Overhead, the sky was every bit as blue as the flower my store was named after—the Forget-Me-Not Flower Shop, located on the corner of Marietta and Main, directly across the street from the gazebo in the middle of Mayfair's town square.

Taking a sip of hot coffee from my thermos, I unlocked the front door and flipped the lights. Most people dreaded Monday mornings, but not me. I, Amelia Rose Woods, loved the beginning of a new workweek. Because I, Amelia Rose Woods, loved everything about my job. Meeting with brides about their big day, designing corsages and boutonnieres for high school dances. Arranging bouquets for birthdays and anniversaries and apologies and just-because-I-love-yous.

Receiving the fresh flowers that arrived each morning in the back of Wally's van. Even coming alongside the grief-stricken as they bid farewell to a loved one.

I turned on the glue guns and the glue pans, set my coffee and the bag of goodies on the front counter, and looked up at the picture hanging behind it—my mother and me standing in front of this very shop before my first day of kindergarten. We shared the same copper hair, the same fair skin, the same spray of freckles over the same small nose, except I had gray-blue eyes instead of brown and a pointier chin. In the picture, I wore a jean skirt with pink hearts stitched into the hem, my hair in pigtails. One of my small hands clutched onto my mother's. The other held a small bouquet of daisies for my new teacher. Earlier that morning, Mom had let me put the bouquet together all by myself. Warmth filled my chest. The deep-down-in-your-soul kind of warmth. She'd be so happy if she could see me now.

With a smile on my face and thanksgiving in my heart, I printed the orders that came in overnight. A bouquet that needed delivering by noon and one more that needed delivering by six. And then there were the four centerpiece arrangements for the annual book club meeting at the public library in Apple Creek. There were no funerals today, and while I had a wedding this weekend, I'd already placed the order. We wouldn't start putting the actual bouquets and arrangements together until midweek. I picked up the phone and dialed my part-time assistant, Astrid. She had worked at Forget-Me-Not for two years now, mostly on an as-needed basis. I left a message explaining that she didn't need to come in, then got to work on the arrangements in the storefront cooler while waiting for Wally and his flower van to arrive.

He came every morning at nine fifteen, leaving me just enough time to clean up and arrange the flowers before opening the doors at ten. I pulled out bad stems, added new ones, refreshed the water, then cleaned all the shelves and doors. By the time I finished, Wally had pulled up outside on the street.

"Morning, Wal," I said, meeting him by the rear hatch. "How are the flowers looking today?"

"As fresh and as pretty as you." He smiled his snaggle-toothed smile. He was a rough-looking fellow. Not at all the type you'd expect to drive a flower van.

I shooed off his compliment and handed him the bag from Eloise's, a giant-sized chocolate chip–pumpkin muffin tucked inside.

He opened the bag and took a big whiff.

I opened the rear hatch and did the same. "Any extras today?"

"Yes, actually. An abundance of alstroemeria." He pulled out the bucket. "I can add it to your next bill if you want some."

They were a gorgeous shade of golden yellow. I stuck my nose in the blooms and inhaled deeply. "Why the abundance?"

"There was a big order cancellation."

"Well, I'll definitely take some."

Wally got to work unloading my end-of-the-week orders from Saturday, along with some unexpected alstroemeria.

Once my bounty was inside, I cleaned and cut the stems, put them in new buckets with fresh water and flower food, stored them in the cooler, and went out front to switch the sign from Closed to Open. I swept up the mess and had just finished the by-noon arrangement when the bell on my front door chimed.

I didn't have to look up to see who it was.

George came every Monday at ten fifteen on the dime to purchase a bouquet for his wife, Sylvia. They'd been married for sixty-four years and he still bought her flowers. I didn't care what Hollywood said, that white-haired, age-spotted, arthritic old man was the epitome of romance. I secured a ribbon around the stems of the bouquet I was finishing. "Good morning, George."

His cane tapped a slow rhythm as he slipped off his hat and made his way to the counter. According to George, that's what a man was supposed to do when talking to a lady—take off his hat. "Good morning, Miss Amelia. That's a fine-looking bouquet you have there."

I held it up. "You like?"

"It's awfully pretty. Awfully pretty indeed."

"Wayne Sawyer ordered it for his wife's birthday." I set it off to the side. "What'll it be for you today, George?"

He rubbed the gray stubble on his chin. "How about something yellow?"

"I have the perfect thing!" I brought Wayne's bouquet back to the cooler and pulled out a small collection of gerbera daisies, daisy poms, and some of the alstroemeria I splurged on earlier, and brought them out to the front to arrange them.

"Those are nice," George said, waving his finger at the alstroemeria. "Yellow is Sylvia's favorite color, you know."

"I think you may have told me once or twice."

"When we first got married, we lived in this teeny tiny garage of a home up in Rhinelander. And do you know what my Sylvia did?"

I did, actually, but I didn't mind hearing the story again. "What'd she do, George?"

"She painted all of our walls yellow. Every single room."

I looked up from my artwork. "Every single room?"

"Yes, ma'am."

"Were you upset?"

"How could I be? Our house looked like the sunshine. It looked like my Sylvia."

I put the finishing touches on the bouquet and handed it over. "Well then, this ought to make her extremely happy."

"Yes, it ought."

I rang George up, wished him a wonderful week, and helped him out the door as he recapped his head and hobbled toward his car with his bright yellow bouquet in hand. Unlike my other customers, who were local residents, George was a bit of a mystery. He didn't live in Mayfair. Most likely he came from somewhere close by, one of the nearby towns without a flower shop of its own.

The phone rang just as George pulled away from the curb in his Lincoln Navigator. I waved one last time, then hurried inside to answer it. It was my delivery guy calling to say he was sick and getting sicker. I ordered him to rest up and get well soon, then called Astrid back, hoping it wasn't too late for her to come in after all. We had two bouquets that needed delivering, along with the arrangements for the book club. But Astrid didn't answer. I drummed my fingers on the countertop for a few minutes.

Normally I'd call up Rachel and she'd make the deliveries without any questions. But Rachel was currently out of commission. I twisted my lips to the side. My brother was working. One of my stepsisters worked as a lawyer in Milwaukee. The other, however, lived in Green Bay, not more than twenty minutes north of Mayfair. She stayed at home with her two young boys. Maybe she'd do me a favor and deliver the flowers for me. I let out a sigh and dialed her up.

She answered on the fourth ring.

"Hi, Crystal. It's Amelia."

"Amelia? Well this is unusual, hearing from you on a Monday morning."

"I'm in a bit of a bind at the shop."

"Oh?"

"My delivery guy called in sick, and I can't get ahold of my other employee. I hate to bother you, but I was wondering if there was any way you could make some deliveries for me."

"Deliveries?"

"I'll pay you back the gas money. It shouldn't take more than an hour, tops."

There was a pause on the other end. "Oh, I wish I could, but Milo and Henry have to nap."

"All day?"

"No, not all day. All afternoon. Plus, Candace is coming in tonight. I want to make sure the house is spic and span for her. You know how weird she is about cleanliness. And right now we're at the park. The boys have been asking all weekend to go to the park. We can't leave."

She was going to be at the park *all* morning long with Milo and Henry—ages one and two?

"Hey, random question. Did you drive by Matt's wedding on Saturday?"

"Matt's wedding?" My face exploded with warmth. So much that I could have heated a small village in Siberia.

"Candace and I could have sworn we saw you outside the church. Your car too."

"No, of course not." More heat. Waves upon waves of it. I cleared my throat, told Crystal I had to get back to work, then hung up the phone like it was a hot potato. Before I could relive the mortifying memory for too long, the front bell chimed and in stepped my brother. Shaggy red hair, my pointy chin, Mom's infectious smile. Her brown eyes too.

"Well, this is a nice surprise." William was a rare customer at my flower shop. Not because he didn't like flowers, but because he worked during store hours. He graduated from Cross Point last spring and had moved to Mayfair afterward to work as a CPA for a local accounting firm. I loved having him so near.

He headed toward me with that smile still in place, set his elbows on the counter, and flipped open a small velvet box in the palm of his hand—one with a diamond ring inside. It took me a bit to process what it meant. A diamond ring in a velvet box? I looked from the piece of jewelry up to him. "Are you—is this . . . ?"

"I'm going to ask her to marry me."

"Bridget?"

"Of course Bridget, who else?"

I blinked. Several times. Stammered a bit. Then did what adoring big sisters should do when they hear such news from their baby brother. I beat my worry into submission, came around the counter, and wrapped him in a hug. "Wow, Will. Congratulations!"

"I'm going to pop the question tonight."

"Wow." I tucked my hands into the back pockets of my jeans, trying to relax the muscles in my face. Will and Bridget were so young, and they'd only started dating at the end of May.

He tipped his chin down and gave me *that look*. "Amelia . . ."

"What?"

"I love her. Madly. I'm telling you, she's the one."

"That's great."

He tipped his chin down farther. "Please don't worry about this."

"I won't. I'm not. Seriously, Will, I'm thrilled for you." My baby brother was getting married. To a woman I barely knew. Could he really blame me if a heavy dose of unease was mixed in with that thrill?

"I was hoping you could make up a bouquet for me to give her tonight?" He shut the small box and slipped it into his pocket.

"Of course! Any particular flower in mind?"

"Red roses symbolize love, don't they?"

"A dozen red roses, coming up."

His smile returned, bigger than before. "Let's make that two dozen."

Chapter Three

William delivered my before-noon bouquet on the remainder of his lunch break. I closed the shop early so I could deliver the before-six arrangements myself. Not a big deal, since I'd had a sum total of four customers walk through the door, and that sum total included my brother. Such was the nature of the floral business. Seasonal fluctuations. My crazy time came between Valentine's Day and Mother's Day. Unless a lot of brides decided to have fall weddings, the fall months tended to be slower ones.

I stowed the arrangements in the backseat of my Honda Accord, plugged the addresses into my GPS, turned on my Lorie Line Pandora station, and began the final part of my day. Maybe when I finished I could grab a hamburger to go from Patty's House of Pancakes, curl up on my couch at home with my tabby cat, Baxter, and watch something romantic. Get my mind off of my brother's impending proposal. He didn't want me to worry, but that was easier said than done. To me William would always be my scrapes-on-his-knobby-knees, dirt-on-his-nose, shoes-on-the-wrong-feet, attached-at-the-hip little brother. He wasn't old enough to get married. And how could he know Bridget was "the one" when they'd only been dating three and a half months?

I delivered the first bouquet quickly, then headed toward Apple Creek—a town fifteen minutes south of Mayfair—distracting myself with a mental list of possible movies I could watch when I finished. *Pride and Prejudice* was always an option, the BBC version, of course. That moment when Mr. Darcy walked out of the lake never failed to make me sigh. Or I could go with something a little older, like *The Philadelphia Story* or *The Shop around the Corner.* Definitely not *Brief Encounter.* I smiled as I thought about Nate Gallagher's e-mail. I could always pop in *Cinderella.*

The early evening sun sank lower in the blue sky. The faint scent of burning leaves swirled through the open window of my car as I drove past the sign for Apple Creek. I turned up Orchard Lane, parked in front of the library, and brought in one arrangement at a time to the librarian, a broad-shouldered woman with a long face.

"Oh, these are lovely!" she said, leading me through the library into a back room with four large round tables. She placed one arrangement in the center of each table. "Do you like to read?"

"Yes, I do." In fact, Rachel believed I read too much. "*It's part of the problem,*" she liked to say. I, on the other hand, saw absolutely nothing wrong with getting lost in a great story.

"Then you should join us! It's a wonderful evening. We

talk about our favorite books from the year and put the ones we want to read this next year on the calendar. There are several women your age. We're a fun bunch."

"It sounds fun, but I already have plans tonight." I could practically hear Rachel sighing in my ear. *"A date with the television and your cat does not count as plans, Amelia."*

"Well that's too bad," the librarian said. "Maybe next time."

"Yes, next time."

She thanked me for the beautiful flowers. I thanked her for the business, then headed outside, toward my car, eager to start my date with the television. I could change into my pajamas and pop some popcorn. Maybe even start a fire. The delectable thought put a hop in my step. I was about to open my car door when something nabbed my attention.

It was Bridget, my brother's girlfriend. In Apple Creek. Strolling up the street. Arm in arm with a man who was not William.

I ducked behind my car, heart pounding inside my chest, and peeked over the roof, positive I'd seen wrong. But there was no mistaking it. Unless Bridget had an identical twin sister, that was definitely her. And unless William dyed his hair brown and grew a few inches, the tall, lanky man whose waist she had her arm around was not my brother. A heavy knot of dread sank through my stomach as the man opened a door to a bar-and-grill eatery and Bridget stepped inside.

I was a pretty nonconfrontational person. But at the moment, I wanted to push up my sleeves and march in after her. In fact, I crouched there for a while imagining the scene. Brave Amelia storming inside the restaurant, giving this woman who was toying with my brother's heart a serious piece of my mind. The knot of dread pulled tighter. Had she already rejected William's proposal and moved on to another man? Or worse, had she accepted his proposal while carrying on a clandestine affair? The thought made me sick and at a loss for what to do. Because as much as I wanted to, I wasn't brave enough to go inside that restaurant.

I needed Rachel's advice in a desperate way.

I climbed into my car, wishing I could call her. Her last e-mail stated that she didn't have a cell phone yet. Even if she had one now, I didn't know her phone number. I squished up my face, trying to figure out her time zone. Seventeen hours ahead. She checked her e-mail in the evening, after her work was finished, which meant hopefully I'd get a phone call by morning. I opened up the e-mail app on my phone and shot her a quick note with trembling fingers.

Subject: SOS, RESPONSE NEEDED ASAP

I need your advice. Is there any way you can call me? Do you get reception where you are? I don't care if it's in the middle of the night my time. Please tell me you have a phone.

—A

When I arrived home, I checked my e-mail on the off chance Rachel had already responded. No such luck. But there was another e-mail sitting in my inbox, sent earlier in the day.

From: gallagher24@gmail.com

To: amelia@forget-me-not.com

Date: Mon, Sep 14, 2015 12:06 p.m.

Subject: Re: Brief Encounter

Dear Amelia,

As much as I would love to make you feel better, I have to refuse. I cannot let your insurance bill go up astronomically on account of a small scratch on my bumper. That would most definitely not make you feel better. So in consideration of your future happiness and financial stability, I can't give you the information you're asking for. *No* means no, Amelia. You're just going to have to accept it.

In response to your postscript question. Yes, I have seen the movie. Several times, in fact. I'm impressed you know it. Not many people watch the old movies anymore. My sister thinks the film is terribly romantic. I think her idea of romance is a little warped. Two married people in post–WWII England falling into a doomed love affair? I can definitely see your point. Perhaps I should have come up with a different subject line.

Now, *Breakfast at Tiffany's*. There's a classic movie I can get behind. And before you ask. No, I have no problem forfeiting my man card with that particular admission. It's a great flick. Audrey Hepburn is adorable.

Best,

Nate

"There are far, far better things ahead
than any we leave behind."
—C. S. Lewis

That night I popped popcorn, started a fire in my fireplace, and watched *Breakfast at Tiffany's*. Twice. Nate was right. Audrey Hepburn was adorable. Considering the circumstances, she did a great job of cheering me up. Baxter seemed to enjoy it too. He raised his tail three times.

Chapter Four

I unlocked the front door of Forget-Me-Not with not nearly as much pep in my step or warmth in my heart as yesterday. No phone call from Rachel. No e-mail either. I hadn't heard from William. I had no idea if he'd proposed and, if so, what happened. Or how to handle the fact that I'd caught his possible fiancée with another man. And whether I was ready for it or not, I would see him tonight, at Crystal and Candace's surprise thirtieth birthday party.

If only pictures could talk. I could have a conversation with my mother right then and there. She'd know what to do. Sighing, I set my coffee and Wally's muffin on the counter and pressed the blinking light on the store's answering machine, expecting an after-hours order from a customer.

"Hey, Amelia, it's . . . well, it's Nate."

I pulled my chin back. Nate, as in Nate Gallagher? The guy who liked Audrey Hepburn and refused to give me his insurance information?

"I just got your e-mail. I'd call you on your home phone or your cell phone, but all I have is this number on the flowery business card you gave me. To answer your questions, yes. I do have reception. I know Yooperland must feel very north to you Wisconsinites, but we do get cell phone service in the Upper Peninsula and I do own a phone." His tone was friendly, teasing. His voice, deeper and smoother than I remembered. "I'm not sure if the e-mail was meant for me or not, but I must admit, I'm highly intrigued. Is everything okay? If you want to call me, my number is 906-224-0505. I'll be around."

The answering machine beeped.

I blinked several times, confusion scrunching inside my head. Cell phone reception? My e-mail? But I never e-mailed him last . . .

Oh no.

I pulled out my cell phone from my purse and opened up my e-mail app. I tapped on the Sent folder and waited for the e-mails to load. A couple seconds later, there it was. SOS, RESPONSE NEEDED ASAP. Only, instead of sending it to galvison_rach@hotmail.com, I'd somehow sent it to gallagher24@gmail.com. The g-a-l must have brought up his e-mail address instead of Rachel's, and I'd been so panicked about the entire incident that I didn't notice the blunder.

I buried my face in my hands and let out a loud groan. First, I hit him with my car and fled the scene like a crazy woman. Then I sent him a cryptic, slightly hysterical e-mail to call me as soon as possible, in the middle of the night if necessary. He probably thought there was something wrong with me. Like maybe I'd been dropped as a baby a time or two. Seriously.

Shaking my head, I hit Compose and tried to explain.

From: amelia@forget-me-not.com

To: gallagher24@gmail.com

Date: Tue, Sep 15, 2015 8:32 a.m.

Subject: so very sorry for the mix-up

Dear Nate,

Once again, I am incredibly embarrassed and horribly sorry. In my previous e-mail to you, I promised that I wasn't typically so scattered and frantic, and yet I'm not doing a very good job of convincing you of that, am I?

The e-mail you received yesterday was sent by mistake. It was meant for my best friend, Rachel Galvison, whose e-mail address (unfortunately for you) starts with the same three letters as yours. You might be wondering why I didn't just call or text Rachel if it was such an emergency. The answer to that is simple. Last month Rachel moved to Fiji. It sounds pretty spectacular, but it's not really. She joined the Peace Corps and is working in some remote village, teaching children English while she learns crazy-sounding languages like Chuukese and Kosraean. Last we e-mailed, she didn't have a phone.

I was a bit (that's a lie—I was a lot) panicked about something and needed her advice, so I sent the rushed e-mail off without double-checking who I sent it to. I'm really very sorry for bothering you.

I'm afraid you are getting the wrong impression. I'm not

prone to drama. My life is actually pretty mellow. That's what I call it, anyway. Rachel likes to say "boring." I am very sorry, and I promise not to let the mistake happen again.

Mea culpa,

Amelia

PS: This e-mail has officially taken me thirty minutes to type out, as I'm sending it from my iPhone. I strongly dislike sending e-mails from my iPhone for this very reason. Most days I want my flip phone back.

From: amelia@forget-me-not.com

To: galvison_rach@hotmail.com

Date: Tue, Sep 15, 2015 8:41 a.m.

Subject: I'm the world's biggest basket case

Rachel,

I am mortified.

I caught Bridget with another guy yesterday, on the cusp of finding out William had purchased an engagement ring. In my panic, I sent you an e-mail. Or at least I thought I sent you an e-mail. Turns out, it didn't go to you. It went to this guy named Nate, who I hit with my car (long story). He must think I'm psycho. Anyway, I need advice on what to do. William is head-over-heels in love with this girl. You saw them together with your own eyes. If I tell him that I caught Bridget with another man, he'll be crushed. But of course, I have to tell him. Better he know now than find out after the wedding, right? Please call or e-mail as soon as possible.

Miss you terribly,

Amelia

PS: I have now officially quadruple-checked to make sure I'm sending this to the right person!!

At five o'clock, I began my closing routine. My delivery guy, who was no longer sick, had taken all the orders that needed delivering before six, except the arrangements for my stepsisters' party. I would bring those with me. I'd received three phone calls from my stepmother throughout the day ensuring that I wouldn't forget them. It was more than we'd spoken all year. I finished organizing the back cooler, then began the task of cleaning out the dirty stem buckets with soap and water. I organized and filed the orders that needed to go out tomorrow and was sweeping the floor behind the counter when the front bell jingled. I looked up from the growing pile of leafy debris.

It was William, looking even giddier today than he had yesterday.

My broom stopped.

He spread his arms wide. "She said yes."

The knot of dread in my gut doubled.

"Your baby bro is officially engaged to be married to the love of his life." William met me at the front of the store. "We were supposed to go to dinner last night, but something came up and Bridget had to cancel. Since I couldn't wait, I ended up surprising her at her school yesterday afternoon. Her students clapped and cheered. And she loved the flowers."

"Wow." I didn't know what else to say. Or do. Bridget had said yes to my brother's proposal, then gone out on a date with another man that very same evening. If I wasn't so filled with concern and heartbreak for William, I would have been steaming hot mad. Seriously, how dare she?

My brother's smile drooped at the corners. "What's wrong?"

"Nothing."

"Amelia . . ."

"No, it's nothing. Really. I'm just . . ." Just what? Shocked? Upset? Conflicted? I had no idea what to say. I needed Rachel! "A little emotional. I mean, you're getting married."

"It's crazy, eh? When did we get so old?"

"Hey, I have six years on you, buddy. If you're old, then I'm ancient."

William laughed. "Is your calendar free for October twenty-fourth?"

"What's October twenty-fourth?"

"The day I nab myself a wife."

If I'd been drinking something, I would have spit it out. Good thing William had waited until the end of the day to tell me. My coffee was long gone. "Why so soon?"

"Because when you're as in love as Bridget and me, there's no reason to wait. We're ready to be married, and since we don't want anything huge or fancy for a wedding, it won't take long to plan. Besides"—William's attention flickered toward the framed photograph on the wall over my head—"October's when Mom and Dad got married. It's a great month. Bridget and I are hoping you'll do the flowers."

He was right, of course. When the weather cooperated, October weddings were beautiful. October weddings between a wonderful, godly man and his cheating fiancée, on the other hand? Not so much. My mind fast-forwarded to the event. I imagined the other man showing up. A huge confrontation in the middle of the church. Bridget trouncing off with her secret lover, leaving my brokenhearted brother at the altar.

"Amelia?"

My eyelids fluttered. "What was that?"

"Can you do the flowers?"

"Oh . . . sure. I'll have to check the calendar, but yes. I should be able to."

"Great. Bridget and I will see you tonight at Mackinaws." He tapped the counter a few times with his palms and shot me a wink. "She'll be the one with the brand-new ring on her finger."

Mackinaws was on Voyager Drive in Green Bay—a restaurant built from huge pine logs and beams with massive vaulted ceilings and six stone fireplaces and impressive animal mounts—the two largest of which were a bear and an eighteen-point buck. My stepmother, Jeanine, had booked their loft for the party. It sat up to a hundred, which seemed like a crazy amount of people for a birthday party, but Candace and Crystal would have no problem filling the space. Whereas I tended to have one or two close, intimate friends, my stepsisters were perpetually popular and kept a big crowd of friends, some hailing all the way back to elementary school.

I stepped inside, holding two of the six arrangements Jeanine ordered a month ago. Bouquets of snow-white roses, lilies, and mums, filled out with wispy baby's breath and silvery dusty miller and plastic pearl sprays. I hated working with baby's breath, mostly because it smelled like cat pee. But Jeanine had cast the vision, and when she cast a vision, nobody could change her mind. So here I was, carrying these two elegant winter-esque arrangements inside a restaurant that screamed north woods.

Upstairs Jeanine was a bustle of activity, simultaneously checking in on guests and micromanaging the two teenage servers arranging the food—trays of smoked salmon, bacon-wrapped chestnuts, fruit, vegetables, cheeses, a taco bar. I wondered how much debt she was racking up on her credit card for this particular soiree. My stepmother was cursed with a rich woman's appetite and a middle-class budget—a common source of contention between her and my father when I was growing up.

She spotted me setting the two arrangements on the nearest table and came over, her face bright. She looked entirely too young to be the mother of thirty-year-old twins. Mostly because she went to the salon every six weeks to hide all traces of gray, worked out an hour each day to keep her physique, wore an entire cosmetic aisle of makeup, and I suspected did Botox, but I wasn't exactly sure on that last one. She gave her hands a few excited claps beneath her chin. "The flowers are here!"

"The rest of the arrangements are in the car."

She rearranged a few of the roses. "The baby's breath looks a little wilted. We better get the others before it gets any worse."

I gritted my teeth and smiled, then told her she could stay here. I'd get the flowers. After two more trips up and down the loft, I escaped into the restroom. All the people in attendance were either strangers or old acquaintances from my days living in Green Bay. The only two who wouldn't be strangers or acquaintances were William and Bridget, but I couldn't be around them tonight. I had no idea how to act cheery or congratulatory when I felt so far from either. I was a lousy faker. And as much as I wanted to unload the heavy burden resting on my shoulders and tell my brother the truth about his fiancée, Jeanine would absolutely throw a fit if I did it before Candace and Crystal's party.

I took my time washing and drying my hands and studied myself in the mirror. I looked more wilted than the baby's breath. "An hour, Amelia. You can handle an hour."

With that, I joined the growing crowd. William and Bridget had arrived during my bathroom break. Jeanine stood next to them by the food table. She fussed over Bridget's ring, then wrapped William in a big hug. The sight set off a pang of sadness in my heart. Even all these years later, I missed my mom.

As if sensing my thoughts, William made eye contact with me over Jeanine's shoulder. They came apart, and he thrust his hand up in the air to wave. He grabbed Bridget's hand and made his way toward me. Thankfully, one of Jeanine's friends intercepted them before they could get very far, and I made a beeline to the other side of the room, where the crowd was thickest. My mature plan of action? Avoid William and Bridget until I knew how to handle the situation.

I squeezed between two groups of people and tapped a gentleman's shoulder to get past. He turned around, his eyebrows going from neutral to high up on his forehead. "Amelia!"

I nearly choked. "Matt?"

"Wow, it's been such a long time." His attention flickered down and up—a quick, innocent check out. "You look great."

"Um, thanks. H-how are you?"

"Good. I just got married, actually." He put his free hand on the small of a woman's back, pulling her away from her conversation. "I'd love for you to meet my wife. Man, it sounds weird saying that."

The petite, dark-haired, blue-eyed, beautiful-skinned woman beside him slapped him playfully in the stomach, then slipped under his arm, where she fit perfectly. "You better get used to it, buddy."

He smiled. "Chelsea, meet Amelia. Amelia, meet Chelsea."

My name made Chelsea's entire posture perk. "Amelia, as in *the* Amelia? I can't believe I finally get to meet Matt's college sweetheart!" There wasn't a trace of phoniness in her tone. She sounded and looked genuinely happy. "I know your sisters and I are friends, but it's great to actually meet you. I feel like I ought to give you a hug."

And so she did. She wrapped one arm around my neck for a brief, friendly squeeze.

I tried not to feel awkward. And reminded myself—on repeat—that they didn't know I'd been spying on them this past Saturday. "Congratulations on the wedding."

Chelsea beamed. "Thanks!"

"Are you two not going on a honeymoon?"

"Oh, we are. I made this guy promise me that." She squeezed his waist. "Right, Matty?"

"We had to delay it a bit because of work. We're leaving on Monday."

I pulled at the collar of my shirt. "Where to?"

"California's wine country," Chelsea said. "I've always wanted to tour a vineyard. Italy was too far for a week, so we decided this would be the next best thing. Have you ever been?"

Matt laughed, a jovial glint in his eye. "When we dated, Amelia hadn't even been on a plane."

"Well, that was six years ago, Matty. I'm sure she's been on a plane by now."

My ears caught fire. Because, no, I hadn't. Thankfully, I was saved from responding by my stepmother, who raised her voice to gather everyone's attention. Apparently the birthday girls had pulled into the parking lot. This many people couldn't exactly hide, so we all became very still and silent. Then Candace and Crystal appeared—identical twin Barbies alongside their handsome Ken husbands—and everyone let out a resounding, "Surprise!"

I had to give Jeanine credit. Her daughters looked truly taken aback.

Candace set her hand against her chest. Crystal's mouth fell wide open. And then they both started laughing and playfully reprimanding their spouses for keeping such a secret. Jeanine got to them first, enfolding them both in a great big hug, dabbing tears from her eyes when she let go. "My babies are thirty. I can't believe my babies are thirty."

I searched for a way to get to them. The sooner I could extend my birthday wishes, the quicker I could get home to my cat.

I stepped inside my quiet, two-bedroom cottage, leaned against the door, and let out a long stream of breath. Exhaustion had etched itself into the base of my neck in the form of a throbbing headache. I'd gotten roped into staying longer than planned. Two hours of small talk with people I barely knew had taken a toll. As had the stilted conversation I'd had with William and Bridget. Judging by the odd looks my brother kept giving me, he suspected something was off.

Baxter jumped down from his favorite spot in the bay window and rubbed up against my leg. I gave him a pet. "Did you miss me, Bax?"

He weaved figure eights around my ankles, arching his back and curling his tail.

"I missed you too." I set my purse on the small table in the entryway and slipped out of the ballet flats I'd changed into after work.

Baxter followed me into the kitchen, where I popped a couple of extra-strength Tylenol and turned on the burner beneath the teakettle. I scooped up Baxter and brought him with me to the kitchen nook, where I often left my laptop. I petted a purring Baxter in my lap and waited for the computer to boot up and the teakettle to whistle.

The kettle whistled first. I poured myself some chamomile tea, then opened up my inbox, hoping to find an email from Rachel.

Unfortunately, I didn't. But there was something from Nate Gallagher.

From: gallagher24@gmail.com
To: amelia@forget-me-not.com
Date: Tue, Sep 15, 2015 5:42 p.m.
Subject: Re: so very sorry for the mix-up

Dear Amelia,

Your mea culpa is not necessary. You're not bothering me at all. Which I wouldn't say if it weren't true. You don't know me, but if you did, you'd know I don't say false things to make people feel better.

You're actually doing me a service. I've been searching for ways to procrastinate, and this is the perfect excuse. People say I'm good with advice. So maybe it's not an accident at all that the e-mail meant for your Fiji-traveling friend, Rachel, ended up in my inbox instead.

Can I help?

Best,

Nate

PS: I actually own a flip phone. My friends all like to poke their fun, but I think they're just jealous that I haven't succumbed to technology's allure.

"There are far, far better things ahead
than any we leave behind."
—C. S. Lewis

Chapter Six

I sat back from the computer while my tea breathed ribbons of steam into the air.

"Can I help?"

First I dented his bumper and he refused to let me pay for it, then he had the courtesy to call me at my flower shop after my embarrassing mess-up, and now he asked if he could help? I rewound my memory to Saturday, trying to recall as much about this Nate Gallagher as possible.

A nice head of thick, dark hair. The kind that men with receding hairlines most likely envied. An athletic build. Not football athletic, but something like tennis or track. Above average height. He'd worn his wedding attire well. My age, perhaps, and good-looking, only I couldn't remember to what degree. I'd been so consumed with getting away quickly before Candace or Crystal could see me that I hadn't paid much attention to the man I hit.

I dipped my chamomile tea bag up and down in the hot

water, then did the only thing any logical girl e-mailing with a nice, handsome man would do. I googled him. I typed "Nate Gallagher" into the search engine and took a sip of tea. Lots of things came up. So many I wasn't sure what to click first. There were multiple Nate Gallaghers in the United States. How could I know any of these pertained to the Nate I rear-ended?

I clicked on Google Images. Pictures loaded onto my screen, several of which were familiar—a man with olive skin, dark brown hair, light brown eyes, straight teeth, youngish, and very, *very* cute. The kind of cute girls not only noticed but couldn't help commenting on. And he was e-mailing *me*, asking if he could help. I clicked on one of his pictures, which led me to a travel article written in 2009 on lesser-known towns in Ireland. I skimmed it enough to know it was well written (witty and charming), and sure enough, at the end where it talked about the author was the familiar picture, along with a bio. Nate Gallagher was a travel writer. Or at least he had been in 2009. Google showed me several other articles, all equally well written, all dated before 2011.

Facebook rendered no results. There were plenty of Nate Gallaghers, but none who were cute men living in Michigan's Upper Peninsula. I did find a profile on Twitter. After scrolling through almost two years' worth of tweets (he posted once, maybe twice a month) that ranged from funny to serious to incredibly random, I started to feel very stalkerish and clicked out of the site. When all was said and done, here was what I learned about Nate Gallagher:

He was cute.

He was interesting.

He was a fan of the Philadelphia Phillies.

We shared the same faith.

I wondered if he'd come to the wedding as a friend of the bride or the groom. If the groom, he must have been a recent friend, since surely I would have remembered if someone like him had been friends with Matt in college. I sat back in my chair. I *did* need advice and I couldn't really count on Rachel, seeing as she was now living in some remote village halfway around the world. And Nate *had* offered.

I clicked the Compose button, stared for a long while at the blinking cursor, took another sip of my tea, and started typing.

From: amelia@forget-me-not.com

To: gallagher24@gmail.com

Date: Tue, Sep 15, 2015 10:36 p.m.

Subject: An Affair to Remember

Dear Nate,

I don't know. Perhaps you can help me. It's a pretty complicated situation. Or maybe it's not and I'm only making it complicated. One thing is for sure: it *is* urgent. And since I have no idea when Rachel will get the message I sent to her in Fiji, I think I'll take you up on your offer.

When I sent you that frantic e-mail, I had just finished delivering some flower arrangements to the public library in Apple Creek, which is a town not so far from my flower shop. Actually, let me back up a little. Earlier in the day, my brother stopped by to let me know he was going to propose to his girlfriend. It caught me off guard, mostly because they've only been dating since the end of May.

Anyway, as I was walking back to my car after dropping off the flower arrangements to the librarian, I saw my brother's girlfriend with a man who definitely wasn't my brother. Let's just say they looked . . . awfully cozy. I was shocked. Absolutely shocked. And so I sent Rachel, or actually you, that frantic e-mail.

To make matters worse, my brother came back to the store this evening and announced that she said yes. Supposedly the two of them were to have dinner last night, but she had to cancel (to have dinner with another man!), so he went to her school (she's a teacher) yesterday afternoon and proposed. I had no idea what to say. Or do. There's not a single person on this planet I love more than my brother. He's head over heels for this girl. This will absolutely crush him. But I have to do something. I can't pretend I didn't see what I saw.

So here I am, sitting in my kitchen with my cat in my lap and lukewarm tea by my elbow, feeling terribly conflicted and at a loss. What would *you* do if this were your brother?

With gratitude,
Amelia

PS: What has you procrastinating?

I brought my hands away from the keyboard. I had saved the subject line for last. At first I titled it *She Done Him Wrong*, one of Cary Grant's earlier, lesser-known movies with Mae West, but then I got paranoid that Nate would have no idea what I was talking about and would simply think I had bad grammar. Not a good thing for a guy who had a sticker on his back window about the Oxford comma. I ended up deleting that subject line and changing it to one of Grant's better-known films, even if it was an affair I'd rather forget.

I reread the message a few times, cracking my knuckles as I did. It was an unattractive habit, I knew, but some occasions simply called for knuckle cracking. Was I really going to send this? It was pretty personal information to send to a person I didn't know. But maybe that was a good thing. Nate didn't know me or my brother or his fiancée. He lived in the Upper Peninsula. There wasn't really any harm in him knowing, was there?

The cursor hovered over the Send button. The sight of it made my hands clammy. Before I could chicken out, I squeezed my eyes tight and clicked.

Chapter Seven

From: gallagher24@gmail.com

To: amelia@forget-me-not.com

Date: Wed, Sep 16, 2015 12:31 a.m.

Subject: Re: An Affair to Remember

Dear Amelia,

You weren't exaggerating. It is complicated. I'm sorry you're faced with such a horrible dilemma.

Here is my honest advice. If I were you, I would talk to my brother's fiancée. Tell her what you saw and give her a chance to explain. Maybe it's not what you think?

I want to thank you for trusting me enough with your problem, and for giving me an excuse to procrastinate. At the moment, I'm currently ghostwriting a book for a celebrity. My contract forbids that I say who, but I will give you two hints. He's rather famous and he's not the easiest fellow to work with, which I think might surprise many of his fans.

And hey, would you mind doing me a favor? If you follow my advice, please let me know how it goes. And if you don't follow my advice, let me know that too. Maybe it's the writer in me, but I have to know how things end. Loose strings drive me crazy.

Best,

Nate

PS: Your subject line made me smile.

"There are far, far better things ahead
than any we leave behind."
—C. S. Lewis

From: amelia@forget-me-not.com

To: gallagher24@gmail.com

Date: Wed, Sep 16, 2015 6:07 a.m.

Subject: Re: An Affair to Remember

I'm glad it made you smile. And wow, a ghostwriter. I don't think I've ever had the pleasure of meeting one of those before. I'm grateful for the advice. You're right. I should talk to Bridget. (That's her name, by the way. I don't think I told you in the previous e-mail.) Maybe I didn't see things correctly. I read once that eyewitness accounts aren't nearly as reliable as we think they should be. I promise to keep you updated on the situation. Wish me luck!

—Amelia

I stepped inside the front office of Mayfair's one and only school. It served grades K–12 all in the same building, with the second story reserved for the high school. I attended in kindergarten and halfway through first grade before my dad moved me and one-year-old William to our new home and family in Green Bay.

Mrs. Berdahl, a short-haired, big-hipped woman who ran the front office when I was there in kindergarten, greeted me with a big smile. "Amelia, what brings you here so bright and early?"

"I was wondering if I could have a quick word with Bridget?" She taught French. This was her first year. If I was going to confront her, as Nate advised, I had to do it as soon as possible. Before I could talk myself out of it.

"Let me get you a visitor badge, and you can go on up to her room." Mrs. Berdahl opened her top drawer and pulled out a lanyard with a badge attached that said Visitor in a bold black font. "You know, everyone was talking about William's proposal yesterday. It was one of the most romantic things I'd ever seen, him walking down to her room with all those roses. Bridget hasn't stopped smiling since."

I forced my lips to curve up, wishing it were genuine. Hoping Bridget had a good, solid explanation for what I'd seen. I wanted to be happy for them.

Mrs. Berdahl handed me the badge. "Say, do you have any yellow roses in stock? It's my aunt's birthday tomorrow. She adores yellow roses."

"I can make sure to have some if you want to swing by and pick up a bouquet."

"Oh, that would be wonderful. I'll be in after work tomorrow."

"I'll make sure to save some yellow roses for you, then." I put on the lanyard, said good-bye, and headed toward the stairwell. It was eight o'clock. Classes didn't start for another thirty minutes. I was technically supposed to be at the shop by now. I nodded hello to a few teachers who spotted me walking past their classrooms. Once outside Bridget's, I wiped my sweaty palms on the thighs of my jeans and took a deep breath, hoping the extra oxygen might give me some courage. When I knocked on the open door, Bridget looked up from some papers on her desk, her eyes going wide at the sight of me.

She stood abruptly. "Amelia? What are you doing here? Did something happen to Will?"

"Oh no. Sorry. William's fine." At least, physically. The state of his heart remained to be seen.

She pressed her palm against her chest, as if to calm her racing heart.

My hands took to fidgeting. "Do you have a second to talk?"

"Sure, I have a few minutes." Bridget straightened the papers on her desk and waved me inside. "Is everything okay? It seemed like you had something on your mind last night at the party. I'm sure this must be a little weird for you—your younger brother being engaged—especially when the two of you are so close."

"No, it's not that. It's just . . ." I stepped farther inside the room. "I saw you."

"You saw me what?"

"When I was delivering flowers on Monday evening to the public library in Apple Creek." I waited for my words to click. For Bridget to realize what this meant. She only looked confused. "I saw you and that . . . guy? Walking arm in arm into the restaurant next to the library."

Her face went completely pale. Her eyelids fluttered and she severed eye contact. "I don't know what you're talking about."

"It was the same night you canceled plans with William. The same day you said yes to his proposal."

"Amelia." She looked straight into my eyes, her face as white as a ghost. "I wasn't in Apple Creek on Monday night."

And there I stood, with no clue what to say. This, I hadn't expected. Sure, eyewitness accounts weren't the most reliable things, but there was no mistaking that the woman I'd seen on Monday night in Apple Creek had most definitely been Bridget.

"I don't know what I was thinking. Of course the great-grandparents should have flowers." Alyssa Green looked at me across the counter with her big doe eyes as I wiped the surface clean with a rag. "And then I couldn't sleep last night thinking about daffodils. I can't believe I left them out of the centerpiece arrangements. They symbolize new beginnings, which is perfect for a wedding."

They also happened to be spring flowers. And this

already happened to be the biggest, most stressful wedding I'd ever done. Ten, yes, *ten* bridesmaids, with hydrangea bouquets. A gorgeous flower, to be sure. But they wilted so easily, they gave me a heart attack. All of which would be manageable if Alyssa wasn't the most exasperating bride I'd ever worked with. She wasn't mean, or even a bridezilla. She was simply high maintenance. Like a polite pregnant lady who constantly changed her mind about what she was craving. That was Alyssa, only with her flower arrangements. It made me long for Lily Emerick, Mayfair's local event planner. Working with Lily on weddings was a cinch. She ordered well in advance and picked up the flowers straight from the shop. Too bad Alyssa hadn't hired Lily.

"Alyssa, the wedding is this Saturday. I can get the boutonnieres and the corsages, but I'm not sure about the daffodils. I already made the order." And the centerpiece arrangements were already under way.

Alyssa's eyes welled with tears.

Maybe if she were a mean bridezilla I could have stuck to my guns. The tears, however, did me in. "I'll see what I can do. I'm sure my vendor can bring in a special order."

Alyssa melted with relief. "Oh, thank you!"

I pointed my rag at her. "But no more changing your mind."

"I promise I won't!"

The door swung open with a jingle and a swoosh. William breezed inside like a thundercloud—all dark and ominous. He nodded hello to Alyssa, then turned to me. "Can I have a word?"

"Um, sure."

Looking between us, Alyssa waved good-bye and slipped outside.

William watched her go, then rounded on me as soon as the door closed. "Did you go to school today to talk to Bridget?"

"Yes."

"She called me in tears this afternoon, saying you accused her of cheating."

"I never accused her of anything. I simply told Bridget what I saw the evening you proposed to her. That's all."

"This is why you've been acting so funny, isn't it?"

"Yes."

William pushed his hands through his hair. It was a stress-induced mannerism inherited from our father. "You're getting the wrong impression of my fiancée."

"Why don't you give me the right one, then?"

"She was having dinner with an old family friend on Monday night. They grew up together. The two are practically brother and sister. He surprised her with an unexpected visit and he's an affectionate guy. It wasn't anything."

The phone rang—a shrill, sharp sound that filled up the silence between us. I let it go to the answering machine.

"William, if that's true, then why did Bridget lie about being in Apple Creek on Monday night? She looked me straight in the eyes and said it wasn't her." The whole thing reeked of guilt.

"Because she panicked. You caught her off guard when you showed up the way you did. She went from thinking something bad had happened to me to thinking you wouldn't believe her. She made a mistake."

I stared at William, wishing I could untie this knot of dread in my gut, wishing I could dispel my doubts.

"I'm not a baby anymore, Ames. I trust Bridget." He set his hands on the counter. "I need you to trust me."

From: gallagher24@gmail.com

To: amelia@forget-me-not.com

Date: Thu, Sep 24, 2015 4:12 p.m.

Subject: The Man Who Knew Too Much

Dear Amelia,

In vain have I struggled. It will not do. My feelings will not be repressed. You must allow me to tell you how much this suspense is killing me. I am dying a slow death here, Amelia. Please put me out of my misery. How did things go with Bridget and your brother?

If you've decided I know too much already and you aren't comfortable sharing any more, please let me know. I promise I'll understand. I just need to know whether or not I should continue checking my e-mail with the expectation of finding something from you. Needing closure is one of my faults, I'm afraid. And so, apparently, is nosiness.

Best,

Nate

"There are far, far better things ahead
than any we leave behind."
—C. S. Lewis

From: amelia@forget-me-not.com
To: gallagher24@gmail.com
Date: Thu, Sep 24, 2015 9:15 p.m.
Subject: Re: The Man Who Knew Too Much

Dear Nate,

I'm so sorry for keeping you in such suspense. I promise it wasn't thoughtlessness on my part. The truth is that I've been terribly busy.

The homecoming dance is this Saturday, so I've been up to my eyeballs in corsages and boutonnieres, and I just finished doing flowers for what was quite possibly the biggest, most stressful wedding of my life on the same weekend as our town's Fall Harvest Festival, which is great fun, but I help out with the decorations. Then there was a funeral yesterday, which is always a last-minute thing. We've had all hands on deck here at the Forget-Me-Not Flower Shop, and that's only two sets, unless you count our delivery guy, who is no good at making arrangements. I've pretty much been living at my store, and if I'm being 100% honest, I didn't really know how to process how I'm feeling about everything. And since I wasn't sure how to process my feelings, I decided to do the mature thing and repress them altogether by diving into my work. If we're going to admit to our faults, I guess that's one of mine.

Here are your loose ends. Whether they've been nicely tied up is still up for debate.

I followed your advice and confronted Bridget. She denied the entire thing. She looked me straight in the eye and said it wasn't her. I had the wrong person. Which wouldn't be the worst thing, except William (that's my brother's name) showed up at my flower shop that same day, accusing me of accusing his fiancée of cheating. Turns out, she called William in tears and said that it *was* her, but she panicked. Apparently I saw her with a family friend who is simply an affectionate guy.

I could maybe believe that had she told me the truth herself. What I don't understand is why she would lie to me about it and then change her story to William. It's fishy, isn't it? William asked me to stay out of it. He trusts Bridget and he wants me to trust him. Oh, but it's hard. I admit, I am rather protective of him. He's six years younger than me, you see, and we're sort of orphans.

Our mother died in childbirth. I was a six-year-old little girl with a grieving father and this little baby for a brother. Being a mother to him made me forget how terribly I missed my own. Our dad remarried too soon, and eight years later, he died too. William and I stayed with our stepmother and two stepsisters, who aren't the warmest of people. Growing up, it felt like it was me and William against the world. We were literally the redheaded stepchildren. (I was wearing a hat when we met, so you might not have noticed my red hair.) And now that same baby brother has gone and proposed to a woman I want to trust but don't. How is he even old enough to get married?

Wow, I am throwing a fabulous pity party for myself, aren't I? As I reread this e-mail, I realize I've painted myself in a very tragic light. My life isn't tragic, really. Yes, I've had my losses. But who hasn't? God has given me a flower shop that I cherish, a younger brother I adore, and this quirky little town that I love. I like my life, Nate. I'm happy with where I've landed. I just wish I felt more confident about where William is landing.

Sorry again for making you wait!

Amelia

PS: Bravo on the Mr. Darcy quote. He's a long-standing literary crush of mine. Your e-mail opening might have made me swoon a little.

PPS: I haven't seen *The Man Who Knew Too Much*. I had to look it up on IMDb. I'll have to watch it. I'm a big fan of Jimmy Stewart and Doris Day.

I woke at five in the morning feeling a strange combination of panic and regret. Nate had wanted to know how things turned out regarding his advice. He'd never asked me about my family history or all of my accompanying feelings. Why had I shared so much? And how much of a freak did he think

I was for divulging all that I'd divulged? I wasn't even sure how it happened. I'd sat down at the computer, it all sort of tumbled out, and now he definitely knew too much—whether he wanted to or not.

Maybe I needed to keep a journal. Maybe if I kept a journal I would no longer pour out my embarrassing heart to cute men. I pulled my pillow over my face and groaned. Rachel was right. I needed to get out more. Meet someone in real life. Perhaps the reason I cyber-dumped on Nate was because deep down Baxter and my flower shop weren't enough. Maybe I *was* lonely, and now I'd gone and scared away the one guy who had charmed me (he quoted Darcy, for heaven's sake!) since Matt.

I slipped into my robe and shuffled out into the dark kitchen with toes curling against the chilly air, my regret following me the entire way. Baxter remained sleeping at the foot of my bed. I sat down in front of my laptop and woke it from its slumber with a click. The luminescent screen lit up my kitchen nook. I opened up my inbox, wishing I had the power to take back the e-mail I sent last night. Wishing I could send him something much cooler instead. Like a here's-what-went-down and leave-it-at-that type of e-mail.

When my inbox loaded, I found a couple orders for the day. Along with two unread, un-flower-related messages.

One from my long-lost best friend, Rachel.

The other from Nate!

Chapter Nine

From: gallagher24@gmail.com

To: amelia@forget-me-not.com

Date: Fri, Sep 25, 2015 1:05 a.m.

Subject: Re: The Man Who Knew Too Much

Dear Amelia,

Thank you for putting me out of my misery. It was a relief to hear the ending of the story. No, the loose ends weren't completely tied up, but I think they're secure enough. If I were you and William were my younger brother, I would respect his wishes. He knows what you saw, so the burden is no longer on your shoulders. He has chosen to trust Bridget, and he's asked that you trust him. I think it's a pretty reasonable request. And I think you can honor it without feeling guilty. There is my unsolicited advice for the day. Feel free to take it or leave it.

As far as younger siblings getting married, I can relate. My little sister is married, which I find incredibly strange.

Thankfully, her husband seems like a pretty decent guy, so all I can do is be happy for her. Then again, my sister and I have parents who are alive and married, which makes my situation a lot less complicated than yours. Most people in your situation *would* throw a pity party, and yet you choose to focus on your blessings. Not everyone would do that, Amelia. It's an admirable quality.

While reading your e-mail I couldn't help but notice something, and I hope you don't think I'm making light of your situation. I promise, I'm not. But it hit me that you *are* a lot more like Cinderella than I thought, complete with the evil stepmother and the two stepsisters. Their names aren't Drizella or Anastasia by any chance, are they? You don't have a talking mouse friend named Gus, do you?

I wanted to thank you for your note. I enjoyed reading it. And I also wanted to let you know that there's no pressure to e-mail me back. Your life sounds very busy at the flower shop. I, on the other hand, am just a writer who spends copious amounts of time at the computer, looking for excuses to do anything but write. I don't want to be a nuisance, and you should feel no obligation to write back. The reason I'm saying this at all is because you seem like the kind of person who might continue exchanging e-mails with a complete stranger even if it is a bother, just for the sake of that stranger's feelings. I promise, my feelings are of hardy stock. In case you decide not to e-mail, I wanted to say that I've enjoyed our little exchanges. You're an interesting person, Amelia, and I happen to like interesting people.

All the best,

Nate

PS: You should definitely watch *The Man Who Knew Too Much*.

"There are far, far better things ahead
than any we leave behind."
—C. S. Lewis

From: amelia@forget-me-not.com
To: gallagher24@gmail.com
Date: Fri, Sep 25, 2015 5:15 a.m.
Subject: Re: The Man Who Knew Too Much

Dear Nate,

I'm incredibly sorry if I gave you the impression that you were bothering me! You are far from a nuisance. I've been enjoying our exchanges too. Please don't feel bothersome. Please continue to write. And please accept my sincerest apology.

—Amelia

From: galvison_rach@hotmail.com
To: amelia@forget-me-not.com
Date: Fri, Sep 25, 2015 2:41 a.m.
Subject: Re: I'm the world's biggest basket case

Amelia! You have to forgive me! The village was attacked by a swarm of fire ants. They ate everything in sight, including some of the animals. All they left behind were the skeletons. We had to flee in the middle of the night and . . .

Okay, I'm lying. That didn't happen. But I did read about it happening in a book once. The less adventuresome truth is that I've been swamped in Chuukese and absolutely consumed with these kids. I love them. Every single one of them. And lest you feel too neglected, Internet service is practically nonexistent here. Tonight it's working, so I am typing as fast as possible before it cuts out again. If I travel to the city, I can call you. Other than that, there's not much point in having a phone.

Tell me what's going on with William! He's engaged to a cheater!? What can I do to help? And you hit a guy with your car!? I tell you what. I leave and your entire life falls apart. Please tell me the flower shop is still standing. Oh, and how's Baxter? Scratch his ears for me.

Love you,

Rach

PS: When are you coming for a visit? It's long past time for you to get a passport.

From: amelia@forget-me-not.com

To: galvison_rach@hotmail.com

Date: Fri, Sep 25, 2015 5:20 a.m.

Subject: Re: I'm the world's biggest basket case

Your help is no longer required! Things are fine with William. He and Bridget are engaged, yes. But she's not a cheater. At least I hope she's not. They're getting married on October 24th, which is in less than a month!

I didn't hit a guy with my car. I hit a guy's car with my car. That's a big difference. He's the one who actually helped me work through the drama with William and his fiancée. He gave me some great advice, and I think everything's looking up. I'm good. More than good, in fact. I'm feeling pretty great. :)

Now tell me more about Fiji! You love the kids. You're learning the languages. Are you ever going to come home?

Missing you like crazy,

Amelia

PS: If I ever get a passport, I should probably go somewhere less intense than a village in Fiji for my first trip. Like maybe Ontario.

From: gallagher24@gmail.com

To: amelia@forget-me-not.com

Date: Fri, Sep 25, 2015 2:12 p.m.

Subject: Re: The Man Who Knew Too Much

Dear Amelia,

I'm not sure I've met anyone who apologizes as much as you apologize. And what's ironic is that you've not done anything that warrants an apology. Are you up for a challenge? I challenge you *not* to apologize for apologizing too much. Think you can do it?

Anyway, thank you for the e-mail. I'm glad I'm not being a nuisance and that you've enjoyed our exchanges too.

So tell me, how did you become a florist?

Best,

Nate

"There are far, far better things ahead
than any we leave behind."
—C. S. Lewis

From: amelia@forget-me-not.com
To: gallagher24@gmail.com
Date: Fri, Sep 25, 2015 7:08 p.m.
Subject: The Shop around the Corner

Dear Nate,

Challenge accepted. I will not apologize, even though everything in me wants to do it. And FYI, hitting you with a car most DEFINITELY warranted an apology. That's all I'll say about that.

How did I become a florist?

I happen to love that question. My mother was a florist. She owned my flower shop (which is actually *on* a corner, not *around* a corner) before I owned my flower shop. Back then it was called The Flower Pot. I have the fondest memories of helping her put together bouquets as a little girl. She started me off on cleaned (no thorns), long-stemmed roses (which are the easiest bouquets to make). Every time I smell them, I think of her. She and my dad used to slow dance in the store. Whenever I sweep the floor, I think of them that way. Smiling and slow dancing. I would sit behind the counter coloring in my coloring book and watch them. They had the best kind of love.

Even though I was only six when she died, not a day goes by that I don't think of her. Random things remind me of her. Like all your talk about Cinderella. She used to read me bedtime stories at night. All kinds. But my favorites were the fairy tales. I'd be lying if I said I didn't relate to Cinderella a time or two in my teenage years, even if my stepmother and stepsisters aren't actually evil.

Anyway, my mother left the flower shop to my dad when she passed, and my dad, I think, had every intention of giving it to me when I was old enough. None of us expected him to pass away as suddenly as he did, least of all him. His affairs weren't in order, and so the flower shop went to my stepmother, who sold it. I was fourteen, which I think is a difficult year for any girl, but most especially when you've lost your father and the place you thought would be yours. I won't pretend I didn't mourn deeply.

Life moved on. Time took away the sting. I went off to college and got myself a boyfriend. And then I graduated and we broke up, and lo and behold, my mother's old flower shop went up for sale. It felt like Providence. I took out a loan, signed on the dotted line, and here I am, the owner of my mother's old flower shop. I thought about naming it The Flower Pot again, but my mother's favorite flowers were forget-me-nots, and so, the name has a double entendre. Her picture hangs on the wall above the cash register. I absolutely love what I do.

Boy, do I get winded when I e-mail you. You must be easy to talk to. I'm actually quite shy in real life. My friend Rachel (the one living in Fiji) is always telling me that I need to get out there and live life. But I think owning and running a successful flower business counts as that, don't you?

Enough about me. It's your turn. What got you into ghostwriting? Not many little boys I know want to be a ghostwriter when they grow up. And are you really not going to tell me which celebrity you're ghostwriting for? Would you tell me if I guessed correctly? Where on the Upper Peninsula do you live? Oh, and I've been meaning to ask. What does the 24 stand for in your email address?

Affectionately,
Amelia

PS: Guess what movie I rented for tonight? I'll give you a hint. Jimmy Stewart and Doris Day play the lead roles.

"If I'm honest I have to tell you I still read fairy tales and I like them best of all."
—Audrey Hepburn

The next morning at the flower shop, while Astrid and I worked and worked on corsages and boutonnieres for the homecoming dance, I couldn't stop smiling.

"What has you so giddy?" Astrid asked.

"Nothing," I quipped.

But then I started humming. Astrid gave me that sideways look of hers and asked again. I laughed and shrugged and couldn't for the life of me stop thinking about Nate Gallagher.

Chapter Ten

From: galvison_rach@hotmail.com

To: amelia@forget-me-not.com

Date: Tue, Sep 29, 2015 1:57 a.m.

Subject: Re: I'm the world's biggest basket case

Wait a minute. The guy whose car you hit is giving you advice? Do you like him? Is he cute? Please, Amelia, I'm surrounded by tribal folk all day, including bare-chested, saggy-breasted women who don't usually have all their teeth. I could use a little bit of normalcy. For the love of all that is holy, SPILL.

From: amelia@forget-me-not.com

To: galvison_rach@hotmail.com

Date: Wed, Sep 30, 2015 6:23 p.m.

Subject: Re: I'm the world's biggest basket case

There's nothing to spill. The two of us exchanged some e-mails. I was a little giddy about it. But he hasn't e-mailed back in a while, and it's his turn.

It's weird, though, because he's always been so fast at responding. This lull isn't like him. Of course it comes after I signed my last e-mail "Affectionately." Affectionately?! What was I thinking? I might as well have told him I loved him.

But you'd think if he wasn't freaked out before then (I've done some ODD things where he's concerned), a little word like *affectionately* wouldn't do it.

Do you think something happened to him? What if he got into an accident and he's in the hospital? Or . . . oh my goodness, Rachel, what if he died? How would I even know?

Never mind. He's not dead. I just did a search for his name in all the obits for the Upper Peninsula (he's a Yooper). Nothing came up. Which means only one thing. He must not be interested.

Oh well. It was nice while it lasted.

—A

PS: Yes, he's cute. In fact, here's a picture. Too good to be true, eh?

From: gallagher24@gmail.com

To: amelia@forget-me-not.com

Date: Fri, Oct 2, 2015 6:46 p.m.

Subject: Re: The Shop around the Corner

Dear Amelia,

Now it's MY turn to apologize profusely. Please forgive

me. I had to take an impromptu trip to New York City to meet with the celebrity. It turned into a long, extended, dreadful affair with all-day meetings at the publishing house. I barely had a moment to breathe, but I promise I thought about you the entire time.

How I became a writer isn't nearly as good of a story as how you became a florist. It was always something I was good at—writing. At least that's what all my English teachers and professors told me. After I graduated college, I had a severe case of the travel bug. And so I tried making a go at travel writing. I was dirt poor, but happy. I had to take on a lot of odd jobs to supplement my income. My parents convinced me that it was long past time to settle down and get a real job, so I entered into a little phase of life I refer to as the "dark" years. I sat in an office and wrote grants. For two years. I still shudder thinking about it.

This particular celebrity, it turned out, was a fan of my travel articles. His agent contacted me about writing his first book, which makes many of my writer friends want to murder me in their sleep. Opportunities like this don't typically fall so decidedly into a person's lap. This is the third book I've written for him. He gets crankier with each one. And no, I can't tell you who it is. Not even if you guessed correctly.

So tell me what it's like running a flower shop. What's your favorite and least favorite thing about what you do? I have this whole picture in my mind of what it's like. It seems like a romantic job. I'm willing to bet you're laughing at me right now. It's probably not at all how I imagine it to be. Things rarely are.

I live in Crystal Falls, which according to MapQuest, is a

two-and-a-half-hour drive from Mayfair. And as far as the 24 in my e-mail address, I'd love to hear what you think it means.

Your parents sound wonderful. Tell me more about your father. What did he do for a living? I love the dancing story. Do you like to dance? And are you as alarmed as I am at how fast this year has gone? Somehow it's already October. I love fall, but I'm not ready for winter.

Best,

Nate

PS: How'd you like the movie?

PPS: Nice Audrey Hepburn quote at the end of your last e-mail. You're turning out to be every bit as adorable as she was.

PPPS: *The Shop around the Corner*? Arguably the most romantic movie of all time. Excellent choice. And, I might add, the two wrote letters to one another. Maybe we'll be the next Alfred and Klara (minus the hating each other in person bit, I hope).

PPPPS: How many postscripts do you suppose are acceptable in one e-mail?

"There are far, far better things ahead
than any we leave behind."
—C. S. Lewis

From: amelia@forget-me-not.com
To: galvison_rach@hotmail.com
Date: Fri, Oct 2, 2015 8:23 p.m.
Subject: Oh my goodness!!!!

He e-mailed me back. The cute man I hit with my car e-mailed me back. He called me adorable. He compared me to Audrey Hepburn! Supposedly, he had to take an impromptu trip to New York to meet with a publishing house, and according to him, he thought about me the whole time?!?

Seriously, Rachel, this guy is too good to be true. He's smart and witty and absolutely charming. He quoted Mr. Darcy! He knows all the classic movies even better than I do. He listens. He asks good questions. He's not even intimidated by my neuroses.

Okay, deep breath. Inhale. Exhale. I'm giddy. Beyond giddy. I'm hopping around in my seat. Baxter isn't even sure what to do with me. I want to e-mail him RIGHT AWAY, but I'm going to wait. I'm going to play it cool. Heaven help me, I really like this guy.

From: amelia@forget-me-not.com

To: gallagher24@gmail.com

Date: Tue, Oct 6, 2015 9:31 p.m.

Subject: Re: The Shop around the Corner

Dear Nate,

Yes, I did enjoy *The Man Who Knew Too Much*. But then, I've yet to watch a Jimmy Stewart movie I haven't enjoyed. I completely agree about *The Shop around the Corner*. I smile like a fool every time I watch it.

My father was a carpenter. When I was a little girl, I thought this made him as good as Jesus. He was a good man. A quiet man. A hardworking, Wisconsin-to-the-bone fellow who loved to hunt and bled green and gold. He was building a house in Green Bay when he met my stepmother. Things happened pretty quickly after that. I don't blame him. He was a working man with a very sad six-year-old daughter and a newborn son on his hands. He wanted me and William to have a mother. I can understand that.

As far as running a flower shop being a romantic notion. Well, some days it feels that way. And some days it feels like I'm a chicken running around with my head cut off. Case in point. My first year on the job, I had this very large wedding. I brought all the beautiful bouquets, which I'd slaved over, to the chapel the night before. Put them in the cooler. And discovered the next morning that the setting was all wrong on the cooler and they'd all frozen. Every single one. The next morning was one giant, panic-stricken scramble with plenty of tears (all from me). It didn't feel romantic at all.

My favorite part, besides the beauty, is probably the customers. I don't just love being a florist, I love being a small-town florist. I know almost everyone who walks in the door. I get to be a part of their lives. I have this one customer in particular—this ninety-year-old man named George. He comes in every single Monday morning to buy his wife a bouquet. He always has a cute, funny anecdote to tell me too. On the adorableness scale, this man has Audrey beat. My least favorite part would be the bridezillas. Thankfully, I haven't had to work with many of those. A week ago I met with Bridget and William to go over flowers for their wedding. It went well. She's not a bridezilla.

I agree with you about the time. I wish I had a magical hour glass that could make everything slow down, especially in the fall. October is a beautiful month in Mayfair. The leaves will peak in color in a week or two. The air is crisp and the town square is decorated in pumpkins and hay bales. We have this darling little chapel that sits kitty-corner across the square from my shop—all white clapboard with a steeple that rises up over the trees. It's where my parents married, and it's where Bridget and William are getting married too. There's this place called Sawyer Farm. Maybe you've heard of it? Along with a pumpkin patch, they have the biggest corn maze in Wisconsin. Every year William and I go. My parents used to take me, so now I take William. This year he's bringing Bridget. I kind of feel like the third wheel.

What's your favorite and least favorite part about writing? To me *your* job sounds romantic. Clacking away at the keyboard in some cabin in the woods, the fire crackling in the fireplace, inspiration flowing from your fingertips, espresso at the ready. Lunches with publishers. Book signings and book tours. Impromptu trips to New York City. Am I close? Travel writing sounds even more romantic. Here's my confession. And you have to promise not to laugh. I've never traveled anywhere. Unless you count Iowa. Or the Upper Peninsula. Most people don't.;)

What about your family? You haven't told me anything about them, except that your sister is married. I'd love to know more.

24 . . . your age when you set up your e-mail account? The number of your favorite sports player? The most postscripts you've written in one e-mail?

Affectionately,

Amelia

PS: It's not that I don't like to dance. It's more that I simply don't do it. I do like watching people dance though.

From: gallagher24@gmail.com
To: amelia@forget-me-not.com
Date: Thu, Oct 8, 2015 12:33 a.m.
Subject: Re: The Shop around the Corner

Dear Amelia,

Points for making me laugh. Out loud actually. I'm not a fan of *LOL*, but it would be true if I wrote it here. The most postscripts I've written in one e-mail happens to be four, and they were all to you. The other two guesses were wrong. Better keep trying.

In other news, it makes me sad to read that you don't dance. Just think of all Cinderella would have missed out on had she watched the prince dance at the ball instead of joining him on the floor. Maybe Drizella would have ended up as the princess. That would have changed the entire feel of the story.

Your father sounds like a great man and you sound like a great florist. Your understanding of a writer's life, however, is not so great. Trips to New York City aren't nearly as exciting as they sound. Book tours are mostly a thing of the past, and book signings are mortifying affairs wherein most authors sit at a table by themselves, often mistaken as store employees. I haven't had the pleasure of experiencing this, thankfully, since I'm a ghostwriter. But I've heard horror stories from my author friends. Mostly my job involves me banging my head against the keyboard and seeing what comes out. No crackling fire or cabin in the woods. My favorite part is being finished, and my least favorite is sitting down and typing. (I jest. It's not that bad.)

My family's pretty run-of-the-mill. My parents are still married and live out east in Pennsylvania. That's where I grew up. The only reason I'm up north is because of my grant-writing job. After I quit, I never bothered moving. My mother bemoans the fact that I'm not yet married. Every year she's more and more desperate to be a grandmother. Thankfully, with my sister newly hitched, she's transferred her pleading elsewhere. They're good people—my mom and dad. We're a close family. My sister is four years younger than me. Fun fact? The day we met was the day of her wedding. That's why I was dressed up so fancy. I was one of the groomsmen. She and her husband just got back from their honeymoon in California. She's always had this obsession with touring a vineyard. They live fairly close to you. I think you and my sister would hit it off. Maybe we can all meet up someday. Grab a bite. Or tour that corn maze. You have me wanting to visit your town.

What do you say?

Best,

Nate

"There are far, far better things ahead
than any we leave behind."
—C. S. Lewis

I sat at the small table near the front window of my shop with a lump in my throat. Fern Halloway and Phil Nixon, my oldest bride and groom to date, sat across from me. Fern was a seventy-four-year-old woman whose first husband died twenty years ago. All of Mayfair celebrated when Phil, the owner of Mayfair's one and only convenience store, mustered up the gumption and asked her on a date last Christmas. Now the two were going to be married exactly a year later at the same chapel as Bridget and William, the same chapel as my mom and dad. A Christmas wedding, and the entire town was invited.

Fern flipped through my portfolio and pointed at various bouquets while Phil squinted through his spectacles, agreeing with everything she said. I let the couple browse in peace while the knots in my stomach pulled tighter and the lump in my throat grew lumpier. I couldn't believe it. Nate—the man who had been consuming my thoughts, the man who had been brightening my days, the man who had made me giddy with excitement every time I checked my e-mail—was Chelsea's older brother. And Chelsea was my ex-boyfriend's new wife. If Nate and I continued this relationship, it was only a matter of time before he found out that the day we met was the day I'd been spying on my ex-boyfriend, who was his new brother-in-law, and then what? He'd assume I wasn't over Matt and end things before they really started. Or worse, he'd tell Chelsea, who would tell my stepsisters, and I'd never ever hear the end of it.

I clasped my hands in my lap, wondering how I'd missed it.

The groomsmen hadn't worn tuxedos. I remembered now how much Crystal had gone on and on about what a classy wedding it had been. How sharp all the groomsmen looked in their suits. I remembered also how Nate had his suit coat draped over his arm, which probably had his boutonniere pinned to it. I would have registered a boutonniere. I would have realized that he had been so much more than a simple wedding guest. He was part of the wedding party!

"I think this is the one," Fern said, tapping on a picture. She held the photo book up closer to Phil. "What do you think, honey? Do you like this one?"

"I like anything you like, dear."

Fern scooted the book over to me. The bouquets were made of spruce branches, dahlias, spray roses, pinecones, and gorgeous viburnum berries. One of my favorite winter bouquets. A bouquet that usually made my heart smile. This morning the only thing smiling were my lips. Not even Eloise's pumpkin muffins could cheer me up. I picked up my pencil and hovered it above my notes for the Nixon-Halloway December wedding. "How many bridesmaids will there be?"

From: galvison_rach@hotmail.com
To: amelia@forget-me-not.com
Date: Sat, Oct 10, 2015 3:12 a.m.
Subject: Re: Oh my goodness!!!!

THAT is the guy you hit with your car?? I don't even care that he's a Yooper, if he's even a quarter as intelligent and charming as you say he is, you'd be a fool not to date him. Enough with the e-mailing, Amelia, it's time for a date already! I'm talking about a real-life, in-person date. Trust me. If he's comparing you to Audrey Hepburn and saying he couldn't stop thinking about you, then he's dropping some major I'm-into-you hints. You better be dropping them right back! If not, then I've taught you nothing.

From: amelia@forget-me-not.com
To: galvison_rach@hotmail.com
Date: Sat, Oct 10, 2015 7:26 a.m.
Subject: Re: Oh my goodness!!!!

Le sigh. I knew it was too good to be true. Turns out, Nate is Chelsea's brother. Who is Chelsea, you ask? Chelsea is Matt's new wife.

Ugh, it's a long, embarrassing story. One I hoped never to have to tell you. When I ran into Nate, it was outside Matt and Chelsea's wedding. Yes, I was spying. Please don't scold me, Rachel. I learned my lesson, trust me. The thing is, I couldn't help myself. Matt and I dated for four years. I thought I'd marry the guy. I wanted a small glimpse of his wedding. For closure's sake. And wouldn't you know, as I was doing my snooping, I rear-ended Nate. I was so flustered, I didn't notice that he was one of the groomsmen. None of that registered at all. And then we started e-mailing, and now I've discovered he's Matt's new brother-in-law.

Needless to say, there will be no real-life, in-person dates.

Totally and completely bummed,
Amelia

From: galvison_rach@hotmail.com
To: amelia@forget-me-not.com
Date: Fri, Oct 16, 2015 2:05 a.m.
Subject: Re: Oh my goodness!!!!

Why in the world not??? Because he's in-laws with your ex? An ex you've been broken up with for SIX YEARS!? This Nate guy sounds fabulous, Amelia. Please don't sabotage it because you're scared. Tell him you're Matt's ex. The two of you can laugh about it on your date.

Scared? Scared!

I placed buckets of sunflowers and mums inside the cooler, setting them down harder than necessary. But seriously, Rachel had no clue what she was talking about. This had nothing to do with me sabotaging anything. This had nothing to do with me being scared. This had everything to do with reality.

I imagined admitting to Nate that I knew his sister, that the only man I ever dated was, in fact, his brother-in-law, and funny story . . . the day we met? Yeah, I was actually driving by to spy on the wedding. I shook my head, brought a bucket of flowers with me out front, and began snipping the stems. I wasn't being scared. I was being practical. Snip, snip, snip. I was so into the therapeutic snip-snipping that I didn't register the jingle of the front door or the customer that had walked through it until said customer cleared his throat.

"Are you upset with those flowers?"

The sound of George's voice had me looking up, and smiling too. Maybe the most genuine smile I'd smiled since reading Nate's e-mail last week. "It's nice to see you here on a Friday, George. What brings you in?"

He leaned his cane against the counter and slid off his hat. "I believe the good Lord did."

"Oh?"

"You've been on my mind, Miss Amelia. Ever since I came in on Monday for my bouquet."

"Well, that's sweet." I set the scissors down and wiped my hands on a nearby towel. "What flowers do you want in your bouquet today?"

"Forget-me-nots."

"Those are one of my favorites. Your wife will love them." I pulled out a bucket of the blue beauties from the cooler. "So why have I been on your mind since Monday?"

"You were in a sad state last time I saw you."

"Oh, George, I wasn't—"

He held up his hand to stop my protest. "I know you were smiling and doing and saying all the right things, but if there's one thing my old age has helped me with, it's sensing a person's spirit. You were going through the motions on Monday, and in all these six years I've been coming into this shop, I've never once seen you go through the motions. So this morning, when the Lord put you on my heart and mind again, I knew I had to come in and check on you. And here I've found you attacking those poor stems there."

"George." I tilted my head when I said it, and blinked away an embarrassing sheen of moisture. He'd touched me. Right in the center of my sad heart. Pricked it with a little rose thorn, because everything he said was on the money and there was no use denying it. I was sad. If I told Nate the truth, he'd think I was pining for Matt, when the actual truth was, I was pining for Nate. A man I'd only ever met once in my life during a chaotic, embarrassing moment.

"Well?" George said.

"You're right. I've been feeling a little blue."

"Like those flowers."

I smiled and put together a small bouquet of my mother's favorite flower for my favorite customer. "I fancied myself in love. Or at least, in the process of falling that way. Things ended rather abruptly."

"That would make a heart sad, all right." He twisted his hat inside his arthritic hands. "Mind if I ask why it ended so abruptly?"

Somehow, as I put the finishing touches on George's bouquet, I found myself telling him the entire story from beginning to end. It was more therapeutic than the snip-snipping. "It's complicated, isn't it?"

He pulled his billfold from his back pocket while I rang him up. "Most of the good things in life are."

"Do you agree with Rachel?" I handed him the bouquet. "Do you think I'm sabotaging a good thing because I'm scared?"

"You want an honest answer from your old friend?"

"Yes, I do."

"I think it can't hurt to take a risk and tell him. I think that if what the two of you have is the early blossomings of love, then that's worth all the embarrassment in the world." He stuck his nose inside the blooms, then handed them back over the counter to me.

"You're not happy with the bouquet?"

"Oh, I'm tickled with the bouquet. I'm just giving them to the recipient."

From: gallagher24@gmail.com

To: amelia@forget-me-not.com

Date: Fri, Oct 16, 2015 12:19 p.m.

Subject: Change of Heart?

Dear Amelia,

I'm sorry if I said something in my previous e-mail to scare you away. I probably made it sound like I was asking you out on a date. If you don't want to meet up in person, I can understand that. That would be a big step in our relationship.

I hope you are doing well. I know this sounds crazy, considering, but I miss you. I have nobody to help me procrastinate now but my dog. I have a dog. Did I tell you that?

Best,

Nate

PS: The subject line fits, but the movie's not all that great. If you haven't seen it, I wouldn't bother. There are better ones out there. However, Shirley Temple makes an appearance. She's always good for a smile.

"There are far, far better things ahead
than any we leave behind."
—C. S. Lewis

Chapter Twelve

From: amelia@forget-me-not.com
To: gallagher24@gmail.com
Date: Fri, Oct 16, 2015 6:57 p.m.
Subject: Re: Change of Heart?

Dear Nate,

I'm sorry. I know I apologize too much, but I feel this warrants an apology. I've been terribly busy at the flower shop. Everyone is suddenly getting married in October. Fall weddings are all the rage, apparently. Still, that's no excuse for my silence. I promise I've been thinking about you often. I at least hope that in my absence, you've been able to get a lot of writing accomplished.

Your previous e-mail didn't scare me. And what you wrote doesn't sound all that crazy. I miss you too.

Affectionately,
Amelia

I hit Send before I could give it too much thought. Nate deserved a response.

But he also deserves the truth, my conscience whispered. And all of what I'd sent him had been a lie, except the missing-him part. I did miss him. So much it left a hole inside my chest.

The flower shop, however, had not been terribly busy, or even busy at all. His e-mail *had* scared me, in all kinds of ways. His relationship to my ex-boyfriend aside, there were less complicated things to consider. Like the fact that I wasn't as interesting in real life as I was via e-mail. When it came to e-mail, I had the luxury of editing. Revising. Putting in the best parts.

And there was the matter of me. I'd been wearing a hat and sunglasses when Nate and I met. I wasn't a ravishing beauty, or even beautiful at all. I had red hair and freckles, something Candace and Crystal had teased me about mercilessly growing up. Some people insisted I was pretty, but those were mostly old, kind men, like George, who were probably just being nice. Never mind Chelsea and Matt and all the accompanying embarrassment. What if Nate and I went on a date and he realized he'd driven all the way to Mayfair for nothing?

I guess Rachel was a little bit right after all.

Bridget fidgeted. William placed an assuring arm around her shoulder. Usually I met with my brides twice. Once initially to make all the plans, then again a few weeks before the big day to make sure everything was squared away. I didn't want any of my brides fretting over a missing corsage for a beloved great-aunt we forgot to consider. I'd had both of these meetings already with William and Bridget. This third one, which really wasn't a meeting at all (more of a stop-by-the-shop check-in), was a courtesy to my brother and my soon-to-be sister-in-law.

According to him, Bridget had started having anxiety dreams, where all manner of things went wrong. Most of them had to do with the flowers and the wedding dress. So William checked on the alterations for her dress and asked if we could meet one last time to check over the flowers.

"We have three bridesmaids' bouquets." One of which I'd be carrying. "And, of course, your bouquet. Three groomsmen boutonnieres and three additional boutonnieres. Two for Bridget's side of the family. One for the pastor. Six corsages—three for William's side." Jeanine, Candace, and Crystal would cause a fuss if they didn't all have corsages. "Three for Bridget's side. The unity candle arrangement, which we'll bring to the reception hall. And then ten centerpiece arrangements."

Bridget continued to nod as I moved down the list in my notebook.

"See, everything's in order," William assured.

"I don't know why I'm so nervous." Bridget fiddled with the hem of her shirt.

"It's only natural," I said, hoping to set her at ease. "Almost all brides and grooms get a little anxious as the wedding approaches."

Bridget nudged my brother. "He's not."

"Yeah well, William doesn't get nervous about much."

He winked at me over the top of Bridget's head. "So we'll see you tonight, right? Out at Sawyer Farm for our annual corn maze adventure?"

I hesitated.

"Come on, Ames, you have to come. It's tradition."

He was right. It was. And it's not like we hadn't brought guests with us before. All through college, I'd brought Matt. But this felt different. William had been so much younger, and younger brothers were supposed to be tag-alongs. I wasn't sure if that rule applied to older, single sisters. I opened my mouth to answer when the door swooshed open, bringing in a delightful breeze of October air.

I expected a familiar face. This particular familiar face, I did not.

Standing in my store, looking even handsomer in person with his hair a bit wind-tossed and his eyes a richer shade of brown than I remembered, was none other than Nate Gallagher. He wore a navy-blue merino sweater with sleeves pushed halfway up his forearms and a broken-in pair of toasted-brown chinos with a braided leather belt and the kind of smile that could make a girl light-headed. He looked like a walking J.Crew advertisement.

I fumbled with the pencil, and in my attempt to catch it, knocked the notebook to the floor. I ducked behind the counter to pick both up with all of Africa's heat gathering inside the confines of my cheeks. Nate Gallagher was in my shop! And I found myself fighting the very same urge I fought when we first encountered one another, only instead of hiding beneath my steering wheel, I wanted to army-crawl into the back room and never come out again. I forced myself to stand and set the notebook on the counter between us. "Sorry about that. Wow, Nate. What are you doing here?"

"It's my sister's birthday. I took her out to dinner last night. I swear I wasn't going to stop by unexpectedly like this, but then I got your e-mail this morning, and well . . ." He stuck his hands inside his pockets and shrugged with the most adorable, self-deprecating expression ever to grace a man's face. "I couldn't resist."

"Oh yeah?" I set the pencil next to the notebook. It almost rolled off the counter again. I made a spastic grab for it, then tucked a strand of auburn hair behind my ear.

Settle down, Amelia.

"Anyway, I was wondering . . ." He looked at William and Bridget—who were both gawking, gave them an apologetic wave, then leaned a little over the counter. "Well, maybe we could grab a coffee or something."

"Oh, a coffee?" Why was my voice coming out so high? Seriously, what *was* that? I cleared my throat and tucked another strand of hair behind my ear. Glanced nervously at my brother, then back at the man who was making my underarms sweaty. "Well, I'm working. The shop doesn't close until one."

He checked his watch. "That's only a half hour away. I don't mind waiting."

I bit my lip, searching for an excuse. Begging the heat in my cheeks to go away already.

"Bridget and I can close down for you," William blurted.

"What?" I let out a nervous laugh. "But you don't know how to close."

My brother made wide eyes at me that thankfully, Nate didn't see. Apparently William wanted me to go on a real-life date as badly as Rachel. "I've watched you do it enough. And Bridget used to work at a flower shop in high school, so if there's a last-minute customer, she can make the bouquet. Right, Bridge?"

Her eyes glittered with curiosity as she looked from Nate to me. "Right. We've got this, Amelia. You should go have coffee with . . . ?"

"Oh, I'm sorry." I let out another nervous laugh. "This is my, uh, friend, Nate Gallagher. Nate, this is my brother, William, and his fiancée, Bridget."

"Ah, William. It's nice to meet you." Nate shook both of their hands with a smile tucked into the corner of his mouth. He knew more about them than either had any idea.

"You too," William said, darting a glance my way. "Hey, if you're staying the night, you should come to the corn maze with us tonight. It's this yearly tradition. Lots of fun."

This time I made big eyes at William. What did he think he was doing?

"A corn maze, huh?" I didn't miss the twinkle in Nate's eyes. "That sounds like fun."

We all stood there for an awkward moment.

Then Nate slid his hands back inside his pockets and pivoted one shoulder toward the door. "Shall we?"

Chapter Thirteen

The air was crisp and clean as I stepped outside beside Nate.

"Eloise's Bakery?" he said.

"It's great, but Eloise doesn't serve coffee. Patty serves coffee."

We walked side-by-side down the wide sidewalk, the smell of fallen leaves and Eloise's pumpkin muffins swirling together in the chilly breeze. I searched for something to say, but my tongue was officially tied. Nate, however, strolled beside me, looking perfectly at ease while taking in our surroundings. He caught me staring and smiled. It was a grin that etched crinkles into the corners of his eyes. "You're right. This place is gorgeous in October."

"Yeah, it is." I scrambled for something—anything—to add, but I was still trying to catch up with the moment. I was actually walking down Main Street with Nate Gallagher by my side.

He motioned toward the sign above Patty's House of Pancakes. "Is this the place?"

I nodded.

He stopped in front of the diner's large picture window and pivoted on his heels to face me. "Amelia, if you don't want to do this, it's fine. I shouldn't have bombarded you like this. I don't want to force you to keep me company."

"You're not forcing me. Not at all. I'm sorry I'm making you feel that way. You just . . . you caught me off guard. And I did warn you that I'm shy. That wasn't an exaggeration." My heart thundered harder the more I rambled. I scuffed my shoe against the cement, wishing I could be articulate and interesting in person. "I'm really sorry."

Nate tipped up my chin with his knuckle. It was a friendly action. Not too intimate. Yet heat stretched inside my belly, extending all the way down into my toes. He brought his hand quickly away. "There you go again."

"What?"

"Apologizing."

A smile spread across my face. And as it did, some of the knots in my stomach loosened. Somehow, simultaneously, this guy set my heart at ease and my senses on high alert. I took a deep breath. Forced my shoulders to relax.

He dipped his chin. "Are you sure you want to have coffee with me?"

"I'm positive." I glanced inside the window, where we'd already garnered the attention of a few familiar patrons. "But I should warn you. If you take me in there, Patty will see us. And once Patty sees us, all the other Bunco Babes will know that I was having coffee with a stranger. And then the entire town of Mayfair will be abuzz."

The twinkle returned to his eyes. "What, exactly, is a Bunco Babe?"

"They're a group of women who get together once a week to play Bunco and swap gossip. They have pink T-shirts and everything."

He chuckled.

The sound of it boosted my confidence. Maybe I *could* be as interesting in person as I was in our e-mail exchanges.

"That's not a problem for me, since I don't live here. You're the one who has to deal with the fallout." He raised one of his eyebrows. "Are you up for it?"

"I think so."

"Okay, then." Nate opened the door and swept the air with his arm, an invitation for me to go first.

It didn't take more than half a second before Patty saw us from behind the counter. Her eyes went extra wide, making them look as white as white inside her dark face. Nearly as wide as she was tall, she waddled more than she walked. "Amelia Woods, coming in on a Saturday before one o'clock?" She eyed Nate approvingly. "And who's this good-looking gentleman friend you have here?"

Every single person in the diner had stopped eating and was now officially staring. Patty's voice carried.

"Patty, this is Nate. Nate, this is Patty."

Nate shook Patty's hand, told her it was a pleasure to meet her, and said the food smelled delicious.

She swatted her dish towel at him, then led us both to

the corner booth, where it was—as she emphasized—more *romantic*. The flush in my cheeks expanded into my ears.

"What can I get you?" Patty asked as Nate and I scooted into our seats.

He deferred to me. "Are you hungry?"

I shook my head. My stomach was currently engaged in a circus routine. I couldn't eat if I tried.

"I guess it'll just be coffee then."

Patty scooted off to get our order, and Nate relaxed back into the booth, looking at me with a big, goofy grin.

"What?" I said.

"Nothing. It's just great to be here with you in person."

The circus performers in my stomach did some fluttery acrobatics. "How's the book?"

"I'm closing in on the end."

"Do you have anything lined up for after?"

"A couple opportunities have come my way." His grin didn't falter.

And it was highly contagious. I'm pretty sure the two of us looked like a couple of grinning fools. "Are you really not going to tell me who the celebrity is?"

He shook his head. "My lips are sealed."

Patty returned, set two mugs in front of us, filled both to the brim, and slipped away.

Nate crossed his arms on the table and leaned toward me. "Your shop is pretty great."

"Thank you."

"I saw the picture of you and your mom on the wall."

"Yeah?"

"You two look a lot alike."

"I definitely got her hair. But she wore the red prettier, I'm afraid."

"I don't think that's possible."

My skin prickled with pleasure, all the way up into my hairline. "So, twenty-four?"

"Any more guesses?"

I took a slow sip of my coffee, keeping eye contact over the rim of my mug. "Number of articles you've written?"

"No, but that's a good guess."

"Countries you've visited?"

"I wish."

"Number of girls you're currently in correspondence with?"

He let out a bark of laughter, then eased his arm over the backrest of the booth. He was perfection sitting across from me—absolute perfection. And he was here. With me. By choice. Laughing like he was enjoying it as much as I was enjoying it. "I like you, Amelia."

The words heated up every square inch of my skin. "I like you too."

"Enough to let me tag along to Wisconsin's biggest corn maze?"

With him looking at me the way he did, the word *no* dropped completely out of my vocabulary.

Nate picked me up in the same car I rear-ended in September. He walked up to my house and rang my doorbell and met Baxter, who liked him instantly. A good sign. The fifteen-minute drive had me hyperaware. Of my body, of his body, the closeness of our arms as they rested on the console. And holy cow, he smelled good. We agreed to meet William and Bridget at seven in front of the barn entrance, where the Sawyers sold their tickets—for the petting zoo, hayrack rides, a barnyard haunted house, and of course, the corn maze.

Gravel crunched beneath Nate's tires as he parked in the makeshift lot. Nate told me to sit tight and came around to open my door. The night was chillier than normal for mid-October. Enough that I'd worn my winter coat and a scarf. Nate had on a corduroy jacket that fit him well. Even though my hands were freezing, I kept them out of my pockets. We walked toward the big red barn, puffs of frozen breath escaping into the dark, our knuckles every bit as close as our arms had been on the console.

I spotted William and Bridget first. They waved hello as we approached. I had called my brother earlier and given the two of them strict orders not to ask how Nate and I met, that it was too embarrassing to bring up. I blew heat into my palms and rubbed my hands together as the four of us stepped inside the barn. There wasn't a very long line. The cold had chased a lot of people away. I reached inside my coat pocket to remove the twenty-dollar bill I'd stuffed inside, but Nate removed his billfold and asked for two tickets to the corn maze. I protested. "You're my guest. That means I should pay."

"But I invited myself, remember? And there's no use arguing. My last name is Gallagher. We Irish are stubborn folk."

I peered up at him. "You don't look Irish."

"That's because I take after my mom, who is Italian. I'm afraid Italians are every bit as stubborn as the Irish, which means I have a double dose of it running through my veins." He winked. "Another one of my faults."

Once the tickets were purchased, the four of us strolled to the maze entrance. Stadium-type lights had been set up around the periphery, casting enough glow down onto the cornfield that we could see. The girl who took our tickets asked if we wanted maps. Nate declined, insisting it would be cheating. As soon as we stepped inside, we were faced with one of two choices—left or right.

"I have an idea," William said. "Bridget and I go left. You two go right. Whoever comes out last buys the other couple hamburgers at Patty's afterward."

Nate looked down at me, that irresistible twinkle in his eyes, as if to say it was my call.

"You have yourself a deal," I said.

William grabbed Bridget by the waist and hurried left. They disappeared to the sound of her giggling.

Nate and I were officially alone. Surrounded by giant stalks of corn.

We started off, this time with my hands in my pockets. Even if the air between us did spark with heat, it was too cold to leave them out. Off in the distance, some teenagers shrieked.

"Number of gum sticks you've stuffed into your mouth at one time."

Nate's brow furrowed. "What?"

"Twenty-four."

He laughed. "Do I have a big mouth or something?"

The darkness had me feeling bold. "You have a nice mouth."

"Yeah?"

"Yeah."

We reached another fork in the path. Nate let me pick. I chose left.

"Number of Audrey Hepburn movies you own?"

He laughed again. "I don't think she's in that many movies, is she?"

"I don't know. You're the classic movie expert."

"You're not an amateur yourself."

The wind rustled the corn. Crickets chirped a slow melody. The cold had slowed down their leg-rubbing.

"What got you interested in them?" I asked.

"My college roommate freshman year. He was a film student and absolutely obsessed with Judy Garland. I'm not kidding. He covered his entire side of the room with posters of her. It was weird. He was always watching the old black-and-whites." We came to another fork. Nate chose right. I don't think either of us was in a hurry to get to the end. "I started watching them with him and discovered they were pretty great. The interest stuck." Nate picked up a stick and dragged the tip along the stalks. "What about you?"

"My dad was a big fan. We used to curl up on the couch together and watch them. One time, when I was in fourth grade, I was sick with the stomach flu for an entire week. He stayed home with me and we had a movie marathon. Started with musicals—*Singing in the Rain, Seven Brides for Seven Brothers*. Then we moved on to some others. He was a quiet man—my dad. But a big romantic at heart."

Nate raised his eyebrow. "Like his daughter."

"You think I'm romantic?"

"A crush on Mr. Darcy? A fan of fairy tales? Owner of a flower shop? I'd say yes, most definitely." He did it so smoothly, so suavely, I barely noticed it happening. One second my hand was tucked inside my coat pocket, the next it was out, my fingers entwined with his. It made my stomach swoop, and every single one of my nerve endings tingle.

"Holy mackerel, your fingers are frozen." He stopped in the middle of the maze, took both of my hands, and rubbed them between his larger ones. I didn't feel the least bit cold. In fact, I felt very, very warm. He must have sensed the change in temperature too, because his rubbing slowed, then stopped altogether.

I looked up at him, my heart racing so fast I was positive he could hear it.

He tucked a strand of hair behind my ear.

My breathing turned shallow.

He set his hand on the small of my back, drew me closer, dipped his chin . . .

And then a laughing couple rounded the corner and the two of us fell apart.

My brain was so fuzzy, my body so hot, I didn't pay much attention to who the couple was. Nate, however, released a disbelieving laugh. "Chelse?"

"Nate?" she said in return.

My breathing went from shallow to nonexistent.

"What are you two doing here?" Nate asked.

"Your little sister wanted to go out on her birthday weekend, and so here we are, at the Sawyer Farm corn maze."

Matt wrapped his arm around her waist. "We're a wild and crazy married couple, I tell ya."

The two of them closed the gap between us. I really, really wished they wouldn't.

"Never mind what we're doing here. What are you doing here?" Chelsea punched Nate's arm, then looked at me, her expression morphing from delighted to startled. "Amelia?"

"Amelia?" Matt parroted.

My mouth went as dry as cotton.

Nate's attention shot from his sister to me to Matt. "You guys know each other?"

Matt rubbed the back of his neck. "Sure we do. Amelia and I . . ."

"Amelia and Matt were college sweethearts." Chelsea tucked her arm around her husband's elbow. "They dated for *four* years. What in the world are you two doing together?"

"We, uh . . ." I swallowed, not at all sure what to say.

Nate looked like a deer in the headlights, watching his life flash before his eyes. Only instead of his life, he was probably replaying our run-in outside the church all those days ago when our worlds collided. Judging by the flicker in his brow, the pieces were coming together.

What a nightmare.

A lump as hard as a rock had parked itself inside my throat. I sat listlessly on my couch in the dark, Baxter curled up in my lap. Nate had dropped me off thirty minutes earlier. I hadn't taken off my coat. I hadn't taken off my shoes. I'd just plopped down on this cushion and turned comatose.

After our run-in with the two people on the face of the planet I never wanted to run into, we ended up completing the rest of the maze with them. Matt and Chelsea went on and on about what a small world it was and how unbelievable it was that we knew each other. Neither seemed to notice that Nate and I didn't have much to contribute to the conversation. I was too busy holding back tears to join in.

Once we came out, Chelsea and Matt said their goodbyes, and Nate and I waited for William and Bridget, who hadn't come out yet. I attempted to apologize, maybe a million different times in the five minutes we waited, but I didn't know how. All the tingling sensations had turned into this rock-hard lump in my throat that refused to leave. It was obvious Nate didn't want to be there anymore. It was obvious I'd made him feel like a complete fool.

When William and Bridget appeared, I feigned a headache and Nate dropped me off at home. Neither of us put our arms on the console during the drive. Now here I sat, alone in my dark house with Baxter on a Saturday night, something I'd always been fine with . . . until now. Now the entire scenario felt too depressing for words. I tucked Baxter beneath my arm and headed into the kitchen nook, booted up my computer, and opened my e-mail.

Dear Nate,

I am so sorry.

I punched the Delete button over and over until the four words were gone, then tried again.

> Well, that was awkward.

Delete, delete, delete.

> I'm sure you are thinking that I still have a thing for my ex.

Delete, delete, delete.

I buried my face in my hands and shook my head. *Lord, what am I supposed to say?* I rubbed my eyes and waited for the words to come. When it was all typed out, I saved the e-mail as a draft and closed my laptop.

Chapter Fourteen

"Your eyes still have that sad look about them." George rested his hat over the handle on his cane. He was waiting for me to finish his Monday-morning bouquet. "The forget-me-nots didn't cheer you up?"

"They did, George. They cheered me up quite a bit." I motioned to the bouquet behind me, tucked inside one of my mother's old vases. They were holding on well. I wrapped his sunflowers in twine. "You know, you've never told me how you and Sylvia met."

His light blue eyes brightened. "Haven't I?"

I shook my head. George had shared plenty of stories over the years, but their meeting wasn't one of them.

A dreamy look clouded his expression, like he was traveling back through time. "The first time I saw my Sylvia was in a dance hall before I went off to war. I saw her across the room." He shook his head and whistled. "I knew at that very moment I'd never be able to love a woman as much I loved that woman right over there."

The story thawed some of the coldness in my bones. "It was love at first sight, eh?"

"And every sight after." He smiled at me.

I smiled back. "How were you sure the two of you were going to make it?"

"Oh, I wasn't." He scratched the top of his bald, age-spotted head. "Walking across that hall, asking Sylvia for a dance was a risk, especially since my heart was already hers. But that's what love is—a risk. It's just a matter of whether or not it's one we're willing to take. With Sylvia, I was willing."

The story left me feeling lighter. Braver. If I was Cinderella, George was my fairy godmother. The thought left me smiling as I handed him the sunflower bouquet. "This one's on the house today."

"Oh, now . . ."

I held up my finger. "I don't want to hear another word. This is on the house, and if you try to argue, no bouquets for a month."

George chuckled, then took the sunflowers and shuffled out of my shop. I held the door open for him and watched him rap-tap down the street. Once he got into his car, I hurried back inside and pulled up e-mail on my phone. I hardly ever checked it at work. But George's imparting wisdom had filled me with a sense of urgency that was impossible to resist. I pulled up the message that had been sitting in my draft folder since Saturday night, added a postscript, then clicked Send.

If any man was worth the risk, it was Nate Gallagher.

From: amelia@forget-me-not.com
To: gallagher24@gmail.com
Date: Mon, Oct 19, 2015 10:34 a.m.
Subject: Hi . . .

Dear Nate,

I'm not sure what you must be thinking. I can imagine, but every time either of us has done that, we've both been wrong.

Still, I feel like I need to play out the scenario.

Here we are, having a great time together in the middle of a corn maze, when your sister shows up with her husband and this bomb the size of Hiroshima. I not only know your brother-in-law, I dated him. For four years in college. Then you remember how we met. Outside the church where Chelsea and Matt got married. And then you remember how frantic I was to get away the day we met. And everything probably clicked from there.

I'm sitting here, trying to think what I'd be thinking in your shoes. I guess I'd probably assume that you were still in love with your ex. Why else would you spy? And why would you keep that from me?

Would you believe me if I told you that's all wrong? Yes, I was spying on their wedding. My stepsisters were actually there—Drizella and Anastasia? You might have even walked with one of them down the aisle. They both look like life-sized Barbie dolls, if that helps jog your memory. I promise, though, I wasn't spying because I'm still in love with Matt. I got over him years ago. I was spying because . . . I don't even know. Curiosity? I guess you aren't the only one with a nosiness problem.

I know you think I have an issue with apologizing, but please allow me to extend one here. I'm sorry. I'm sorry for avoiding you when I found out my ex was your new brother-in-law. I'm sorry for lying when I told you that the reason for my silence was due to busyness. I'm sorry for putting you in such an awkward position at the corn maze. I'm sorry for not being able to say any of this in person, on the drive home. And most especially, I'm sorry for making you feel anything less than the wonderful man you are.

Regretfully,

Amelia

PS: I know this is probably a crazy proposition right now. But I'm going to throw it out there anyway. As you know, William gets married on Saturday. I don't have a date for the wedding. Any chance you'd want to join me? Despite the way it ended, I had a pretty fabulous time with you this weekend.

Leaves crunched beneath my feet as dusk slipped into darkness and the last of the sun sank behind the horizon. Wind blew up the path, rustling the colorful leaves that remained on the trees. It tangled with my hair, sticking wisps against my lips. When I reached the spot, I knelt down and placed the bouquet of forget-me-nots in front of my mother's tombstone. I peeled the wisps of hair away and blinked at her name etched in stone.

"Hey, Mom." I picked a few blades of cold grass. "William gets married tomorrow."

I wasn't sure if they'd make it—William and Bridget. Sure, they loved each other madly now. The question was, was it the kind of love that would flame hot and fizzle, or would it grow throughout the years? Like George said, it was impossible to know. I still wasn't sure if Bridget had really been visiting with a friend that evening or if something more had been going on. But that was a moot point. What mattered was that William had chosen the woman he was willing to risk his heart with. All I could do was pray that he'd chosen correctly.

"I wish you could be there," I whispered.

I sat for a while longer, until the wind grew too sharp and the chill too crisp. My frozen fingers reminded me of last Saturday, almost an entire week ago now. I sent Nate that e-mail on Monday, and so far I hadn't heard back from him. His silence spoke volumes. With a long sigh, I got back on my feet and made my way to the car. The county cemetery was mostly deserted, so the lone, hunched figure standing in front of a tombstone not too far from my vehicle stood out like a shining beacon. The old man had his head bowed, a hat in his clasped hands, a cane resting against his hip, his posture so familiar I did a double take. "George?"

He looked up.

And sure enough, it was him, standing at a tombstone surrounded by bouquets. I took a few steps closer, peering at the name on the stone.

SYLVIA STOCKDON

BELOVED WIFE AND MOTHER

BORN 1927

DIED 1996

My eyes widened.

"Well, Miss Amelia, it sure is a fancy seeing you here."

I looked between him and the polished marble. All this time—all this time he'd been coming into my shop to buy his wife bouquets?—she'd been gone. "I had no idea."

"Oh, I don't see why you would. I've never gotten used to talking about her in the past tense. I'm not sure if I ever will." He twisted his hat. "She's been gone almost twenty years now, and there's not a day goes by I don't miss her fiercely."

I understood. More than he knew. Only the ones I missed were my parents.

"You know what I always think about, though, when I stand out here?"

"What's that?"

"All the pain of losing her? I'd experience every last drop of it all over again for one more day." He gazed at the ground. "One more dance with my lady."

The words brought tears to my eyes. "Hey, George?"

"Hmm?"

"Would you be my date tomorrow for my brother's wedding?"

"A wedding and a pretty gal? Now that's an offer I could never refuse."

I kissed his pouched cheek, told him I'd see him at the chapel on the square at two thirty tomorrow afternoon, and left him alone with his memories. When I sat inside my car, I pulled my phone from my purse and dialed Nate. He'd given me his number when we shared coffee at Patty's. I had been too flustered to write it down after his earlier message on my answering machine. Nerves jumped around in my belly as the phone rang in my ear. I wasn't sure what made them bounce faster—the idea of him picking up, or the idea of him letting the call go to voice mail. When a recording sounded in my ear, I deflated in my seat.

"Hi, Nate? It's Amelia." I inhaled a rattled breath. "I wanted to let you know that I understand. I get why you haven't e-mailed me back. Our relationship would have been a complicated one. I wanted to apologize one final time—for not telling you about Matt once I realized Chelsea was your sister. I guess I couldn't figure out how to get the words out. I'm not sure if that's ever happened to you or not. And I also wanted to say thank you. For the e-mails. For the advice. For the friendship. They made a pretty fall in Mayfair even prettier, and for that, I will always be grateful."

Chapter Fifteen

The floorboards creaked beneath my open-toed orange pumps as I made my way to the back room of the small chapel. The ceremony would begin soon. The pews were getting full. And since the bride and groom had already seen each other for pictures, I asked them to meet me back here ten minutes beforehand. The satin of my navy-blue dress swished as I walked. Bridget had chosen knee-length A-line dresses for her bridesmaids—a classy cut that I probably could wear again. It looked gorgeous with the bouquet of orange ranunculus I held in my hand.

I stopped before the doorway and took a deep breath, then poked my head inside. The site of William and his bride-to-be made that same breath swoosh away. He looked absolutely dashing in a charcoal tux, and Bridget . . . Bridget was stunning. She wore a V-neck mermaid cut chapel train dress with gorgeous beadwork and a bounty of lace and held a bouquet of white ranunculus. She truly *was* radiant with charms.

When William saw me, he let out a low whistle. "I have a couple of gorgeous ladies on my hands."

I shook my head and wrapped him in a big hug, holding on tight for a long beat, savoring this moment. When I pulled away, I held up a black handkerchief. "I thought you might want to put this in the inside pocket of your tux. It was Dad's."

He took the gift in his hands, rubbing the silk between his thumb and forefinger, then folded it up and tucked it inside his pocket.

I straightened his tie, remembering the time I straightened his collar before his first day of kindergarten. It felt like yesterday. "They'd be so proud of you, you know."

Moisture gathered in his eyes.

It had me dabbing at my own.

Before we could get too mushy, I turned to Bridget. But a lot of help she was. Her eyes had filled with tears too. I swiped a knuckle beneath my eyelashes and held out my gift to her. A vintage brooch—sparkly with rhinestones and pearls in the shape of tiny flowers. The perfect size for a bride's hair. "My mother wore it on her wedding day."

"Oh"—Bridget set her palm against her chest—"I can't take that."

"Sure you can. It'll be your something borrowed."

A tear spilled down her cheek.

She turned around, and I slid the brooch inside her hair. Then she hugged me tight and whispered in my ear, "It's okay, Amelia. I promise to take good care of him."

I sat in a white plastic chair while George finished his cake beside me. It had been a gorgeous wedding. I wrapped one leg over the other, folded my hands over my knee, and watched everyone on the dance floor. The bride and the groom. Bridget's parents and her grandparents. My stepsisters and their husbands. Jeanine and the date she'd brought with her from Green Bay. Phil Nixon and Fern Halloway. Wayne and Sandy Sawyer. Their nephew Jake and his wife, Emma—she was Baxter's vet, and they were the town sweethearts. A whole floor of people who loved each other enough to take a risk.

George set his plastic fork on his plate, stood slowly, and held out his hand. "May I have this dance?"

I hesitated, wondering . . .

At what point in my life had I stopped dancing? Was it after my mother died? Or maybe after that, when my father followed? I guess it didn't matter when. What mattered was that I'd stopped. Somewhere along the way, I decided to stay off the dance floor. To watch instead. Maybe Rachel was right. Maybe it was time to get off the sidelines. To stop watching and start experiencing. I looked up into George's eyes, proof that living life meant pain would be inevitable. But maybe all the pain would be worth the *life* I'd experience along the way.

I took George's hand. He wrapped my arm around his elbow. The two of us made our way onto the floor and began swaying to Ben E. King's "Stand by Me."

"So whatever happened to your beau?"

"My beau?"

"The one that had love blossoming. Did you decide he was worth the risk?"

"I did."

"And?"

"It didn't work out."

"That's too bad. What was his name?"

"Nate Gallagher."

"Now there's a fine Irish name."

"His mother is Italian." I sighed. "Honestly, George, he was too good to be true."

"We all are in the beginning." The two of us shuffled back and forth, old George feeling frail in my arms. How much longer until he no longer came into my shop every Monday morning? "The good stuff comes when you decide to stick around long enough to learn each other's faults. That's what true love is all about."

"Hey now, I thought you said you loved Sylvia at first sight. You couldn't have known her faults then."

"I did love her right away, but it wasn't *true* love yet. It wasn't that deep-down, feel-it-in-your-bones kind of love. That kind's a lot messier. A lot better too. And it only comes with commitment and time." George's swaying slowed. Something behind me had caught his attention.

"Well, I wish I could have had some more time with Nate."

"There's a wish I think I can grant." He gave a nod over my shoulder.

I turned around and my breath hitched.

It was Nate. He stood behind me looking absolutely disheveled. Windblown hair, skewed tie, shirt front slightly untucked. He was even a little out of breath, like he'd run all the way from Yooperland. And absolutely, irresistibly adorable.

"What are you doing here?" I asked.

George patted my hand and slipped away.

"I didn't get your voice mail until this afternoon." He tugged at his tie. "And I must say, it absolutely confused me."

He came all this way to say that my message confused him? "I don't understand . . ."

"I never got an e-mail from you. I was waiting on one. Hoping for one. But after what happened, I was determined not to pressure you. I mean, it seemed pretty clear to me that you weren't very interested last Saturday."

I shook my head. He couldn't be more wrong. "Nate . . ."

"But I never got one. No e-mail in my inbox. And then you left that message alluding to an email, and I was absolutely confused." Nate pushed his fingers through his hair. "So I checked, and somehow your e-mail went to my spam folder. Maybe it was the lame subject line."

"Hey, now."

He smiled. "As soon as I read it, I grabbed my keys and hit the road. Then I got here and realized two things. I'd forgotten my stupid flip phone at home, and I had no idea where the reception was."

I cupped my hand over my mouth.

"I walked around town square asking anyone I could find, until someone finally led me here. To you."

"Stand by Me" gave way to another song—"I've Got You under My Skin" by Frank Sinatra. More people joined the dance floor, pushing Nate and I together.

"Since I came all this way"—he spread his hand on the small of my back and drew me closer—"would you let me have at least one dance?"

I slipped my hand in his, smiling so wide I wasn't sure I'd ever stop. His nearness made my insides tingle. I felt so light I thought I might float right off the dance floor. And oh my goodness, his cologne. Seriously, what was it called—heaven in a bottle?

"So, twenty-four." He flung me out, then pulled me back in again. "Any more guesses?"

"Number of cats you'd like to own someday?"

His chest rumbled with laughter.

"Am I at least getting close?"

"Not by a long shot." We swayed to the beat, his tempo flawless. "You were right, what you said on the phone. This could be complicated."

I held my breath.

"But I have to say, Amelia, I'd rather have a complicated relationship with you than an uncomplicated relationship with anybody else."

The words were too good to be true. *He* was too good to be true. And he really was. Of course he had flaws. Real flaws (not the charming ones he admitted to in his e-mails), the kind that might really, as Frank Sinatra sang, get under my skin someday. I couldn't wait to get to know what they were.

"Hey," he murmured into my hair.

"Hey, what?"

"Cinderella's finally dancing at the ball."

Our pacing slowed, no longer in tune with Frank's beat.

Nate drew my body to his, slid his broad hands up my

ribcage, and kissed me in the middle of the dance floor at my baby brother's wedding. A fire-in-my-belly, light-headed, world-spinning, weak-in-the-knees kiss. The kind fairy tales were made of. I clasped my fingers around Nate Gallagher's neck and kissed him right back.

Acknowledgments

Seriously y'all. I'm not typically a fan of writing first drafts. They tend to feel unwieldy and messy and sort of like oh-my-goodness-this-is-going-to-be-the-end-of-my-writing-career-because-this-is-so-horrendously-horrible. I usually lament this thought once or twice (or a hundred times) to my husband and my best friend, Melissa, both of whom remind me that I say this with every single story and, so far, my career hasn't ended. Anyway, that's usually how my rough drafts go down.

For whatever reason, this wasn't the case with *The Perfect Arrangement*. Let's just put it this way: If *The Perfect Arrangement* were a baby, it would be one of those incredibly endearing, low-maintenance, perpetually smiling babies that makes mamas everywhere feel like they're winning.

For that, I feel all kinds of gratitude toward the two main characters—Amelia and Nate—for their blessed cooperation. I had a blast bringing you two to life on the page.

And now that I've expressed my gratitude toward two imaginary people, I probably ought to express it toward the real-life ones.

Immense thanks go to . . .

My village, without whom I'd not be able to write an ever-loving word. My husband, for everything he does so I can pursue this dream. My children, for letting mommy escape to the office in relative (it's all relative, isn't it?) quiet. And my family, who are always willing to take said children so mommy can escape to the office in *actual* quiet.

Becky Philpott, Karli Jackson, Elizabeth Hudson, and all the other people at HarperCollins who've had their hands in this particular story. You're wonderful to work with! Same goes with my fabulous agent, Rachelle Gardner.

Terri Nelson and Terri Werkhieser, for not only answering my questions about the floral business, but for inviting me inside your adorable shop in Orion so I could gather some first-hand knowledge.

Katie Coleman, for kindly naming Amelia's business. The Forget-Me-Not Flower Shop fit perfectly. Oh, and all my Facebook fans, for helping me name Nate and Amelia! If you're reading this and not on my Facebook page you really should join in the fun. People help me name things all the time.

Amy Haddock, for sharing some funny flower-arranging anecdotes, one of which I used in the story.

Jesus. Because, well, you're everything.

And then, of course! My fabulous readers with an extra-special shout-out to the Ganshert Gang. You take the joy that is writing and increase it exponentially. Thanks for filling this adventure with so much encouragement, support, and love! I hope you enjoy reading my latest every bit as much as I enjoyed writing it.

1. Who was your favorite character and why?
2. Amelia has dealt with some pretty significant losses, and yet she says her life isn't tragic. Could you say the same thing if you were her? Are you more likely to focus on the good or the bad?
3. Who are you more like—Amelia, or her best friend, Rachel? How so?
4. Amelia feels very protective of her brother, William. Is there anybody in your life you feel extra protective of? Why?
5. Do you think William's fiancée, Bridget, was being honest? Do you think Nate's advice to let it go and respect William's wishes was good advice? Why or why not?
6. George tells Amelia that love is a risk, it's just a matter of who you're going to take the risk with. How do you know when somebody is worth the risk?
7. Just for fun—what do you think the 24 stands for?

Award-winning author Katie Ganshert graduated from the University of Wisconsin in Madison with a degree in education and worked as a fifth grade teacher for several years before staying home to write full-time. She was born and raised in the Midwest, where she lives with her family. When she's not busy penning novels or spending time with her people, she enjoys drinking coffee with friends, reading great literature, and eating copious amounts of dark chocolate.

You can learn more about Katie and her books by visiting her website katieganshert.com or author Facebook page.

Love in the Details

BECKY WADE

For the One who makes all things possible, even novellas. Thank you for entrusting me with this ministry and for equipping me to write each and every page.

Prologue

Josh,

Since I broke up with you, I can't stop crying. Can you please forgive me? I love you. I'm certain I'll always love you.

Today would have been our eight-month anniversary. When you left for MIT a month and a half ago, I never imagined that we wouldn't keep dating or that I wouldn't see you again at Thanksgiving. The long-distance thing has been miserable but our marathon phone calls and our back-and-forth e-mails throughout the days were getting me by.

Now I've lost all of it, and I'm heartbroken without you.

Here's what you don't know and what I can't tell you. Your mom came to see me. She drove to UT San Antonio, met me in my freshman dorm room, and took me to lunch. She cried, Josh. She cried because she's so upset over the fact that you're unhappy at MIT. She said you told her that you wanted to leave and come back to Texas to be near me.

She's a single mom and you're her only son and she loves you. My heart went out to her.

You've worked so hard. You're a genius and you've earned the financial aid scholarship that MIT offered you. Please understand I don't want anything to get in the way of that, especially me. You deserve to go there and you have to make the most of this opportunity because your mom can't afford to pay for you to go to college anywhere else.

She held my hands and, with tears streaming down her face, asked me if I'd break up with you. She said that so long as we were dating, you wouldn't be able to pour your whole focus and determination into your education. She said you'd always be torn between two places.

Maybe I should have stood up to her and refused to break up with you. Maybe I should have told you about my meeting with her, even though she begged me not to.

Your mom has always been wonderful to me, Josh. I respect her and I care about her and I couldn't turn her down. So I called you and ended our relationship without giving you any good reason other than that my feelings had changed and that I wanted to be free to date here at UTSA.

My feelings haven't changed, Josh. I don't want to date anyone but you. And I can't stand the fact that I let you think otherwise. Since our breakup, I haven't taken your phone calls and I haven't returned your e-mails and I won't mail this letter. But it's not because I don't love you. And that's why I can't stop crying.

You might not know it yet but you're going to do great things. I know it. I love you. And I'm very, very, very sorry for hurting you. Can you ever forgive me?

With all my heart,

Holly

Chapter One

The moment Holly had imagined, dreaded, and obsessed over had arrived. Josh Bowen—oh, my goodness it really was him, *Josh*, um, holy smoke!—was walking toward her down Martinsburg's Main Street sidewalk. Josh had returned to town temporarily, and thus, she was about to come face-to-face with her high school boyfriend for the first time in eight years.

Holly came to a halt, sensing the coffee inside the three to-go cups in the cardboard tray she held sloshing at the suddenness of her movement. Her heartbeat sped into nervous panic mode.

He hadn't spotted her yet. She could dash into the candy shop and hide. Or maybe the children's boutique . . . Only, she'd known for some time that Josh planned to visit Martinsburg, Texas, for Ben and Amanda's wedding. She'd been giving herself pep talks about this very moment, steeling herself to confront him again, practicing, even, what she would say. She shouldn't hide. She should deal with this, with him.

Thank God, she'd actually taken a bit of time on her appearance this morning. While her jeans, white top, and well-worn-in brown leather jacket weren't what she'd have picked for this reunion, they were decent enough.

Josh.

He looked much like he had at eighteen, except taller, his facial features less soft, his whole bearing more international. He no longer dressed like a graduating senior from a small-town Texas high school. In a navy pea coat open down the front, gray sweater, and flat-front charcoal pants, he gave off a hip and urban vibe. He *was* hip and urban now. Since she'd seen him last, Josh had leveraged his brilliance into a ridiculously successful tech company and moved overseas.

A piquant mixture of sweet memories and bitter heartache rose within her.

He glanced at something in a store window, giving her a view of his clean-lined profile. Then he turned his face forward and his attention intersected with her squarely. His expression went blank. His stride faltered.

Oh, boy. Holly attempted a pleasant smile. God had been merciful to her by allowing her to see him first, at least.

Josh seemed to recover himself and continued toward her at a slower pace.

A good number of people, mostly tourists, strolled the sidewalk. At a quarter past ten in the morning on this third day of November, many of the shops on Main had just opened for the day.

Holly stepped to the side, close to a section of brick in between two storefronts. Here, they could say hello to one another without blocking traffic like a boulder in the middle of a stream.

Josh came to a stop facing her.

She could hyperventilate, say something, or run. She chose the second option. "Welcome back."

"Thank you."

"It's good to see you again." The intimacy they'd once shared had been as enormous as China. In the face of that, her paltry sentence felt as small as Luxembourg.

His brown eyes assessed her with a tiger-like intensity that caused all the things she'd planned to say to slide out of her brain. There was something in those eyes that hadn't been there before. A shadow. A shadow of guardedness and hostility.

What had she expected? They'd loved each other once. Then, without warning or explanation, she'd shut him out of her life.

"Ben told me that you were planning to come to Martinsburg early for his wedding," Holly said.

"Yes."

Josh and Ben had met in the ninth grade, become best friends, and remained close. Ben's dad had never been a part of his life, and Ben's mom had always been overstressed and cash-strapped. Holly couldn't imagine her handling any mother-of-the-groom responsibilities for Ben's wedding. None.

So Josh had relocated to Texas from now until Ben's Thanksgiving weekend wedding so that he could give his friend the kind of support that counted. Ben had told Holly that Josh had taken over the planning and the funding for both the rehearsal dinner and the bachelor party weekend. Based on the Josh she'd known, his show of generosity and loyalty did not surprise her. "It's nice of you to make the effort to be here for Ben."

No affirmative reply.

"I'm Trinity Church's volunteer wedding coordinator. Since Amanda and Ben have decided to get married at Trinity, I'll be working with Amanda's professional wedding coordinator behind the scenes, representing the church . . . Anyway, I'll be helping out on Ben and Amanda's big day."

His tiger eyes continued to assess her with such absorbed concentration that her mouth went dry. Wrongly, her heart seemed to be gaining speed instead of steadying.

She bit the inside of her lip to keep herself from babbling about the wedding or—at all costs—from blurting out that she was sorry. These many years later, that's what she most wanted to say to him. It was a sentiment that had often filled the letters she'd written him and never sent, how horribly sorry she was for ruining what they'd had, when what they'd had, she'd realized more and more clearly over time, had been rare and beyond price. "How have you been, Josh? I've heard you've done very well."

"I've been okay," he said carefully.

"I'm glad."

"How about you?" He asked it seriously, like he actually cared about the answer.

"Great." She gave him a bright smile. He was super

smart. He could probably see through it. It was a smile overly, falsely bright. "I write young adult novels."

"I know."

"You do?"

"Yes."

"I. . . ." How did he know about her novels? "I . . . really love writing. When I'm not on a deadline, or banging my head against my keyboard, or out of ideas. Which is most of the time."

In answer, his lips indented upward on one side. Josh had a face perhaps a bit too angular and a nose perhaps a quarter of an inch too long to be considered classically handsome. His was an arresting face, grave and interesting, appealing to Holly in ways hard to define. His straight dark brown hair had fallen across his forehead when they'd been dating. Now it looked as though he warmed an expensive men's hair product in his palms, parted his hair on the side, then combed it back with his fingers to keep it in place.

Holly held onto her cup tray like a kickboard in a choppy sea. She really hoped her mascara hadn't smudged or that the sip of coffee she'd taken before she'd seen him hadn't left whipped cream on her lip.

"How's your family?" he asked.

"They're all fine. None of them live in Martinsburg anymore. My dad sold his construction business so now he and my mom only stay in their house here a few months of the year. The rest of the time they're at the lake house or their apartment in Austin cuddling Mark's baby—did you know that my brother got married and had a little boy?"

"I did know."

Was Ben filling Josh in about her the way that Ben filled her in about him? "And Jessica's in law school."

He nodded.

"So I'm the only one left in town." She gave a little shrug as if to say, *I'm still living in Martinsburg, despite that my parents, older brother, and younger sister have all moved on. But I really don't mind because I like it here and I'm very content and secure. Very!* "How's your mom?" Josh's father had died when Josh was twelve.

Warmth slightly softened the austerity of his expression. "She lives in Colorado now, near her sister."

"Is she retired?"

"She can retire whenever she wants." Which Holly translated to mean that Josh had set her up in such luxurious style that she'd never have another financial care in her life.

"But she doesn't like to sit still," he continued. "She's working at a charity that helps unemployed women find work."

"That's good to hear." Before Josh's mom had moved, Holly had run into her around town from time to time. Each meeting had filled her with complicated emotions of affection and pain. She didn't blame his mom for asking her to break up with Josh all those years ago. How could you blame a person for advising you to do the right thing, the thing that had become the springboard for all the success Josh had achieved afterward? On the other hand, Josh's mom couldn't have known how very much Holly had loved Josh or how much losing him had devastated her. So, deep in her heart, she couldn't bring herself to hold his mom completely blameless, either. She inhaled, seeking calm, rooting around for another topic of conversation—

"Well." He flicked a few fingers in the direction he'd been walking. "I'd better be going."

"Sure." She didn't allow her disappointment to show as she edged closer to the wall to let him pass. "I'll see you around."

"Bye."

"Bye."

He moved off.

Somewhat dazed, she watched him go.

His steps paused.

She jerked her face toward her tray and made a show of straightening the cups.

"Holly?"

"Hm?" She pretended to be surprised to discover that he hadn't left.

"I'm planning Ben's rehearsal dinner and I need to find a venue. I'm not familiar with Martinsburg anymore. Would you be willing to help me look for a place?"

He was asking *her* for assistance? "Sure."

He produced his phone. "May I have your number?"

She gave it to him.

"Thanks. I'll contact you." He nodded curtly, then strode down the street.

She was going to search for rehearsal dinner venues with Josh? Because of the wedding and the smallness of Martinsburg, she'd known that she'd cross paths with Josh during his time here. But she'd envisioned their interactions as short and formal. She hadn't expected to spend real time with him. Or share real conversations.

She made her way along the sidewalk in the opposite

direction, passing an art gallery, a wine shop, and a women's clothing store before coming to the home furnishings store she lived above. A narrow alley between buildings took her to an exterior staircase. From there, a hallway led to her building's three second-story units. She left Rob's coffee outside his doorway. He worked late every night as a sous chef and typically woke around this time. She knocked quietly on Mrs. Chapel's door. Her elderly neighbor opened the door the width of the inner chain she always kept latched.

"Here you are, Mrs. Chapel." Holly squeezed a cup through.

"Thank you, dear. Did you remember to put in one and a half packets of sugar?"

"I did."

"The cup feels cold."

"Sorry about that. I ran into an old friend on the street. Just zap it in the microwave for thirty seconds."

Mrs. Chapel patted the cup accusingly with arthritic hands. "If you're going out again later, I could use a new pack of Depends."

Holly laughed. "Now Mrs. Chapel, you know I'm just your friendly next door neighbor and coffee delivery girl."

"Fine." The old lady winked sagely at Holly. "I'll guilt one of my daughters into picking up the Depends for me."

"Good plan." Holly dashed around the corner to her door before Mrs. Chapel could ask her to buy Ensure or Vitamin K.

She'd scored the best apartment of the bunch. It overlooked Main and boasted lots of windows and spacious everything: living room, kitchen, bedroom, bathroom.

The moment she set aside her tray, she dug her phone from her purse and texted her girlfriend, Sam Sullivan. *Lunch today, 12, Taqueria.*

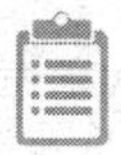

Josh continued along Main Street until he was sure he'd left Holly far behind him, then ducked blindly into a store. One sweeping view of the place told him that the shop sold Texas nuts.

The middle-aged woman behind the counter caught his eye. "Welcome. May I help you?"

"I'll take whatever's most popular." He hadn't come in for pecans. He just needed a few minutes of privacy.

"Certainly. Our hickory smoked trail mix is our most popular item."

"Fine."

She held up an empty sack. "Two-pound bag all right?"

"Yes."

Josh took up a position near the front window, his back toward the shop, his shoulder set heavily against the side wall.

There was a reason he'd avoided returning to Martinsburg.

And his reason had the most infuriatingly beautiful gray-blue eyes.

He'd spent his college summers taking courses and working close to the MIT campus. For the most part, his mom had come to visit him in Massachusetts. The few times he'd stayed in Martinsburg for Christmas, he'd gone to great lengths to make sure he never saw Holly.

Seven months ago, Ben and Amanda had gotten engaged

and announced that they'd be marrying in their hometown of Martinsburg, Texas, population 10,000. Shortly afterward, Josh had made plans to return to Martinsburg for the four weeks prior to Ben's wedding. So long as he had his technology with him, he could work away from his home base in Paris for up to a month.

He'd told himself it would be fine. He'd told himself that the thing with Holly had happened in another lifetime. He'd had seven months to get his head straight, to prepare himself.

Seven months hadn't been long enough.

Eight years hadn't been long enough, either.

"Here you are!" The store employee displayed the trail mix like a fine wine. "Our best seller."

"Thanks."

"Would you like to come to the counter for a nut tasting?"

"No. I . . . just need a minute to myself." He gave her a level stare.

"Ah. Okay. I'll have this at the register for you when you're ready."

He scowled back out the front windows.

Holly Morgan. The Holly who'd once been his.

Josh had never done anything halfway. It wasn't in his makeup. He hadn't done academics halfway in high school or college. He hadn't done his business halfway. He'd always worked like a machine and still did. In fact, part of what had initially fueled him in his career had been his desire to prove to Holly that he was worth something, that she'd made a mistake when she'd cut him loose.

No, he didn't do anything halfway.

Unfortunately for him, he hadn't fallen in love with Holly halfway, either. Theirs had not been a lighthearted romance. They'd kept it pure, but it had also been intense.

Holly had been smart and kind, creative and genuine. She hadn't had the sort of in-your-face, commercial prettiness that had characterized the popular girls in their high school. But to him, she'd been more gorgeous than any woman he'd ever laid eyes on before or since.

When he'd known her, she'd worn her light brown hair straight down her back. Now it fell a few inches longer than her shoulders, layered slightly, wavy, with some shiny dark blonde strands in it. Her thoughtful, heart-shaped face held a sweetness that couldn't be faked. She had great cheekbones and little brackets that formed at the corners of her lips when she smiled.

He'd continued to gain height in college. She hadn't. She stood about six inches shorter than he did now, her build slender but not skinny.

When he'd caught sight of her on the sidewalk just now it had knocked the air from him. He turned his hands palms up and watched the tremor in them. Fisting his fingers, he buried his hands in his coat pockets.

He'd lost two people in his life that he'd never recovered from. His dad and Holly. There hadn't been a day that had gone by that he hadn't thought about them both.

The last time he'd seen Holly, they'd hugged each other in an airport terminal like they never wanted to let go. The departure time for his flight had drawn closer and closer. His mom, who'd already gone through security and was waiting for him at the gate, had started calling his cell phone. He'd held onto Holly for as long as he could. When their time had run out and they'd kissed for the final time, his heart had felt like it was breaking clean in two.

He'd looked back at her from the security checkpoint line. At first, she'd given him wobbly smiles and brave waves. The final time he'd looked back, tears had been running down her face.

He'd worked hard to earn his scholarship to MIT, but once he'd arrived there, he'd wanted, desperately, to give it up and return to Holly. Without her, school seemed pointless, his loneliness endless. He'd been certain he'd be able to make a success of himself regardless of which institution issued his degree. He'd wanted to make a success of himself with Holly. But before he could follow through on his desire to leave MIT, she'd broken up with him.

People drifted by on the far side of the shop's window.

Martinsburg had been founded in the Hill Country of central Texas in 1848 by Germans who'd come for economic and religious freedoms. These days, tourists were drawn here by the town's old-fashioned charm, surrounding wineries, hunting, wildflower fields, B&Bs, and underground caverns.

Upon arriving two days ago, his strategy had been to limit his interaction with Holly as much as politely possible. But, a few minutes ago, when he'd had the chance to walk away and leave her behind, just as he had in that airport terminal all those years ago, he'd failed. In that instant, he'd wanted some tie to her, some small link. So without thinking it through, all instinct and no logic, he'd asked for her help searching out a rehearsal dinner location.

He shouldn't have done that. She'd shattered him when she'd ended things between them. The memory caused his pride to twist and burn.

It had been unbelievably painful to talk with her this morning, and their conversation had only lasted for a few minutes. Why had he signed himself up for more?

He could cancel. Or go on one outing with her and call it good. Pulling free his phone, he brought her name and number up on his screen.

Holly Morgan.

It shamed him that he still hadn't gotten ahold of himself. He needed more time to recover, standing here in a nut shop.

Seven months. He'd had seven months to prepare himself for his reunion with her.

And it hadn't been long enough.

"Hola!" Sam slid into the booth at the Taqueria opposite Holly, bringing a light waft of Chloe Eau de Parfum with her. "What's something we can say to one another in honor of this fine Mexican food establishment?"

"Uh, chimichanga?" Holly offered. "La Bamba? I should have taken Spanish in high school, seeing as how I live in a state that borders Mexico. Instead, I took French." Holly scooted the chip bowl toward Sam. "I've never once visited France."

Sam scooped salsa onto a tortilla chip.

Sam and Holly had made it their New Year's resolution to eat at every restaurant in Martinsburg over the course of twelve months. Their town offered a total of one hundred and three restaurants. So far, they'd made it through eighty-seven.

"So?" Sam asked. "Why the urgent summons? It's Tuesday and we weren't supposed to have lunch here 'til Thursday."

"I saw Josh today."

Sam's manicured eyebrows lifted. "As in your high school love Josh?"

"The same."

"High school love turned billionaire Josh?"

"Yes."

"Already arrived in Martinsburg to ride to the rescue of his loyal pal Ben."

Holly nodded.

"Tell me all."

Holly recounted her meeting with Josh, starting with his appearance and ending with his request for her help searching out rehearsal dinner locations.

Sam had the sleek dark hair, oval face, and beautifully pampered skin of a woman born and bred on the East Coast, which, in fact, she had been. She'd married a man Holly affectionately referred to as Mr. Perfect two years ago and moved to Martinsburg when Mr. Perfect's engineering expertise had scored him a job with Martinsburg's largest employer, a clean energy company. Sam worked as a CPA and had chosen a navy pin-striped suit for today's work ensemble.

"He must have it bad for you," Sam said. "Otherwise why ask for your help?"

"He isn't familiar with Martinsburg anymore. Maybe he just needs a local to offer up ideas."

"A man that rich can hire someone to scout locations. Also, how come he hasn't already booked a place for the rehearsal dinner? Amanda and Ben's wedding is what, three and a half weeks away?"

Ben's fiancée, Amanda, was the beloved daughter of Martinsburg's wealthiest family. Her upcoming wedding had become one of the town's favorite topics of conversation. Not above football, of course. But it had edged past the ongoing dispute about whether Billy's barbeque rub was better than Johnny Earl's.

"Maybe he's been busy?" Holly suggested.

Sam snorted. "Busy dreaming of a reunion with his high school girlfriend. Did you set a date to scout rehearsal sites?"

"No, I gave him my number."

"Holly, Holly, Holly." Sam shook her head pityingly. "Now you've handed him all the control. You're going to have to sit around on pins and needles waiting to hear from him."

"Does the sitting around have to involve pins and needles?" Holly took hold of a lock of her hair and wound it around her index finger. The truth was that seeing Josh had already turned her brain to mush and made her stomach so jumpy she doubted whether she'd be able to consume even a single cheese enchilada. More's the pity. She liked Mexican.

"You should have asked for his number," Sam informed her. "Or you should have said that you'd be free on, say, Saturday from two to five."

"This is why you're married to Mr. Perfect and I'm dating no one."

Sam pointed a tortilla chip at Holly. "My husband is indeed perfect."

"Yes. I realize." Mr. Perfect made good money, dressed

like someone who knew how to sail, cooked, shopped for groceries, cleaned their house, and frequently showered Sam with gifts.

"He made chicken piccata last night," Sam said, "and told me to rest while he cleaned it up."

"Boo! I ate cereal for dinner."

"I'm now going to leverage the man IQ I used to land my husband to help you land your high school love turned billionaire—"

"No! No, no, no."

Sam waited for her to explain her reluctance while mariachi music played softly and the scent of cilantro sifted over them with the air conditioning. A few banners of colorful cutout tissue paper rectangles swagged above them.

"I can't fall for him again, Sam."

"Why not?"

"He lives in Paris, you realize. He'll be leaving town right after the wedding."

"Not all long-distance relationships are doomed to crash and burn."

"Okay, setting aside the long-distance part, if I let myself care about him again, then I risk putting myself through all the heartache I went through the last time we broke up. I can't do it again."

Sam's face softened. Not usually given to physical displays of affection, she reached across the table and wrapped her hand around Holly's forearm. "My first man IQ lesson? Nothing ventured, nothing gained. Do you want Josh?"

"No."

"Yes you do. And this is your chance! You have proximity."

She squeezed Holly's arm to underscore the urgency in her words before sitting back in her booth seat. "I counsel you to mount a full-scale assault on his heart."

"I typically only mount full-scale assaults on my To Be Read pile of books."

"Man IQ lesson number two: you have to start thinking of yourself as superior to him."

Holly laughed. "What?"

"I'm just telling it like it is. In order to catch this guy, you're going to have to believe that *he's* the one who will come to care about you so much that *he'll* be heartbroken when your time together runs out. Are you following me?"

"Um . . ."

"What's the problem? You *are* superior to him. You're wonderful in every way."

"Not in every way. I have allergies and go to work in my pajamas and still haven't earned the affection of Rob's lab. Aren't labs supposed to love everyone?"

"You're a bestselling author."

She gave Sam an unconvinced look. A few of her dystopian YA novels had snuck onto the very bottom of the *USA Today* list. She'd written two books a year since college. Not all of them had done as well.

"Your novels star a fearless eighteen-year-old girl," Sam said, "who never hesitates to take names and kick bootie. *You* are your heroine."

Holly wrinkled her forehead. "She's like the superhero cartoon version of me. She's amazing with a rapier, for pity's sake."

"Well, you're going to need to channel more of her in order to convince your billionaire to put a ring on it."

"He's not my billionaire and I don't want to convince him to—"

"Also, you might want to think about wearing tighter clothing, more makeup, and getting a gel manicure every two weeks. Just sayin'." Sam shot her a big grin.

"Now I know you've lost your mind."

She was supposed to be writing.

Holly had returned to her apartment hours ago after lunch at the Tacqueria. She'd stationed herself at her desk, which faced a glorious old window overlooking Main. She had her computer document open in front of her. Her environment cocooned her appropriately with quiet. Her pumpkin-spice candle was flickering and she'd answered her e-mail. She should be writing. But all she'd been actively doing was waiting for a text or call from Josh.

Sam would not approve.

Beyond the window panes, the sun melted toward the horizon, casting amber light over Martinsburg—

Her phone rang. Holly lunged for it like a woman in sugar withdrawal lunging for the final truffle at a chocolate shop.

The screen announced the incoming caller as Amanda's mom. Spirits sagging, Holly set the phone down and let it go to voice mail. Because of her volunteer position as

Trinity Church's wedding coordinator, either Amanda or Amanda's mom called her almost daily. Holly found it more efficient to compile all their questions and address them at one time.

The cursor on her computer screen blinked, awaiting excellence. She tucked her feet underneath her crisscross style and swiveled her chair to face the interior of her home. It had taken her a good deal of time to exchange out all the old furniture her parents had loaned her for these new pieces she'd purchased for herself. Nowadays, her little place looked like the residence of an actual grown-up. Area rugs over the hardwood floors. Quality furniture she'd scored in back-of-the store bargain rooms. The sofa and padded ottomans were pale gray, brightened by one fabulous yellow raw silk chair, and several navy and white trellis-patterned throw pillows.

She'd built a home for herself in Martinsburg totally independent of her family and Josh. The home she'd made included her writing career, this community, her church, friends, relatives.

It hadn't been easy to get herself to this place. It had been hardest of all during the months following her breakup with Josh. She could remember praying daily back then, hourly even, asking God what she should do, whether she should contact Josh.

Every time she'd prayed about it, she'd sensed God steering her to leave things as they were. Not to contact him.

The tremendous success Josh had enjoyed since then proved that God had been working out His plan for Josh's life through the guidance He'd given her.

So how come she'd felt their old chemistry when she'd seen Josh today? She'd been faithful to God's leadership way back when. So why hadn't God done her the favor of taking away her feelings for Josh?

She planted an elbow on her chair's armrest and leaned the side of her head into her hand. She'd been on plenty of dates with good guys, guys who were genuine and sweet and sometimes even very cute. Why hadn't any of her adult relationships moved from interest/attraction to that thing much harder to attain: love?

The Sunday school answer was, of course, that God had been busy teaching her to be totally content in Him alone. Which was well and good, except that the pesky, romantic bent of her soul refused to quit hoping for a husband and one day, children. She was forever striving to balance peace with her singleness against her ongoing prayer asking God to prepare her for someone and someone for her.

Experience had taught her that heart-tugging, love-inducing men were scarce. She'd had one. Maybe she'd used up her quota.

Her phone chimed. She swung her chair back around and scanned the new text message. *Are you free on Thursday afternoon to visit rehearsal dinner locations? If not, we can go whenever it's convenient for you. Thanks, Josh.*

Oh, bother. Here came all those unwelcome feelings again—giddiness, fear, excitement. She pushed one finger at a time into her palm, stopping just short of cracking her knuckles, while she pondered the gracious tone of his message. Appropriately grateful.

She channeled Sam and decided to wait an hour to

reply. He didn't need to know that she'd pounced on his text. She'd certainly reply in the affirmative even though a Thursday afternoon appointment would mean missing her favorite Zumba class.

Zumba would be available forever. Thursday's outing with Josh presented her with a rare opportunity to achieve something with Josh she'd long wanted.

Closure.

If, when Josh left town in a few weeks, she could part with him on amiable terms, then perhaps she'd be able to close the chapter of her past with his name on it and move on to the *someone* God intended.

Chapter Three

She spotted Josh from half a block away. Casual and still, he leaned against the side of a black Range Rover, waiting for her. Even in jeans and a black crew-neck shirt, he gave off the impression of power, competence, and leashed intensity. He'd pushed his hands into his pockets.

Had he—this sophisticated man—really loved her once? It seemed a distant, fuzzy impossibility. *You're here for closure*, she reminded herself. And to lend assistance to an old friend.

She'd contemplated taking him out in her car, since she was the one who knew the area. But she hadn't been sure what twenty-six-year-old tech gurus were driving around in these days. She'd feared her aging Mazda Miata convertible too dated for him, its quarters too cramped.

She'd instead suggested he drive and that they meet here, at Smith's Smokehouse. Parking around Main could be tricky for nonresidents without assigned parking spots. Smith's had a big lot and a location near her apartment.

She stopped a few feet from him. "Hi."

"Hi." Josh studied her. "Thanks for helping me with this. I appreciate it."

"I'm happy to. It's a nice day for a drive." The temperature had stretched all the way up to a crystal bright seventy-five. "You've given me a good reason to get out from behind my desk." He opened the passenger side door for her. Buttery tan leather upholstery immediately embraced her.

He started the car and pulled onto the road. "Should we go see one of my picks first or one of yours?" he asked.

Via text they'd agreed that they'd each come up with two potential rehearsal dinner venues for today's outing. "Either one."

"Ladies first."

"In that case, turn right at the light." Holly took her wedding coordinator's notebook from her purse and settled it on her lap. "Let's start with the Texas Olive Oil Company's farm. It's just ten minutes outside town and they have a wonderful barn."

A few moments of quiet. "The Texas Olive Oil Company you said?"

"Yes. I heard a rumor that they've started renting out their barn for functions. So I called them and asked if we could stop by for a tour." She'd spent an hour or two brainstorming and researching fresh new rehearsal dinner ideas before deciding on her top choices. No one wanted to eat at the country club for the thousandth time.

"Would I need to rent tables and chairs and have the food catered if I hold it there?"

"Yes. Approximately how many guests are we talking about for the rehearsal dinner?"

He glanced across his shoulder at her. "Seventy."

"I suppose that's about right, considering the ten bridesmaids, ten groomsmen, the house party, the ring bearer, and seven flower girls."

"Plus out-of-town family. Do you think this barn of yours will be big enough?"

"This barn of mine, I do believe, will be big enough."

He rolled down his window and rested a bent arm on the door. Sunlight shimmered against his TAG Heuer watch and made clear the details of his beautifully masculine forearm, wrist, hand. His firm, aristocratic profile could have belonged to an Italian prince.

Try to think of him in a kindly fashion, Holly. Not so much prince-like as pleasant-old-friend-like. "So, you live in Paris now."

"I do."

"What brought you to Paris?"

"I lived in New York after college, when my company was a start-up. But I knew I didn't want to live there long term. I can headquarter just about anywhere."

"Your company specializes in apps for smartphones and tablets?"

"You know about my company?"

"You knew about my books."

"True."

Holly's knowledge about Josh's company derived from two sources: Ben and her own thorough study. Over the years, she'd read every article on Josh and his business—both in print and online—that she could get her hands on. He'd been on the cover of *Forbes* once. Numerous times, he'd been given awards or asked to deliver speeches.

Josh's mind had always fascinated her. Most of the kids in high school had been far more impressed by athletes who'd excelled at football or basketball. They'd viewed Josh—their very own version of Matt Damon's character in *Good Will Hunting*—as somewhat of a mystery. Josh had been so off-the-charts brilliant that even his AP math teachers hadn't been able to teach him anything he didn't know. He'd crushed the SAT and ACT, and his GPA had been far enough above a 4.0 that no one, not even very-brainy Jim Wong, had come close to challenging Josh's status as valedictorian.

Holly had been a relatively smart high school girl in her own right, just open-minded and quirky and mature enough to appreciate intelligence over how a guy's bottom looked in football pants. Her strengths, however, had centered around subjects like English and history. Like most writers, she was anti-math. Nor was she terribly technological. She couldn't comprehend the things that went on in Josh's brain and yet his brain awed her just the same. "Since you can headquarter anywhere, why did you pick Paris?"

He scratched the side of his upper lip with his thumb.

"Because of the crepes?" she asked.

His dark gaze flicked to hers, glinting with humor. "The crepes aren't bad."

"No. I imagine the croissants and soufflés and macaroons aren't terrible either."

"Have you been to Paris?"

"Never. But I might have to go one day. For the crepes."

He drove quietly.

"You decided to live in Paris because?" she prompted. He still hadn't explained why he'd chosen it.

"It interests me. It's historic and busy and full of art and beauty."

"You love it there."

"I like it there but I'm not tied to it. I may move somewhere else in a year or two. Berlin or London or Zurich."

"But not back to the United States?"

They'd come to a light. He assessed her, his eyes saying a lot of things, all of which were shielded so carefully that she couldn't decipher a single one. "Not anytime soon."

For some reason, his answer saddened her. She issued more directions on how to get to the farm.

The outskirts of town ebbed away, replaced by the famous scenery of the Texas Hill Country. Rugged land, populated with cedar and live oaks, punctuated with outcroppings of granite and limestone rolled against a cerulean sky.

"Where are you staying while you're in town?" Holly asked.

"My assistant rented a house for me in the Hollow."

The nicest neighborhood in Martinsburg had been nicknamed the Hollow so long ago that no one remembered why. The home Holly had been raised in, which her parents still lived in part of every year, was located there. "What about this car? Also arranged by your assistant?"

"Yes."

"It must be nice to have an assistant. Do you think I could find one who'd work for me for five dollars a day?"

"No."

"Which explains my lack of one."

"If you were willing to pay an assistant more you wouldn't have to get your own coffee."

He was referencing the coffee tray she'd been carrying the other morning. She refrained from mentioning that if she didn't go out for coffee, she'd lose her mid-morning reason to change out of pajamas. "I'm willing to pay more; it's my puny bank account that isn't."

They pulled into the olive farm. Bushy, thin-leaved trees that looked like something straight out of Galilee spread away from the barn and outbuildings in neat rows.

Josh and Holly climbed from the car and made their way toward the barn. Across the property, a middle-aged farmer lifted his head from a piece of machinery he'd been working on. "Hello there! I'll be right with you."

"No hurry," Holly called back.

She and Josh waited by the two huge metal door panels that slid on tracks to open the front-facing side of the barn. A large flagstone patio extended from where they stood, overlooking a view that sloped gently down to Lake Cypress Bend.

Holly peeked up at Josh. He wasn't admiring the view. Instead, he was watching her.

Warm, discomfiting attraction tugged within her. "What do you think?" She extended an arm to encompass the scenery. "Beautiful, isn't it?"

He gave it an obligatory scan. "It is."

"If the weather's nice, you could serve drinks or appetizers or dessert out here." The nearby trees formed canopies over the open ground between rows, like charming tunnels of nature.

He returned to looking at her. "Tell me about your writing."

She remembered that he'd always been quick to change subjects. He'd never had the patience to chitchat about things that didn't interest him when he could jump the tracks to things that did. "What would you like to know?"

He asked educated questions about the business of publishing and about her writing process. It touched her that he cared to know about her whimsical and cherished profession.

She relaxed by degrees as they talked, just the two of them surrounded by air that smelled like fresh soil and the lavender growing around the base of the barn. It was a unique spell, this. A hawk rode the faraway wind—

"Hi there, y'all."

She'd been so engrossed in their conversation that the arrival of the farmer came as a small surprise. A friendly man with a John Deere hat and a sun-worn face, he pushed open one of the sliding metal doors and ushered them inside the barn.

Unlike many of the leaning, ramshackle barns dotting the Texas countryside, this structure had likely been built in the last five years. It had plenty of windows, exposed wood walls, and wonderful cross-timbered beams spanning the peaked ceiling.

"A while back the boss had the idea of renting this place out for parties and such." The farmer nodded toward the olive pressing machinery. "We put all the equipment on these here rolling platforms so we can move it out when needed."

"Is it available Friday, November twenty-seventh?" Josh asked.

"Let me go get the book." He bustled out.

"You like this barn of mine," Holly stated, because she could see that he did. "You can see its potential."

"Definitely."

The farmer returned, holding a big and dog-eared calendar. Computerized calendars had not, it seemed, made their way to the Texas Olive Oil Company. "What date did y'all say?"

"The twenty-seventh."

"Shoot. It looks as though the barn's already booked that night."

"*It is?*" She was a Martinsburg insider. As far as she knew, this site had only been used for a few high-end events in the past several months, mostly corporate. She hadn't once doubted its availability.

"It sure is. I'm real sorry about that."

Josh appeared unperturbed as he shook the man's hand. They both thanked him and set off for Josh's car.

Holly took one last, heavily disappointed look back at the barn. Such an ideal setting! Drat, drat, drat. "I apologize, Josh. I should have asked over the phone whether this place was booked that night and saved us the trip. They just began to hold events here and hardly anyone knows about it. I thought this place was still a secret."

"Don't worry about it."

They drove next to Holly's second choice, a historic

dance hall outside of town still used for the occasional visiting singer or county-western dance night.

Then on to Josh's very unoriginal first choice, the country club. Thank goodness, the Ladies Golf Association already had it reserved the night in question. Lastly, they visited Josh's second choice, a luxurious restaurant on the outskirts of town called the Lodge.

At each stop, Josh treated everyone with excellent good manners. He also took very little time to survey his options. Both the dance hall and the Lodge were available on the twenty-seventh, but he remained noncommittal.

"You don't seem to be feeling the same urgency that I am about booking one of these places," Holly commented as he steered the Range Rover toward downtown Martinsburg.

"I haven't found what I want yet. I don't like to settle."

"Um, do you realize how particular Amanda can be?" Amanda would have wanted engraved rehearsal dinner invitations in the mail a week ago, minimum.

"I realize." He smiled slightly, looking ahead at the road.

Holly considered that smile. Self-assured, unintimidated. "Very well then." She refused to angst over the rehearsal dinner. She had her hands more than full already with wedding details.

It was enough that she'd started to accomplish today what she'd hoped for with Josh: a more upbeat ending to an important relationship that had ended on a huge downbeat the last time.

Their conversation had flowed easily enough and she'd come to feel mostly comfortable in his presence—which was above and beyond what she'd hoped for before he'd arrived in town. If their light interaction this afternoon felt shallow somehow, that was to be expected. Of course it felt shallow: it didn't come close to addressing the magnetism, tension, and pain that lay between them.

During their last phone call before the breakup, they'd whispered words of love to each other. Now they were two independent adults in the latter half of their twenties, discussing things like whether a room had enough space for ten round-tops.

They drew near the north side of the Hollow. "Would you mind stopping by my parents' house?"

"Not at all."

"Do you remember Shadow?"

"The cat?"

"She still lives at the house. She's the only resident when my parents are out of town."

He quirked a brow at her.

"I know, it's weird. When my parents bought the place in Austin we decided that Shadow would move in with me. But she ran away twice—" She had to catch herself from telling Josh where to turn. He turned in the right place without assistance. He remembered the way. "Both times Shadow ran away, I found her back at my parents' house. So I installed a cat door. I stop by every day to feed her."

"It seems like you could leave more than a day's worth of food. Then you wouldn't have to come by as often."

"But then, you see, Shadow wouldn't get enough social interaction."

He parked in the driveway of her family's stately 1930s two-story. If Holly did say so herself, the house had been kept up well, its shingles painted a pretty beige, its rock chimney standing proudly straight.

"How come you don't live here with Shadow?" he asked.

"Because I'm not eighteen anymore. It would seem sort of . . . I don't know. Sorry? To live here alone at this point. I like my apartment." She gave him a questioning look. "Would you like to come in? It'll just take a minute."

"I'll stay here. I have some business I need to check." He motioned toward his phone, sitting in the middle console.

Holly nodded and let herself inside the house.

Josh had no doubt that text messages and business e-mails awaited his attention, but he hadn't asked to stay outside because of them. For a man who didn't lie—he preferred blunt, straight-up communication—he'd become quite the liar where Holly was concerned.

Just sitting in the driveway of this house brought up a storm of old memories. He had no intention of going indoors and seeing the places where he'd held hands with Holly, talked with her parents and siblings, picked her up for prom.

In case Holly caught sight of him through a window, he set his phone on his leg and looked down at it.

He was pretty sure he was losing it because he wanted more time with her. She made his mind, body, and senses rush to life in ways they hadn't in too many months to count. Whenever he met her eyes, attraction snapped like electricity between them. Her smile left him wordless.

He could buy many things in this world, but he couldn't buy the way she made him feel.

He dealt in math and science and computers. If someone had asked him last week whether magic existed, he would have said emphatically that it didn't. But Holly was like magic to him. Somehow, she was. She made his cynical heart want the one thing he'd be an idiot to pursue. Her.

When she'd broken up with him, she'd done it over the phone, without warning, in under ten minutes. Kindly cool on her side. Heatedly upset on his side. She'd said the sort of clichés that people always say at breakups. She hadn't given him any reason that made sense to him, that he could accept. Then, afterward, she'd refused to speak to him or return his e-mails. She'd betrayed his faith in her, and the last thing he wanted was to make the mistake of caring about her or placing his trust in her again.

He turned his phone in slow half-circles on his thigh, frowning, his forehead grooved.

Did anyone in this town have any idea how talented she was? He'd read every one of her novels. He always preordered them, then read them obsessively, not working or sleeping until he'd finished the final page. They were beautifully written, wise, hopeful, filled with adventure and courage. He had no idea how she did it, how she dreamed up worlds and people and plots out of thin air.

He'd been to Martinsburg's one bookstore. There'd been no big display about their famous local author. They'd had only one copy of her latest release, on the shelf spine out in the YA section. From what he could tell, the people of Martinsburg had overlooked her entirely.

Holly returned, sliding into her seat. "Thanks for bringing me by. You saved me from having to make a trip back later today."

"How was Shadow?"

"As entitled as usual." The afternoon rays pouring into the car from behind Holly turned a section of her hair to glowing honey. She was so achingly pretty that his chest squeezed.

"Since we didn't find a site today"—the level tone of his voice hid his steely determination—"I'm thinking we'll need to try again soon, if you have the time." He was not a good person.

"Okay. I . . . have the time."

The bond between them pulled and the moment grew heavy. He longed to tell her things he had no business telling her. Namely, the truth about how much she'd hurt him and his frustration with himself regarding the resentment he still harbored toward her because of it.

He backed down the driveway, silently calling himself *stupid*, *fool*, *self-destructive*, and much, much worse.

Chapter Four

Right about now, the Saturday-at-eleven Zumba class Holly sometimes attended was probably merengue marching and shimmying to their heart's delight. There wouldn't be any shimmying for her this morning, thanks to a wedding meeting with Amanda, Amanda's mom, and their professional wedding coordinator.

Holly crossed her arms and rested her hip against a pew while watching the bride and mother of the bride trail their coordinator around the sanctuary of Trinity Church.

Mitzi, the woman they'd hired to orchestrate the big day, looked every inch as serious as her name was not. In a sleek gray suit, with earrings as big as doorknobs and an auburn hairstyle a First Lady would have envied, she gave off a chic and able impression. Somewhere in her mid-fifties, Mitzi's body bore the ruthlessly thin, muscled stamp of someone who pounded the asphalt every morning in a pair of Nike Airs.

Mitzi had never before toured the church. Since arriving

thirty minutes ago, she'd spent a good deal of time whisking her tape measure in and out and looking vaguely displeased. Which had Holly, here on Trinity's behalf, fighting back a case of defensiveness.

Trinity Church possessed a tremendous amount of charm, but there was no hiding the fact that the building was *old*. It had been constructed out of stone in 1890 by Germans who'd brought with them their motherland's excellent taste in church architecture. The building boasted a soaring steeple and arched front doors crafted of heavy oak. Inside, rectangular stained-glass windows marked the side walls and an understated altar stood on a dais three steps above the level of the pews.

Holly experienced a rush of fondness and respect every time she entered the place. She'd grown up here. God spoke to her here. Even though the median age of the membership at Trinity probably hovered at ninety, it had never occurred to Holly to switch congregations. Where would she go? That big new box of a church with the thumping music and a bustling marriage mart otherwise known as a singles ministry? Oh my, no. Jumping ship at this point would feel like high treason.

A year ago, sweet Violetta Mae Gaskins had retired as Trinity's longtime wedding coordinator and personally asked Holly to take over her duties. Holly had immediately assured her that she would. The truth? She enjoyed her role. It satisfied something within her, to help arrange other people's happy endings. It made no difference whether those people were real, here at Trinity, or fictional within the pages of her novels.

So far, Holly had presided over six weddings as the church's representative in all things nuptial. A few of the brides (those on tighter budgets or planning more intimate weddings) hadn't brought in professional coordinators. In those cases, the bride, Holly, and sometimes the mother of the bride had managed the big day themselves.

None of the prior weddings had been nearly as ambitious as Amanda's would be, however. This wedding, scheduled to take place in just twenty-one days, was destined to test Holly's skills. It had already begun to test her patience.

Mitzi launched into an animated monologue about floral arrangements.

If Mattel ever decided to roll out a Yellow Rose of Texas Barbie, Amanda could serve as a blueprint. Her long and highlighted blonde hair always looked shampoo-commercial worthy. She wore leather boots and a print dress beneath a fitted jean jacket.

Amanda Warren had been born with extraordinarily good taste. At one week of age, she'd probably begun selecting her own smocked onesies and coordinating baby caps. Goodness knows, Amanda had sailed through adolescence without an awkward stage. She'd been named Fraternity Sweetheart and Homecoming Queen at SMU before returning to Martinsburg to start her own interior design business.

In a life of excellent decisions, Amanda's best by far was her choice of groom. Tall, strapping, ginger-haired Ben Hunt was outgoing, warm, quick to laugh, and genuinely interested in everyone he met.

Holly picked a tuft of lint off her ivory cable knit sweater. She and Amanda were the same age and their parents had been members here at Trinity in the same era. She and Amanda had been pushed together since toddlerhood with the expectation that they'd play together in a mannerly fashion and become bosom friends.

They'd certainly played together in a mannerly fashion. In fact, there'd never been a cross word between them. Yet, they'd never become bosom friends. They lacked that mysterious link that leads to confidences and transparent affection. To wit, Amanda had selected ten bridesmaids and a house party of six for her wedding. Holly had not been invited into either camp.

"Sorry for the long wait, Holly." Amanda approached, the older women in tow.

"No problem. Take as long as you like."

"I think we're ready to talk through a few things with you."

"Sure. We can sit down here," Holly indicated the pews, "or we can use one of the meeting rooms."

Mitzi opted for a meeting room, so Holly brought them to the nearest one. A table dominated the plain space. Holly sat on one side with her pen and notebook in front of her, and the other ladies took chairs opposite her. Amanda lowered an accordion file as large as a carry-on onto the table. Mitzi propped up an iPad attached to a small keyboard and began typing furiously. Amanda's mom, Christine, met Holly's eye.

Christine resembled her daughter, except thirty years older with a chin-length bob. She presided over the Ladies Golf Association at the country club in Lilly Pulitzer clothing and small-heeled sandals with gems on them. The bulk of her communication consisted of "Mm" and a well-bred smile that could as easily mean *I'm thoroughly charmed by you* as *I hope you rot in your grave*. Holly could never tell. She was a little bit afraid of Christine.

"We're concerned about how many people the sanctuary can accommodate," Mitzi stated, glancing at Holly without fully lifting the angle of her face.

"Mm," Christine concurred.

"The sanctuary seats three hundred," Holly said.

"We're expecting at least that many."

"You're welcome to use the choir loft." It functioned much like a small balcony in a theater.

Mitzi and the others theorized over how many bodies they could squeeze into the choir loft.

"Do you have any other suggestions?" Mitzi asked.

"I'm sorry, I don't." Holly understood their concern. Amanda and Christine were going to have a tricky time fitting Martinsburg's ten thousand residents into Trinity Church. Apart from asking guests to sit on each other's laps or straddle each other's shoulders, Holly had no solutions.

"Do you think the pews could accommodate three hundred and fifty?" Mitzi squinted one eye.

"Only three hundred," Holly answered.

"I'd like to give the ushers some specialized training the night of the rehearsal," Mitzi informed Christine and Amanda.

"Sounds good," Amanda answered, still wrestling with the accordion file.

"What does the church have in the way of tables?" Mitzi asked Holly, her earrings clunking the sides of her neck.

"What kind of tables?"

"We'll need a table in the foyer for the guest book and another for the wedding programs and a flower arrangement. We're going to want tables that are suitably special."

"Mm," from Christine, paired with what might have been an I'm-thoroughly-charmed-by-you smile.

"I'd be happy to show you what we have," Holly said.

"If we can't find what we're after here," Mitzi said, "we'll import our own."

"You're welcome to."

"And I do believe we've decided to bring in our own musicians and organist as well."

Holly's loyalty pricked. "Our organist, Doreen, is great." Doreen would hate to miss the opportunity to brag to her friends about playing the organ at Amanda's wedding.

"I think Doreen's great too," Amanda said. "But my dad's second cousin's wife plays the organ professionally in Vienna, so she's going to play for the wedding, if that's okay."

"Of course." *Doreen*, Holly wrote in her notebook, to remind herself to bring Doreen a bucket of caramel corn (Doreen's favorite) when she broke the bad news.

"We're going to want," Mitzi declared, "to take down all the tacky papers and posters and announcements and such that are currently featured in the public areas of the church."

Holly chewed the inside of her lip and wondered if she was too young to start drinking Alka-Seltzer. Thank goodness she had a rehearsal dinner scouting session scheduled for this afternoon with Josh. Otherwise, today might've turned into a real pothole.

Josh. A mental image of him, standing beside her and

turning his face to watch her, took shape. That dark hair. The sleekly muscled body. His height and strength. Those unwavering eyes, focused solely on her . . . *You can't let yourself care about him!*

"Holly?" Mitzi asked.

"Ah . . ." *What was the question? Oh, yes.* "You can take down the announcements in the public areas at ten on the day of the wedding. We'd just ask that you put them back up after the ceremony."

Mitzi's fingers paused on the mini-keyboard. "We have a large staff coming. A floral designer and her team, a lighting designer, a group of ribbon specialists, a garland expert, a videographer, the photographer, not to mention the musicians."

What about a flock of cherubs? No cherubs?

"It would be extraordinarily helpful," Mitzi continued, "to have access to the premises at least twenty-four hours prior."

Amanda and Ben's wedding would take place at five o'clock on the Saturday following Thanksgiving. After which, guests would make their way to the reception at a local winery. "I'm sorry, but we have a prayer meeting every Friday night and a lady's Bible Study every Saturday morning. The church will be available at ten."

"Mm." Christine's smile took on a I-hope-you-rot-in-your-grave tinge.

Holly stuck her pen behind her ear and inhaled deeply. This was going to be a long meeting.

Holly and Josh went location shopping that afternoon, and every other afternoon for the week that followed. With each passing day, the weather turned cooler and crisper. Amber leaves began their downward dance from Martinsburg's trees. The scent of wood smoke tipped the air. Holly brought out throw blankets from her linen closet. The bakery started carrying their eagerly awaited autumn walnut cake with apricot preserves. And Josh *still* hadn't booked a rehearsal dinner venue.

Twelve days before Amanda and Ben's wedding, on her way back from her morning coffee run, Holly set Rob's black coffee at his door, then knocked on Mrs. Chapel's. "Good morning!" She edged the cup through the gap between the door and the jamb.

"Thank you, dear. Did you remember to put in one and a half packets of sugar?"

"Yes, indeed."

"Will you be going out again later?"

"I expect to."

"I'm in need of some Efferdent Plus for my dentures."

"I see. Is it an urgent type of thing?"

"Very urgent."

"In that case, I'll see what I can do." Holly waved and moved toward her door.

"Remember to get the Plus. The Efferdent Power Clean Crystals aren't worth the packaging they're sold in."

"Got it," Holly assured her. "Efferdent Plus."

Inside her apartment, she settled herself and her caramel nutmeg latte at her desk. Between fielding calls from Christine and Amanda, the time she'd spent with Josh in person, and the much larger amount of time she'd spent thinking about Josh, she hadn't accomplished much work of late. Her deadline had made an appearance on the horizon. She'd need to make steady progress toward it in order to avoid becoming a basket case the month before the manuscript was due. She pushed up the sleeves of her cotton shirt, determined to pound out some genius.

One minute dragged into five, then ten, while she squinted at the document open on her computer screen.

Well, it didn't look like genius would be forthcoming today. She'd settle for mediocre hogwash. Then, at least, she'd have something to work with. Hard to edit and revise blank pages.

Work, Holly. Focus.

She ended up sipping her latte instead, her attention sliding toward Main Street while she thought some more about Josh.

They hadn't made headway with a rehearsal location, but their friendship had progressed. Whenever they were together, they spent the whole time talking, slowly catching one another up on the events of the past eight years, accustoming themselves to the people they'd become.

More and more powerfully with every meeting, Holly had grown attuned to Josh's movements, the timbre of his voice, his expressions, his clothing.

There were moments, very fleeting, when she suspected her awareness of Josh might not be one-sided. In those moments, her breath would still and her hopes would tangle with her weighty sense of caution. Then the moment would break.

Afterward, she'd tell herself that he most likely didn't like her in *that way* anymore. If by some miracle he did feel the same magnetism toward her that she did for him, she was pretty positive that he'd never act on it. Josh was a very controlled person, private and complex, with a fair amount of pride.

They never spoke about their dating relationship or how it had ended. She'd begun to wish that she could tell him the truth about why she'd broken up with him. She wanted to explain.

But did she want to explain for his sake or for her own selfish reasons? It would be cathartic to unburden herself, yes. But would dredging up the past be of any benefit at all to Josh at this point? She couldn't very well throw his mom under the bus. And how exactly was she supposed to bust out old confessions, anyway?

"This restaurant has an excellent wait staff, Holly."

"I feel badly about breaking up with you when we were teenagers, Josh! Let me tell you why I did it!"

No. They were friendly with each other and she was helping him find a rehearsal dinner site. That was it. Josh had moved on. He wasn't her eighteen-year-old first love anymore, he wasn't someone she confided in anymore. He was flourishing.

She was the one she should be concerned about. Her heart needed every possible layer of protection against him—

No. It was all right. She'd been doing a good job at keeping things straight in her head. So long as she didn't let herself go all gooey over him on the inside, it was safe enough to help him with dinner venues. Their outings together were too uncommon and wonderful in their poignant way to pass up.

She could afford to spend a little bit more time with him while he was in town. Just a little bit more.

Chapter Five

Holly entered Das Lokal, restaurant number ninety-one in their Year of Restaurants. Sam followed her inside, as did Holly's neighbor Rob. A rush of warm air greeted her as she unwound her scarf and hung her coat on the rack.

Das Lokal enjoyed its status as a town favorite. People, the clink of silverware, and the mouth-watering dinnertime smells of steak, frites, and apple strudel packed the small pub-like interior. Holly scanned the space, looking for an empty booth on the far side—

Her gaze collided with Josh, who'd already caught sight of her. "Oh." He and Ben sat at the bar, a plate of buffalo wings between them. Josh's vision remained steadily leveled on her. Solemn and glittering. Her heart thumped, then skittered into a fast rhythm.

"'Oh' what?" Sam asked.

Holly didn't want Rob to hear, so she leaned near Sam's ear. "Josh is here."

"Your high school love turned billionaire?"

"The very same."

"What? I'll be subtle, but I demand that you take me to him immediately. Immediately! Make haste."

Holly threaded through the crowd toward Ben and Josh's position. Running into Josh around town unexpectedly, outside their scheduled meetings? Fine. She was cool with it. She could handle it. No problem.

He had on a simple white business shirt with the collar open one button at the neck. He always looked at ease in his clothes, even though his garments had likely come straight from an expensive French clothier. The Texas sun had lightly tanned his strong, masculine features. As usual, his hair looked sexily finger-combed.

She'd really like to finger-comb that dark hair with *her* fingers—

"Holly!" Ben hugged her. "Good to see you."

"You too." Holly stepped aside to include her friends in their circle. "Do you both know Sam and Rob?"

"Sure, sure." Ben smiled and shook hands. He knew everyone in town. If he ever decided to run for mayor, he'd win.

"This is Josh," Holly said to Sam and Rob, hoping the he's-an-extremely-cute-math-genius-and-my-first-love part didn't show in her expression.

"Nice to meet you," Sam said, then, bless her, adeptly steered the conversation toward Ben and Amanda's wedding. She gave no indication that she knew or cared anything about the intimate details of Josh's history.

Rob gently bumped Holly's shoulder with his. "I see a booth opening up. I'll go grab it for us."

"Okay, thanks."

The rest of them watched Rob's progress as he commandeered the table. He took a seat, then gave them a salute.

"Does he work at Donovan's?" Ben asked.

"Yes," Holly answered. "He's a sous chef." Holly and Rob had become friends when he'd moved into her building. He was twenty-four, rarely missed a workout, wore his shoulder-length blond hair in a ponytail, and could panfry a mean salmon. Rob had yet to ask Holly out, despite Sam's predictions that he would, and soon.

"Rob's more than a sous chef." Mischief lit Sam's smile. "He's a *handsome* sous chef. And luckily for Holly and me, he's off tonight."

Josh frowned.

Ben chuckled. "You're married, Sam Sullivan."

"I'm not the one Rob's interested in, Ben Hunt." Sam gave Holly a pointed stare. "Like every other man in this town, he's into Holly."

Holly burst out laughing at the absurdity of Sam's statement.

"Why are you laughing, Holly?" Ben grinned. "It's true."

Bantering about Rob in front of Josh. If she ignored all the internal clanging and panic then this situation was still no problem. None at all. "Yes, goodness knows I've always had to beat men off with a stick. Such is my lot in life. At least this one can cook."

"A man who can cook is never to be underrated." Sam

headed toward their booth. "I'll go keep the handsome sous chef company until you arrive."

Sam's departure opened a pocket of quiet between them.

"How was your day?" Josh asked.

She moved her full attention to him. Those dark brown eyes! They were so sharply intelligent and at the same time, burned with emotion.

"I had a good day. I was able to get some work done. Plus, I saved Mrs. Chapel from a lack of denture cleaner and spoke with Amanda for thirty minutes about the parking attendants for the ceremony. You'll be pleased to know, Ben, that the attendants will be receiving a tutorial directly from Mitzi the day before the wedding."

"Thank my lucky stars! Now I'll be able to sleep at night." The reddish freckles that matched his hair made Ben's cheerful face even more endearing. He gestured to the buffalo wings. "You want one?"

"No thanks."

"So." Ben glanced back and forth between Josh and Holly. "This clearly isn't the first time you two have seen each other since Josh came back to town."

Josh seemed to stiffen. "No."

Josh hadn't mentioned to Ben, his best friend, the groom, that they'd been scouting venues for the past several days?

"Should we go ahead and order dinner—" Josh said at the exact moment that Holly said, "We've been driving around town looking for rehearsal dinner sites together—"

Ben regarded Holly with confusion, then placed his palm on his chest. "What? For my rehearsal dinner?"

"Yes," Holly answered slowly.

"Amanda's excited about having it out at the Texas Olive Oil Company," Ben said. "It's going to be awesome. Can't wait."

"The Texas Olive Oil Company?"

"It's up north of town. They have a barn." Ben pushed to his feet. "Excuse me for minute. A buddy of mine from work just came in."

He left, leaving Holly alone with Josh. The two young women sitting on Josh's far side cut disgruntled looks in her direction, letting her know they weren't pleased with her for hogging the attention of Martinsburg's most eligible visitor.

"I booked the Olive Oil Company," he said calmly.

"But someone else already had it reserved."

"It was reserved by a group who were planning to hold a charity fund-raising meeting there. Turns out they were willing to move their meeting back a week in exchange for a sizeable donation to their charity. Look, I . . . I'm sorry you found out about it this way. I should have let you know sooner that I'd booked a location."

"No, it's okay." She refused to feel hurt. She wasn't the event's cohost. She was just the person who'd offered up some venue suggestions. "When did this happen?"

"Recently."

"All expertly arranged by your assistant, I'm guessing."

A lazy smile started on one side of his mouth and grew. The sight of it warmed Holly in ways that had nothing to do with the room's temperature. "Exactly," he said.

"That's wonderful." It *was* wonderful. The Olive Oil Company barn couldn't have been a more perfect location.

But this development also meant that she and Josh had lost the one pursuit that connected them. She swallowed against a foolish sense of disappointment. "If you recall, the Olive Oil Company was my very first choice."

"I recall."

"So what this means is that you went with *my* choice." She smiled.

"You're obviously very gifted with both weddings and rehearsal dinners."

"Obviously."

"How are you with caterers?"

She paused. Was he asking her for more help? "How am I with choosing a caterer? Inexperienced."

"My assistant has already chosen a caterer."

"Of course."

"I'm wondering how you are with choosing a caterer's menu?"

"You mean to tell me that your assistant didn't already select the rehearsal dinner menu?"

"She lives in Paris and is unavailable to sample dishes."

"I'm relatively experienced at sampling dishes. Sam and I have been to more than ninety of Martinsburg's restaurants since January."

"Then you're more than qualified."

"*You're* more than qualified, Josh. You've probably eaten at the finest restaurants on every continent. You don't need my help."

"No," he said bluntly, "I do."

He had a tiny scar on his jaw from a bike riding accident when he was a kid. She could remember kissing the spot.

She *could not* go gooey over him! If only he wasn't so distractingly handsome. If only he'd quit looking at her so intently. It made her feel . . . lovely, when she wasn't. "You don't need my help." Her voice came out confidently, loyally covering her internal weakening. "You didn't need my help with the rehearsal dinner location either, it seems."

"I might not need your help, but I want it."

She was playing with fire! She should turn him down. More contact between them was not wise.

"Please," he said.

She caved. "All right. I don't really have the willpower to turn down"—*more time with you*—"a trip to a caterer's shop to sample delicious food."

"Good. Now that I think about it, we'll probably have to go twice. Once to select appetizers and salads and once to select entrees and desserts."

Ben returned to his bar stool, breaking the bubble for two she and Josh had created. All the sounds and colors of the bar rushed back. "I'll be in touch," Josh said.

"See you guys soon." She made her way to the booth and slid in next to Sam.

"What's something we can say to each other in honor of the German heritage of this restaurant?" Sam asked.

Rob slid down slightly in his booth seat and gave them a mock scowl. "For the record, I think it's goofy when y'all do that." He'd been to several of their Year of Restaurants meals.

"It's so much more fun when we have someone here to find us goofy," Sam insisted. "My husband is home mopping the kitchen floor—"

"—being perfect—" Holly noted.

"—so you're all we have, Rob."

"*Guten* appetite?" Holly ventured, holding up her water glass.

"*Danke schön*." Sam murdered the pronunciation with her thick East Coast accent. "Wiener schnitzel! Dachshund!"

They all laughed and even Rob reluctantly clicked his glass to theirs.

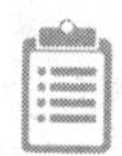

"Dude," Ben murmured. "You're going to have to stop staring at her. She'll notice."

Josh twisted on his stool to face the dinner one of the servers had slid onto the bar. He and Ben both had burgers and shoestring fries in front of them. Josh didn't even remember ordering. He'd lost his appetite.

"I knew you'd fall for Holly again once you saw her," Ben said. He dipped a few of his fries in ketchup. "I remember how crazy you were about her."

"Yeah." His lungs felt hollow. Who was Rob? Holly couldn't actually like that guy, right? With the ponytail? His thoughts shifted in pessimistic patterns, turning his mood sooty and dark. Of course she could like him. Rob was more handsome than he was. Rob kept smiling at Holly like she'd hung the moon. Plus, he lived here.

Not everyone in Martinsburg had overlooked Holly. Rob hadn't.

"Holly's even prettier than she was in high school," Ben said. "She's made a success of her career and she's nice to everyone in this town. She's sort of like our glue. You know?"

Josh took in an uneven breath. "I know."

Ben's face communicated sympathy. "Why don't you tell her how you feel about her?"

"Because I don't want to get involved with her."

Ben whistled. "You could've fooled me. You've been watching her ever since she came in."

Josh pushed the heel of his hand against his forehead. "I'm an idiot."

"Tell her that you're an idiot for her. Women like that kind of stuff."

"I'm leaving soon."

"Relocate here."

"I don't want to live here, Ben." Everything in this town reminded him of the kid he'd been.

After his dad had been killed by a drunk driver, his mom had moved them to Martinsburg so that she could take a secretarial position a friend had offered her. Josh had arrived in Martinsburg grief-stricken and mad at the world. A loner. Desperate inside. He'd been terrified and ashamed of his terror because he'd been fourteen years old and his mom had needed him to be strong. He'd been all she had left.

His mom had insisted he play on the JV soccer team, and looking back, he was glad she'd insisted because that's how he'd met Ben. Ben was the child of a single mom, too, but unlike Josh, Ben had a naturally outgoing and optimistic personality. He'd befriended Josh when Josh hadn't had anything likable to offer. He'd been Josh's closest friend ever since.

All through high school, Josh and his mom had lived paycheck to paycheck and barely had enough to cover rent and groceries. To help out, Josh had worked loading and unloading inventory at a warehouse after school and in the summers. The money he'd made had never gone far enough. He'd realized early that if he wanted a better life for his mom and himself he only had one option: to ace his academics and earn his ticket out of Martinsburg, a town that had become, for him, a symbol of hardship and shame.

The second semester of his sophomore year of high school, he'd sat two chairs behind Holly Morgan in AP English. She'd entered his gray life like a bolt of sunshine. And almost from the first day of that semester, he'd loved her.

It had been as simple and as fast and as inexplicable as that.

He'd loved her.

Holly's manner had been easy and the kindheartedness she'd extended to him sincere. The fatherless and sullen kid, who had plenty of smarts but just one friend, had fallen helplessly for her. She'd been his point of hope, the one aspect of life in Martinsburg he treasured. She'd treated him as a friend for the next two years but his feelings for her had never wavered.

Then one night in the winter of their senior year, when he'd been helping her study for a math test, he'd sensed that things between them had shifted. He'd gathered his courage and taken hold of her hand. She'd squeezed his hand in response. He could still remember the way his heart had pounded and his thoughts had blown out of the water, sitting there next to her at that table with a math textbook open between them, her hand in his.

He'd been introduced to faith as a kid, but Holly was the closest thing to a miracle his teenage self had ever experienced. During the months they'd dated, he'd looked into her eyes and seen God's love for him looking back. She'd taken him to church and talked through spiritual things with him.

Then the girl who'd strengthened his belief had also become the one who'd most tested it when she'd broken his heart. It had taken him a few years to find God again after that. But eventually, he had. His relationship with God had been his life's anchor ever since.

Josh sliced a glance across the restaurant and saw Rob lean toward Holly to say something. Holly tilted her head to listen.

Pain and wanting washed through Josh so powerfully that he had to brace against it.

"Look away," Ben said.

Josh did.

"How come you didn't tell me you'd seen her?" Ben set down his burger and wiped his hands on a napkin.

"Because I haven't been able to decide in my own head if seeing her is a good idea or not."

"What was she saying about looking for rehearsal dinner locations? You've had that Olive Oil place booked for six months."

"I lied to her. I ran into her on the street and I asked her if she'd help me look for a location. I wanted to see her again and that was the only reason I could come up with on the spot."

Ben's forehead creased. "Let me get this straight. You've been driving around town searching for a place to hold the rehearsal dinner when you already have a place? Because you want to spend time with Holly?"

"Yes."

Ben clapped a hand on his shoulder. "Tell her the truth. About all of it."

"I can't. I don't want to get involved with her."

Ben's expression turned pitying. "You've got it bad, dude. Seriously bad."

Chapter Six

"This is delicious." Holly pointed her fork at a plate containing melt-in-your-mouth spare ribs. Oh, how she adored spare ribs. Maybe today hadn't been the best day to wear a snug belt with her jeans.

Josh finished chewing. "I agree."

Five days had passed since their discussion at Das Lokal, two since their first visit to the caterer.

Josh had picked her up in his Range Rover an hour ago (She'd blown off Zumba class again, but really, who could think about exercise at a time like this?) and driven them thirty minutes to his caterer's shop in the nearby town of Hollis. Compared to a big city, Hollis was a pipsqueak. Compared to Martinsburg, a flashy metropolis. Just like at their first visit, the caterer had seated them at her one table, which was framed by a deep bow window. On the far side of the square-paned glass, the afternoon crouched gray and chilly. Inside, the shop brimmed with bright and cheery warmth. It didn't hurt that the dear lady who owned the place kept bringing them plate after sampling plate of wonderful food.

Josh leaned back in the white iron filigree chair he'd been given, a chair so girly that it made him look extramanly in comparison. He wore a chocolate-colored sweater that had a very slight V at the neck. The sweater's austerity, and the way it fit close to his body, suited him. "I'm not much of a party planner," he said.

"I imagine you're pretty busy, what with being a technology mogul and all."

"True." The wry humor in his eyes made her mouth go dry. "I'm very important."

"Very. And armed, lest we forget, with an assistant who seems skillful at everything, including party planning." *Holy smoke, these ribs should come with a warning label.*

"I have a party planning question."

"You could speed-dial your assistant."

"I'd rather ask you."

Her lips quirked. "All right."

"Amanda told me she's having a sit-down dinner at her reception. Should I avoid having a sit-down dinner at the rehearsal dinner?"

Holly considered his question while setting aside her fork. "Your rehearsal dinner is going to be *very* nice, Josh. I'd counsel you to avoid doing anything similar to what Amanda's doing at the reception. It'd be a shame to show up the bride."

"Point taken." He speared a bite of buttermilk fried chicken. "How would you recommend I serve the meal?"

"Food stations? They're classier than a buffet, and in keeping with the rustic, Texas feel of the evening."

"I'm listening."

"I'm guessing you'll want to begin with appetizers and drinks on the patio at sunset. Weather permitting, of course. It's Texas. It could be freezing or it might be perfect."

"Did you try this chicken?"

"Yes. It's amazing."

He indicated the brisket. "What about this?"

"Outstanding," she said.

"You were saying? About the appetizers . . ."

"Right. I'd serve them on the patio. Then, you can have food stations set up inside the barn with the main course dishes, salads, cheeses, fruit, bread. I'm guessing Amanda and Ben will want to say a few words to their guests at some point during the evening?"

"Yes."

"So maybe dessert could be served to everyone individually, at their tables, during that portion of the evening."

The caterer, a woman in her early forties wearing a floral apron, bustled in. The kitchen heat had flushed her face but done nothing to stifle her proud smile. "What do you think?" She placed her hands on her hips.

"I think you should apply for Master Chef," Holly said. "You'd win."

She beamed. "Have you decided which dishes you like best?" She directed the question to Josh, knowing full well he was the one in possession of a Visa Black Card.

"Whatever the lady decides."

"What?" Holly held up her hands. "I'm just a writer and

a volunteer wedding coordinator and the girl who feeds my family's cat."

"She also brings her neighbors coffee and denture cleaner," he told the caterer.

The caterer nodded, amused.

Josh angled toward Holly. Unhurried, he hooked a hand around the top of her iron filigree chair. "What do you like best? Whatever it is, that's what I'm ordering."

She wasn't used to anyone putting so much stock in her opinion. She could probably get used to it, if forced. She looked over the assembled main dishes. During their last visit, they'd decided on appetizers and salads that had a Southern flair, so she'd continue in that theme. "I love them all, but if it were up to me—"

"It is," Josh said.

"I'd choose the spare ribs, the fried chicken, and the . . ." she wrinkled her nose and closed one eye. Saying good-bye to any of these dishes felt criminal. "Turkey pot pie."

"Excellent." The caterer began stacking the plates on a tray.

"Are you sure you're okay with those?" Holly asked Josh, under her breath. "Because—"

"I want what you want," he assured her.

He hadn't moved his hand from her chair. Having his hand there, such a simple thing, really, caused a crippling longing to break open within her.

The caterer propped her tray on her hip and paused to speak to Josh about rehearsal dinner logistics.

Holly and Josh had shared an uncommon intimacy once.

Holly had never again been able to attain that sort of intimacy with a boyfriend. On the contrary, she'd hardly had a boyfriend serious enough to want to go to the movies with.

She ached to have someone that was hers to share her feelings with, to hug, to laugh with. She'd been hoping and waiting and praying for that person, the person God had in mind for her.

Just—just not him, Lord. I can't feel this longing for Josh.

She looked down at her hands, clasped in her lap. She'd been a fool to come here. Up until today she'd been managing her feelings for him. But just now, those feelings had leapt over the line. She was falling for him. Again.

Josh straightened in his seat, removing his hand from her chair. She was in serious trouble, because she was sorry, not glad like she should have been, to lose the sweetness of that small connection.

The caterer swept from the room and returned moments later with five plates of dessert. Josh smiled at Holly, anticipating her delight.

"Oh. My. Goodness," Holly breathed. Red velvet cake, sheet cake, apple pie, two different cobblers.

They made steady progress, taking time to savor each bite and debate the merits of one dessert against the others. She definitely shouldn't have opted for a belt today.

When it came time to make the decision, Josh once again asked Holly for her choice. She picked apple pie à la mode. Flaky, cinnamony, and perfect for fall.

The caterer thanked them and disappeared into the kitchen with the plates and silverware.

"I'm going to be gone this weekend," Josh said, "for Ben's bachelor party weekend."

"Where are you headed?"

"I'm taking the guys to Lost Pines Resort outside Austin to golf."

"It's beautiful there. Should be fun." It said a lot about Josh that he hadn't just thrown money at Ben's wedding events then blown in on a private jet for forty-eight hours. He'd come to Martinsburg to spend real time with his friend and to handle the details himself.

"I'm expecting two straight days of humiliation," he said. "I'm a terrible golfer."

"Not many golf courses in downtown Paris?"

"Not many. Any chance that you have time to meet me up at the Olive Oil Company when I get back? To discuss how we should arrange the tables and food stations?"

She wanted to say yes more than she wanted an appearance on the *New York Times* bestseller list. But she had to say no. "I'd like to, but I can't. I'm booked solid next week."

Josh searched her face, then nodded. "No problem." He set aside his napkin, rose to his feet, paused. As if second-guessing himself, he returned to his seat, facing his body toward hers. "Can I ask you something?" Consternation stitched through his brow.

"Of course."

Seriousness, the sort of seriousness that hadn't entered any of their prior conversations, fell between them. Her pulse began to quicken.

"Have you been helping me because you're friendly and took pity on me?" Ruefulness curled one corner of his mouth and caused a dimple to flash briefly in his cheek. "Or has any of it been because you wanted to spend time . . . with me?"

Was he asking because he'd guessed that she'd developed feelings for him and wanted to gently disabuse her of any crazy notion of a romance between them? Or maybe he was asking because *he* wanted to spend time with *her*?

No, no, no. He hadn't given her any indication of that.

She smiled breezily and adjusted her position to put more space between them. "I've been helping you because I'm friendly and also because I wanted to spend time with you." Through dint of will, she kept her voice sunny. "It's been nice to catch up with you. I always hoped you were doing well, Josh. Ben told me you were but it's been really nice to have the chance to see that for myself." She'd used the word *nice* two times and in so doing, damned their current relationship with faint praise.

He concealed his thoughts expertly. She could see no change in him outwardly. None. He was an astute businessman, after all. The owner of a company. He hadn't gotten to where he was in the world by having the transparent feelings of a girl scout.

And yet . . . she could sense the shadow of sadness that lived in him deepening. Which made her regret her smokescreen approach. She should have replied to his honest question with an honest answer. He'd given her an opening and hadn't she been half-hoping, maybe three-quarters-hoping, for just this kind of an opportunity to talk to him about the past?

She should be brave—right now at this very moment—and

tell him the things she'd been yearning to tell him for eight years. She spoke before she could lose her nerve. "Josh, I . . ."

"Yes?"

She had a hard time getting the rest out. "I want you to know that I'm sorry for any hurt I may have caused you when we broke up."

He gazed at her, his features guarded and grave.

Why wasn't he replying? Doubt assailed her. "It could be, of course, that I didn't cause you any hurt. In which case, you can ignore what I just said."

"You did hurt me, Holly."

His bluntness came as a relief. It bolstered her courage. "Okay. I thought so. Are you still angry with me?"

She could hear a distant dog barking and the quiet conversation of the caterer and her employee, cleaning up together in the kitchen.

"There's a part of me that is," he admitted.

Her stomach dropped. She didn't want him to be angry with her, and yet, if she put herself in his shoes she could understand why he was. She fought to order her spiraling thoughts into words. "Here's the thing. I didn't tell you the truth back then about my reason for breaking up with you."

Several taut seconds dragged past. "You told me something about how your feelings had changed and that you wanted to be free to date other people," he said.

"Yes, that's exactly what I told you, but neither of those things were true."

He frowned, his eyebrows drawing down in the center.

"Should . . ." The concerns that had kept her silent on

this topic until now rose to the fore of her mind. "Should we just let bygones be bygones? Or do you think there's value in revisiting what happened at this point?"

"There's value in it for me, Holly. Even now."

She slowly inhaled. "Do you remember, back when you first started MIT, that there was a time when you considered returning to Texas?"

"Yes."

"Your mom . . ." She swallowed. Was this really a good idea? Maybe the bygones thing was better.

"What about my mom?"

"She was upset about the possibility of your leaving MIT. She couldn't afford to send you anywhere else. But more than that, I mean, *MIT*, Josh. It was the best possible school for you and she and I both knew it. You were brilliant. You deserved a chance there."

"And?" he asked grimly.

"Your mom came to see me at UTSA and asked me to break up with you. I—"

"What?" He spoke the word quietly, almost whispering it. Nonetheless, it vibrated with menace.

"She asked me to break up with you so that you'd stay at MIT and focus on your studies."

His brown eyes blazed as he struggled to process what she'd said, to reframe their breakup through a different lens.

"I still remember her tears," Holly said. "She cried when she came to see me. Your mom liked me, I think. I definitely liked and trusted and respected her. It wasn't easy for her to ask me to end things, but she did, and she made a very strong case."

Josh bent his head and stared at the table as if trying to decipher a code in its surface. "You should have told me that she came to see you." He lifted his chin again to meet her eyes.

"Maybe. I didn't because I promised her I wouldn't."

"If you had told me, we could have talked it out."

"Yes, but would you have stayed in school?"

"I don't know."

"See? By breaking up with you, at least I could be fairly certain that you'd excel in school and in your career. Those were the things that your mom and I wanted for you."

"What about what I wanted?" His frank question caused her whole body to still. "Did you or my mom ever stop to consider that?"

"We . . . I mean, we thought that you wanted to leave MIT and come home to Texas."

"Would that have been so terrible?"

"Yes!"

He cocked his head to the side an inch, waiting.

"Look at you," Holly said. "You're a tremendous success."

"Business success isn't everything in life."

She parted her lips to defend—defend what? Defend his own outstanding accomplishments? Business success *wasn't* everything in life. She couldn't take the position that it was, especially since she didn't know how fulfilled or unfulfilled his own success had left him. "I broke up with you because I wanted what I thought was best for you more than anything else. Do you believe me?"

"Yes."

"Can you forgive me?"

She nearly had cardiac arrest while she waited for him to

answer. He was a thoughtful man. A man who could not be slowed when his mind had been made up or rushed when he needed time to think.

He gave her a small, sad smile and placed his hand on his knee, palm up. An invitation.

She placed her hand in his and his fingers tightened around it. She was holding his hand! Sensory details rushed through Holly's nerves, buzzing and spinning, wondrously sweet. He'd offered her his hand in a gesture of camaraderie, a nostalgic acknowledgment of all they'd shared when they'd been young and bound together by first love.

"It's forgiven," Josh said. "I just need time to . . . process."

"Sure." Hot moisture pushed against the backs of her eyes. All this time, she'd wanted to tell him that she was sorry. What she hadn't realized until now? How crucial it would be to hear him say he'd forgiven her. "Thank you."

"How's anyone supposed to stay mad at you? Is there a mean bone in your body?"

"There are a few. I can be downright cruel to fictional bad guys."

He did not appear impressed.

"I have uncharitable thoughts about Mitzi, Amanda and Ben's wedding coordinator."

"Huh."

She got lost in his beautiful eyes, in the texture of his strong, warm fingers around hers. "It took me a really long time to get over you," she murmured before she'd thought through the comment or given herself full permission to speak it.

"But you eventually did?"

"Eventually." Maybe that answer was close enough to true not to be a lie? Or maybe that lie would become true next month or next year?

He stood, breaking the link between them, then helped her scoot out her chair. They chatted about the weather while they collected their outerwear. He shrugged into his navy pea coat.

That dratted coat. It made him resemble a hero in a romantic movie. Six-plus feet of intelligent, unattainable handsomeness. She had an overpowering urge to grab the lapels of that coat and rise onto her tiptoes to kiss him. She wanted to ruffle his hair and his mastery of himself, and she really wanted to shatter the careful good manners between them.

That wayward thought, coupled with her uninvited affection for him, sent a stab of fear through her.

What was that famous groundhog's name? Punxsutawney Phil? Every time he saw his shadow and returned to his hole, folks could expect six more weeks of winter. She did not want Josh to become her Punxsutawney Phil. She refused to face eight more years of heartache every time she saw him. She'd done one bout of heartache courtesy of Josh. She could not do another eight years. No thank you.

They drove back to Martinsburg, the car filled with subdued conversation about her next book release and his favorite brands of coffee. Inwardly, though, Holly was already beginning to wonder whether she'd done the right thing when she'd told him her schedule was booked. She'd done what she'd had to do for the sake of self-preservation.

Still, their outings had been wonderful. Talking with him, teasing him, seeing him smile. Those things had been a joy, the sort of deep joy that didn't often cross her path. The days ahead, days empty of him, already looked like a desert.

Holly, he must have fabulous women with names like Babette or Amelie available to him in Paris. He might even have a Parisian girlfriend at this very moment. She did not expressly know that he didn't. He probably did. She was simply a high school girlfriend from long ago.

She'd longed for closure and the talk they'd just had had given her exactly that. Everything she'd hoped to say to him, she'd said. He'd told her he'd forgiven her.

It was enough.

It had to be enough.

Chapter Seven

*On Saturday, Holly sat cross-legged on the floor of her par-*ents' kitchen, Shadow in her lap. Nothing but the sun easing through the windows illuminated the chilly interior, which they warmed to sixty-five for Shadow's comfort in the fall and winter months.

The cat lifted her head and purred while Holly scratched under her chin. "Nice home you got here, Shadow."

The feline gave her a haughty look that said, *It's no less than I deserve*.

"Quite right." More chin scratching.

She hadn't heard from Josh since their outing to the caterer. She hadn't expected to. Yesterday, he would have left town for Ben's bachelor party.

He didn't live in Martinsburg. In fact, Josh had only returned to Martinsburg eighteen days ago. So it infuriated her that she was so strongly aware of his absence this weekend. Everywhere she went felt devoid of excitement. The colors muted. More lonely. Why? Because she knew that *he* wasn't here anymore.

"This is why I can't get any more twisted up over him than I have already," she told Shadow, whose eyelids were drooping closed. "The time I spent with him has messed with my head enough."

Meow, Shadow said. Which Holly translated to mean, *Get a grip, girl.*

"Get a grip is precisely what I need to do. I'm going to leave here and go home and write like the wind. I'm really . . . I'm just going to pour out some great, great pages that will keep readers up late into the night. I left my heroine in a den of cutthroats with nothing but her rapier for defense in order to come here, you realize. Now I need to go home and rescue her."

Shadow cracked one dubious eye.

"Have I given you enough socialization?"

The cat gave a terrific stretch, which meant she wanted more petting. "Fine." Holly stroked her family's cat and reminded herself that this was how she spent her weekends. This was her destiny.

Was this really his destiny?

Josh sat in the driver's seat of a golf cart, watching one of Ben's college fraternity buddies hit a drive. The twenty guys on the trip hadn't been content with eighteen holes. They'd played eighteen this morning, stopped for lunch, and were out on the course again for another eighteen. To be honest, he'd far rather be discussing asynchronous JavaScript and XML with one of his programmers. "Nice shot."

Another of Ben's friends moved toward the tee box.

In the distance, Josh could see Ben putting on the green. It had been satisfying to watch Ben and the others enjoying the weekend, despite that he felt like a spectator to their fun rather than a participant.

He'd been in an irritable mood since the day he and Holly had last gone to the caterer's. After their conversation, he'd made himself wait a day so that he could organize his thoughts and emotions before calling his mom. She'd confirmed everything Holly had told him and reiterated all the reasons Holly had voiced. She'd even gone so far as to tell him that she'd always felt guilty about the grief she'd caused him and Holly.

She'd expected both him and Holly to rebound and start dating again after their breakup, she'd said. They'd been eighteen years old. She'd thought that they'd recover faster than they had. She'd apologized to him and asked him to pass along her regret and heartfelt best wishes to Holly.

He tightened his grip on the steering wheel, rubbing the side of his thumb against it.

Despite his mother's good intentions when she'd asked Holly to end things with him, there was no possible way that she could ever fully know what it was she'd screwed up. She'd viewed his relationship with Holly the way most parents probably viewed the relationships of their teenage children, as light and passing and juvenile.

He and Holly were the only two people who knew how

much they'd loved each other. And only he knew the scars Holly's loss had left on him.

None of them were completely without fault. He'd been shortsighted to want to leave MIT. His mom had been wrong to take matters into her own hands. And Holly should have told him about his mom's visit the day it had happened.

Did he fault Holly the most, though?

No. Back then, his mom had been a forty-five-year-old woman armed with a mother's fierce protectiveness of her only child. Holly had been a college freshman living apart from her family for the first time. He understood why she'd been swayed, and he believed her when she told him she'd done what she thought best for him.

It was going to take practice to think of Holly without the bitterness that had accompanied his thoughts of her for so long. But it also felt right to try. She'd explained and apologized. He'd forgiven her.

Who's to say, anyway? The way things had happened might actually have been the best thing for him. He'd built his company into the stuff his dreams had been made of.

Josh adjusted his Nike ball cap, slanting it lower.

He hadn't needed Holly to shop for rehearsal dinner locations with him, nor to visit his caterer once, much less twice. She'd been humoring him. He'd made up something about visiting the Olive Oil company next week, solely so that he'd have another reason to see her. She'd turned him down. Even so, when she'd whispered that it had taken her a long time to get over him, stupid hope had gripped his heart.

He hadn't planned to say anything to her, that day or

any day, that would make him vulnerable to her again. But he'd asked her if she'd gotten over him eventually.

She'd looked at him with that painfully beautiful face, her dusky blue eyes kind, her skin clear, faint pink on her cheekbones, a long strand of glossy, light brown hair falling in front of her shoulder. Instead of saying *not yet* or any other answer he could have worked with, she'd said that she had. Gotten over him.

He wished he could say the same for himself.

Her words, spoken in the sweetest possible way, had hit him like a slap because they'd shown him just how different her emotions were from his own.

Josh's passenger pushed his driver into one of the bags strapped to the back of the cart and took his seat. Josh drove them toward where he'd hooked his ball.

He was here for Ben. In Texas during the month of November, and also on this weekend trip. It frustrated him that he couldn't seem to think about anything except Holly, the woman he'd been trying not to love for eight years. He was weary of trying not to love her.

He wasn't someone who gave his trust and affection easily. He had a cautious personality, a tendency toward solitude, and just a few close friends and family members. He was powerfully self-controlled.

Was. Because none of that held true around Holly. When he was around her, he wanted to buy her things, and take her places, and hold her in his arms. He'd cared about her more than she'd cared for him all those years ago. And he cared about her more again now. What was his problem?

His problem was that she was his weakness.

He'd succeeded at a lot in this life. How could it be that he'd failed, and was continuing to fail, at not loving her?

For weeks, Sam had been telling Holly that Rob liked her and that it was only a matter of time before he made his move. Late on Sunday afternoon, he finally did.

When she heard the knock on her door, Holly immediately thought, *Josh?* Even though Josh had never knocked on her door and wouldn't even know where to find her apartment. She answered the door in a state of breathlessness.

She found Rob standing in the hallway. He had a Thor vibe going, what with the muscles and the long blond hair. He'd paired a white T-shirt with a pair of those baggy pants that chefs favored. His white coat lay folded over his shoulder.

"Hey," Holly said. Of course it wasn't Josh. She had no reason to feel let down. "On the way to work?"

"Yeah. Since it's Sunday it'll probably be slow. I'm thinking I'll be done around nine-thirty."

"Cool."

"Would you like to meet me afterward at Vinnie's for dessert?"

Whenever she and Rob had gone places in the past, they'd gone in a group that included Sam. Sometimes Mr. Perfect or one of Rob's buddies joined them. "Sam and Mr. Perfect are shopping at Pottery Barn in San Antonio today." Which is pretty much how Holly imagined young married couples without kids spent the bulk of their time.

"I know." He gave her a cute I-was-hoping-to-get-dessert-with-you-alone smile.

"Oh. Well." Her thoughts darted in five nervous directions. "Sure. You know me. I never pass up a chance to eat Vinnie's chocolate pie."

"Good." He turned on his heel. "I'll text you."

"'Kay."

Holly spent the next hour pacing her apartment. Josh had asked her to go with him to the Olive Oil Company and Rob had asked her out for dessert. Two men had issued invitations in the space of a week. Single, handsome men! Instead of elated, however, the invitations—one she'd turned down, one she'd accepted—had left her feeling troubled.

She grabbed her coat, scarf, hat, and reversed her Miata from its parking space. Twenty minutes passed before she realized she'd driven by many of the places where she and Josh had spent time together during their romance. She'd taken herself on a Josh Memory Tour without meaning to.

At the Brenners' house, she and Josh had sat inside Bryan Brenner's Jacuzzi during Bryan's graduation party. Green light had illuminated the still, hot water surrounding them. She could remember how Josh had looked, staring at her through the steam.

A bank and a 7-Eleven now occupied the plot where Josh's apartment building had once stood. She could taste the microwave popcorn, seasoned with paprika and parsley, that had been his mom's specialty. They'd eaten it while watching X-Men DVDs in the small living room.

Their high school hadn't changed in any way, except for the new sign out front. Josh had first said *I love you* to her on one otherwise normal day during the spring semester of their senior year. They'd been in the hallway together. The bell had already rung and kids had been hurrying past them. She and Josh had been about to part and go in opposite directions when he'd pulled her back to him.

"I love you," he'd said. And he'd said it with the most solemn seriousness, as if he'd been unable to wait another minute to tell her, as if he was about to be shipped overseas to fight a battle, as if he was dying. And Holly had felt like she was dying, too, except from bliss and lack of oxygen because he'd stolen all her breath.

Then he'd smiled a crooked smile at her. She'd known she loved him before he'd said the words. But it was that crooked smile there in that school hallway that had settled the matter in her heart.

Sam would definitely *not* approve of her Josh Memory Tour.

Sighing, Holly turned onto the road that wound past a park and picnic area at the edge of Lake Cypress Bend. The sun had just set but full darkness hadn't yet descended. She parked and went to sit on top of a vacant picnic table.

The bulbs on the light posts glowed through the hazy evening, making their illumination appear soft, round, enchanted. Several families dotted the area, some at the playground, some at the lakeshore or on the dock, fishing. Everyone had bundled up to ward off the chill. The children's voices carried on the same breeze that spun leaves from their branches.

She and Josh had sat here, on this exact table, numerous times. This had been their spot. Sometimes they'd come here to eat. Sometimes, just to hang out and talk. She'd sat here with him, her head resting on his shoulder, contentment weaving circles around and around her. She could recall how he'd kissed her, and how her body had rushed in response with the joy and awe of it.

A twig cracked behind her and she swung to face the direction with a gasp. *Josh?*

The twig had been broken by two kids, kicking up leaves.

Rob just asked you out. Your neighbor and friend, Rob, who is a very decent person and good-looking to boot. Think about Rob, Holly. Think about Rob.

Holly came to understand, in very clear detail, why Sam scorned the idea of waiting by the phone for a man to call. Sam scorned it because living that way stunk.

Even though Holly knew Josh wouldn't call, she took her phone with her everywhere. It was ridiculous. Josh had no reason to call her. He no longer needed help planning the rehearsal dinner.

Nonetheless, when she slipped into bed at night, she rested her cell phone within arm's reach on her bedside table. She double-checked it frequently throughout the day to ensure that it was charged and prepared to receive a text message or a call from Josh.

Neither came.

She looked for him when she drove around town and each time she entered a shop or restaurant, without success.

Her rational mind knew that remaining separate from

him was the best possible thing for the preservation of her well-being. Her irrational heart, however, couldn't get over the fact that she'd never again have this sort of proximity with him. Josh's time in Martinsburg was vanishing.

The days leading up to Thanksgiving, beautiful days gilded with autumn, should have been too full to dwell on Josh. Her wedding coordinator duties had kicked into fourth gear thanks to Mitzi's astonishing doggedness. Her work on her book had intensified too. Like a round stone that had topped a rise and begun to roll downhill, her plot was picking up speed. She had blog posts to write for her website and marketing to catch up on.

In pursuit of their Year of Restaurants quest, Holly and Sam hit Martinsburg's only Indian food joint and then the most girly sandwich/salad/soup restaurant the town had to offer.

Holly and Rob's dessert date had gone smoothly. In fact, it had been much like their group outings, minus other humans. There'd been chocolate pie, but no romantic feelings on Holly's part. Rob had asked her out again afterward, but since she didn't know how she felt about more one-on-one dates with him yet, she'd declined.

The day before Thanksgiving, Holly's immediate family (and her sister's fabulous new boyfriend) poured into Martinsburg. In tandem with their arrival, great, low-lying banks of clouds rolled over central Texas and coated the town with a steady drizzle. The precipitation escalated on Thursday to rain that alternated from light to downpour.

As was their tradition, the Morgans sat down together in their family home for a formal Thanksgiving meal of turkey and all the fixings, served on Holly's mother's Lennox wedding china.

Afterward, they gathered in the living room in front of the fireplace. Holly's dad coddled the fire into snapping peaks of flame. The smell of pumpkin pie hung in the air and football played on TV. Drowsy from the tryptophan she'd just consumed, Holly daydreamed about where Josh might be spending the day while the rest of the family engaged in their two most popular pastimes: cooing over Holly's older brother's gorgeously chubby toddler and revering Holly's younger sister for her pursuit of a law degree.

The only member of the family not present? Shadow. The cat had hidden under Holly's parents' bed in mute protest of the invaders who'd overtaken her residence.

Late that night, Josh was fighting insomnia and thinking of Holly, when a sudden suspicion slid into his mind. He sat up in bed, paused for a few seconds to think, then dashed aside the covers.

He hoped he was wrong. He really hoped he hadn't overlooked something so important. Surely, he hadn't.

In his plaid pajama pants, he padded down the stairs of his rented house into the kitchen. His laptop waited on the granite counter. Scowling, he pulled up his assistant's final guest list document for the rehearsal dinner.

He scrolled down the list of alphabetized names. The tile floor chilled the soles of his feet and cold air blew across his bare back.

Holly wasn't listed. She'd spent hours driving over the Hill Country with him to look at locations. She'd shared advice and ideas with him. All for a rehearsal dinner he'd forgotten to invite her to. She hadn't mentioned his oversight to him the two times they'd gone to the caterer. She'd remained quiet and polite about it while helping him pick out the menu, for pity's sake.

Josh blew out a breath, disgusted with himself.

It had occurred to him, after that night at Das Lokal when he'd told her he'd booked the Olive Oil Company, that he needed to ask his staff to double check the guest list, and if she wasn't on it, to mail Holly an invitation. He'd made a mental note of it. Planned to do it. But the list in front of him proved that he hadn't followed through.

He'd been distracted and forgetful lately. He'd been distracted and forgetful because his mind was so occupied with Holly.

The rehearsal dinner would take place tomorrow night. He straightened, pushing both hands into his hair as he stared down at the glowing screen.

He was a jerk. A jerk who needed to make things right.

Chapter Eight

"Thank you, dear," Mrs. Chapel said to Holly the next morning, as she accepted her coffee through the door. "Did you remember to put in one and a half packets of sugar?"

"I did."

"I'm in need of some Bengay for my poor back. Would you be able to pick some up for me later, do you think? If you wouldn't mind?"

"I wish I could help you, but I'm not going to make it to the store today. My family's in town so I'm spending the day with them before the wedding rehearsal up at the church."

"Speaking of the big wedding, Doreen told me that someone else is playing the organ." Mrs. Chapel pinched her lips and shook her head disapprovingly.

"That's true."

"She said that you brought her caramel corn to help her recover from the slight."

"Also true."

"Good girl." She gave a decisive nod, her rheumy eyes regaining their twinkle. "And don't you worry about the Bengay. I'll shame my younger sister into buying it for me."

"No one's more of an expert at shaming than you are, Mrs. Chapel."

"Why, thank you!"

Holly moved toward her apartment.

"Some things were delivered for you while you were getting coffee," Mrs. Chapel called after her.

"Oh?"

"By a *handsome man*."

Holly shot her a questioning look.

"I think he's still there," the old lady whispered, loudly enough for passersby on Main Street to hear.

Holly walked around the hallway corner and found Josh—*Josh!*—leaning against the wall next to her door, an array of items covering her doormat. He pushed to standing at the sight of her.

He wore a shirt and tie beneath a sweater vest. With his tall frame and lean physique, he could pass for an Armani model. A sheepishly smiling one. One that moonlighted as a professor of Unfathomable Math.

"Hi," he said.

He'd either become more gorgeous since she'd seen him last or she'd forgotten how gorgeous he'd been to begin with. Her heart, her poor heart, was melting at the sight of him. "Hi."

He lifted a hand and flipped an envelope face up as he extended it to her. "I brought you this." He'd written her name on it in handwriting that hadn't changed much since high school.

"Thank you." She took it from him.

"Here." He lifted the coffee carrier with her lone drink from her hand. She'd forgotten she'd been holding it.

She began to pull open the flap on the heavy stationery. "Is this when you inform me that you've secretly been buying up all the real estate in Martinsburg?" A smile played across her lips. She'd thought to herself once that he'd have no way of knowing where she lived. She'd been wrong. "Are these my eviction papers?"

"I typically save my evil real estate plotting for towns large enough to merit a Walmart."

"Ah." She uncovered an engraved invitation to the rehearsal dinner.

"It didn't occur to me until last night that I hadn't made sure that you were invited," he said. "I'm sorry."

She moved her attention from the lovely invitation to him. "There's no reason to be sorry. I'm just Trinity's wedding coordinator. I'm not actually in Ben and Amanda's wedding."

"I'd like for you to come."

"I—"

"I'm the one paying for the rehearsal dinner and you're the one who helped me with the planning. You're coming. All right?"

She bit the side of her lip. "If you like."

"I would."

"Then I'll be there." She examined the collection of things sitting in front of her door. "What's all this?" A huge vase of flowers. Three flavors of ground coffee. A sheet cake from the caterer. (It had been her favorite, despite that apple pie had been a better fit for the rehearsal dinner.) Five packages of denture cleaner for Mrs. Chapel. And a twenty-four-pound bag of Meow Mix.

"A few thank-you gifts. And a few gifts to apologize for the fact that your invitation was delivered so late."

Delighted laughter broke from her lips. "You didn't have to do this."

"Do you like any of it?"

"I like all of it." She was so touched and surprised by his thoughtfulness that she almost wanted to cry over it. "Thank you." Her voice emerged wobbly with emotion. "How did you know that Shadow eats Meow Mix?"

He lifted one masculine shoulder. "I remembered from eight years ago. I'll help you carry it in, then I'll get out of your way. I know your family's in town." He must have heard, of course, every syllable of her exchange with Mrs. Chapel.

She opened her door and dazedly tried to lend a hand, while he, in actuality, did all the work.

She stood in her small kitchen, the counters covered with his gifts, the invitation in her hand, quiet resting over them as they smiled at each other. Thank God she hadn't left wadded up panties or something on her floor.

"I'll see you tonight at the rehearsal," he said.

"See you then."

He held eye contact with her for a drawn-out second, then let himself out.

Holly blinked at the items. Did Josh like her? Hope,

worry, and confusion battled for control of her mind. Hope, because she dearly wanted him to like her. Worry, because giving him power to hurt her terrified her. Confusion, because she didn't know which was stronger.

The hope. Or the worry.

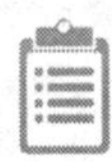

Where was Holly?

Ben and Amanda's family and friends had arrived at the Texas Olive Oil Company and gathered on the patio for drinks and appetizers thirty minutes ago. Josh hadn't joined them. He stood alone inside the barn, wearing a suit and watching the side door that had been left open for arriving guests.

He glanced at his watch, frowning. Concern tightened around his chest and lungs.

Earlier, at the rehearsal at the church, Holly had welcomed everyone to Trinity and offered a prayer. The minute she'd finished praying, Mitzi had taken over. Mitzi had made them run through the routine they'd follow during the ceremony three times.

Holly had stood off to the side the whole time, close enough that Mitzi or Amanda or Amanda's mom could ask her questions. She'd been wearing business clothing instead of party clothing and holding a pen and the notebook she'd brought with her when they'd looked at venues together. Each time Josh had glanced at her during the rehearsal, she'd either been looking carefully elsewhere or down at her notebook.

Josh turned, taking in the view beyond the open sliding doors of the guests and the scenery. The stormy skies had disappeared around noon. They'd left behind clear, still weather ideal for everything Holly had imagined this night could be. He couldn't accept that she wasn't here to see it.

"Josh," one of the bridesmaids called to him. "Come on out. I have some people to introduce you to."

"Be there in a minute."

He returned his gaze to the side door. Holly had told him she'd come tonight. But maybe she'd chosen to skip it at the last minute. She might be tired. Or maybe she'd made plans with Rob.

Should he call her to make sure she was coming?

He was an idiot. A ridiculous—

Holly appeared in the doorway.

He froze at the sight of her. She wore a dress of burgundy lace on a flesh-colored background fabric. She'd pulled her hair into some kind of loose bun at the back of her neck. High heels.

She looked like a princess.

Need, sharp and painful, broke open inside him. At eighteen, he'd been fatherless, poor, without influence, and sure of just one thing. His love for Holly. Years had passed, but that truth had not changed. The man who didn't do anything halfway still loved her.

He made his way toward her. She approached him with a smile.

"I was worried you weren't going to come," he said.

"I took time to change and redo my hair after the rehearsal."

"You look beautiful."

"Thank you. Is everything going well so far?"

"Yes." He offered the crook of his elbow and she set her hand in it. He guided her through the barn.

"It's like magic," she said. "I can't believe the transformation."

The equipment had been moved out and round tables brought in. Linens, votive candles, and large flower arrangements decorated each table. The caterer had suggested they hang lanterns staggered at different heights from the overhead beams, and he'd agreed. "Do you like how it turned out?" It mattered to him that she did.

"I absolutely love how it turned out. Everything's even better than I expected."

If only she'd let him, he'd throw her parties like this, or buy her jewelry, or take her on trips, or hire someone to socialize Shadow, or whatever else made her happy. "Anything you'd change?" he asked. "If so, I might still be able to make it happen."

"I wouldn't change anything about this rehearsal dinner. Nothing at all."

I wouldn't change you, he thought.

They made their way through the guests to the far edge of the flagstones. When they came to a stop, she stepped gently away from him. Conversations and laughter surrounded them with a friendly hum. Rows of string lights extended from the roof of the barn over the patio, like a canopy.

"Can I get you something to drink or eat?" he asked.

"Maybe in a minute. Wow, look at the view."

In the distance, the lake reflected the glow of sunset like a bronze coin. The fading light made her earrings sparkle and her skin glow.

"I thought the rehearsal went well at the church," he said, making an effort to steer his thoughts toward safer ground.

"Yeah. I thought so too." She glanced up at him out of the corners of her eyes. As usual, the gray-blue depths shone with wry humor. "You did a good job charming the flower girls."

"I try."

"You kept them calm when they started to get rambunctious."

"It was the least I could do."

"Heroic. What're you going to do next?" She angled her chin toward the edge of the patio. "Take a running leap off this thing so we can all watch your cape unfurl as you soar off to charm more five-year-olds?"

"No." One side of his lips rounded upward. "I don't like capes."

She chuckled, then took a moment to let her attention sweep slowly over the guests. "How does this party compare to the ones you attend in Paris?"

"Favorably."

"Really? But there aren't any French women here."

"No."

"French women are famously chic and beautiful."

"Are they? I hadn't noticed."

"You mean to tell me you don't have a French girlfriend?" She arched an eyebrow.

"No."

"Are you sure? Does the name Genevieve ring a bell?"

"No."

"Margaux?"

He shook his head. "Would you be happier if there were French men here?"

"I prefer Texan men."

"Texan men who can cook?" The question showed too much of his hand. He sounded like a jealous boyfriend, except that he was only one of those things. Just the jealous part.

She sized him up, looking highly entertained. "Cooking skills are optional."

Two of Ben's groomsmen joined them. The guys clapped him on the back and introduced themselves to Holly. He watched her shake hands with them, then nod and listen to the story one of them was telling about how badly Josh had played on their golf trip.

Josh had almost made it through his time in Texas. He was leaving day after tomorrow. One more day. He only needed to survive one more day without doing or saying something stupid to Holly and making a royal fool of himself.

She'd been kind to him, but there was a big jump between feeling kindly toward someone and loving them.

One more day. Could he manage to hold back the words inside of him for one more day?

The first rule of mingling on a flagstone patio: avoid accidentally wedging a high heel into a crack between stones. Holly focused on exactly that while chatting with Ben and Amanda's guests. She knew many of them because such a large number lived in Martinsburg.

Even Mitzi had come, something of a surprise. Holly would have expected Mitzi to spend the evening before Amanda's wedding running twenty miles, drinking organic green tea, and working feverishly on her iPad.

The sun vanished below the horizon line, putting on a great show of artistry and color before the light ebbed away and the temperature dropped.

When they moved inside, Josh showed her to a table at the front. The name cards revealed that he'd assigned her the seat beside his.

"I don't have to sit right here next to all the action," she murmured. "Really. You could have put me at a table in the back corner. I wouldn't have minded."

"I'd have minded. I like talking to you more than I like talking to anyone else here. Sit and let's eat some buttermilk fried chicken."

She gave him a bemused look.

"What?"

"I've been waiting all my life for a good-looking man to order me to eat fried chicken. I guess I can cross that off my wish list."

The dinner commenced in a blur of happiness, delicious southern food, and rustic Texas charm. It had been ages since Holly had had a reason to don her Spanx or shoes more formal than TOMS wedges. She'd been browsing through a boutique months ago when she'd found the burgundy lace sheath she had on. At the time, she'd had nowhere to wear it. She'd bought it anyway, because her intense dress-crush had outweighed practicality. She was very, very glad she had.

During the meal, Josh frequently left Holly's side to attend to his duties as host. Whenever they were apart, she could sense his whereabouts. She'd spot him across the room only to have him look over as if her gaze had called his attention to her. Each time that happened, she returned to the table's conversation with a warm glow spreading through her.

When the last bite of apple pie had been eaten and the final toast given, everyone rose to exchange subdued chitchat and good-byes. The euphoria that had hovered over Holly all evening began to dissipate. She didn't want the night to end. But it was ending, with or without her go-ahead.

When just ten or so guests remained, Holly found herself alone with Josh. She picked up her purse. "I'd best be going."

"I'll walk you out."

They headed toward the patio. "I had a wonderful time," Holly said.

"I'm glad. Thank you for all that you did to help me plan the dinner."

"You're welcome." Such dismaying formality! Next, she'd be curtsying and he'd be bowing crisply like a soldier.

The outdoors greeted them with a very faint fog of rain. Holly glanced upward toward the moon, glowing dimly through clouds.

"Let me see if I can find an umbrella for you," Josh said.

"No, that's all right." The water hadn't formed into droplets. Instead it seemed to hover in the air, misty and magical. "I like it." She smiled up at him.

Laugh lines fanned out from his eyes as he returned her smile.

Thunk. One of her high heels wedged between two flagstones. She swayed a little and Josh immediately caught her forearm and helped right her balance. "You okay?"

"Fine." She blew a strand of hair out of her eyes, got both shoes on a level stone, and laughed. He still held her arm protectively. "I was just thinking earlier that I needed to avoid doing that very thing." *But then you smiled at me, and I couldn't tear my eyes away from you, and so I lost my concentration.* "I was kind of hoping to make it through the entire night without falling on my face."

"You did."

He was standing so close that she could feel his body heat. "D–did what?"

"Make it through the night without falling."

Literally, perhaps. But not figuratively. She'd fallen, all right.

His expression turned utterly serious and for the first time since Josh had returned to Martinsburg, Holly could see past his defenses. She saw tenderness in his eyes. Tenderness for *her.*

Warm goose bumps spread over her body. He *did* still like her. More, he was going to kiss her. He stepped closer.

He was going to kiss her! She wanted him, physically and in every other way. He was her Josh. The one she'd never gotten over. Anticipation coursed through her. Her breath went shallow with desire—

Wait.

What was she doing? Instinctive worry clashed with confusion. And, abruptly, she stepped away.

His hand dropped from her arm. He looked down and to the side. As if irritated with himself, he gave a slight shake of his head before returning his attention to her. Awkward silence solidified between them. "Holly. I was—"

"Excuse me," the caterer said as she approached, wearing her floral apron. "Sorry to interrupt. I have a quick question for you, Josh."

He inclined his head to listen to the caterer, keeping his vision on Holly.

She could practically feel her heart shriveling. He'd been about to kiss her and she'd stepped back. She'd rejected him even though they'd had the most perfect dinner in the history of perfection. Even though she'd been married to her cell phone for days on the off chance that he'd call. He liked her and goodness knows she liked him. He'd told her himself earlier that he didn't have a girlfriend.

So why had she stepped back?

Two of the women in Amanda's house party walked from the barn onto the patio. "Want to walk out with us?" They looked from her to Josh.

Um. She wanted to stay and let Josh finish his sentence.

"Go ahead," Josh said to the women. "Holly and I will follow in a second." He exchanged a few more words with the caterer, then he and Holly fell in step several paces behind the women, who were in the midst of a discussion about the benefits of Brazilian blowouts.

"I'll look for you tomorrow at the wedding," he said.

Gamely, Holly tried to act as if she hadn't just ruined her one chance at kissing him. "I'll be the one at the wedding impersonating Mitzi's lap dog."

"Someone has to."

"That someone is me."

"I'll be the one in the tuxedo."

"I'll do my best to recognize you, seeing as how men in tuxedos all look alike."

His lips bowed into an imitation of humor. He wasn't actually amused, she knew. His eyes remained troubled.

Remorse twisted hard within her.

Josh slowed his progress. "Good night," he said, loud enough for the ladies in front to hear.

The other women fell over themselves thanking him, flirting with him, and wishing him goodnight.

He responded with his trademark politeness. His suit jacket spread open as he thrust his hands in his pants pockets. He nodded to Holly right before she was bustled toward her car by the women's excitement and chatter.

She drove home with a lump in her throat and tears stinging her eyes, trying to understand what had just happened.

She'd been working so hard to battle back the love for Josh she'd always harbored. Nonetheless, her time with him had softened her heart toward him. It had. When he'd dropped his guard just now, she'd seen that her feelings weren't one-sided. He cared about her too. She'd felt the attraction behind his intentions and experienced the leap of her own response.

So what had gone wrong inside of her? What had sabotaged her?

Fear. That's what had derailed her. She'd been afraid. Not of Josh. Of what, then?

She reached her building, climbed the exterior staircase, and let herself into the hallway. Rob, gone. Mrs. Chapel, long asleep. Loneliness waited for her within her dark and solitary apartment. Beyond her apartment's windows: people coming and going. Inside, emptiness.

She didn't bother turning on lights. The depressing mood of the place suited her. Slipping out of her heels, she walked to her cold fireplace and stood before it, her arms crossed tightly.

Ruthlessly, she raked through her thought patterns, trying to get underneath her fear. Why was she afraid?

She was afraid because she didn't think a romance between Josh and her could possibly end well. She wanted to blame that certainty on the fact that he lived overseas, or on the fact that they'd run out of time in which to cultivate a relationship, or their past history.

But none of those things were the real, hard truth. The real truth was that she didn't think it could end well for them because she didn't believe she was . . . enough for him.

How humiliating! Maddening. She had good self-esteem. She liked herself and she liked her life. But somewhere along the line, a small voice had started whispering to her that Josh was too good for her. Maybe the voice had been there long ago, when they'd been dating, which would partly explain why she'd followed through on his mom's request that she break up with him. In her heart of hearts, perhaps, she hadn't thought herself worthy of him.

Or maybe the voice had begun in those dark days after they'd broken up, when she'd told herself their romance never would have worked anyway, in an effort to make herself feel better. Or maybe all the years of disappointing dates, of watching her family members move on to bigger and better things, of humble middle child syndrome, had given the voice credence. Unlike what they said about a lot of people of her generation, Holly was not filled with a sense of entitlement. No. Quite the opposite.

Somewhere along the line she'd become like Shadow the cat, content to remain alone in the place where she'd always lived, because this was where she felt she belonged and what she deserved. Martinsburg was safe and familiar. She'd closed herself off to opportunities for change. For adventure.

For love. Tears brimmed on her lower lashes before seeping over.

"Holy smoke, Holly. Enough already. Quit it." She swiped the tears from her cheeks.

That sly voice that had been whispering to her wasn't God's voice. She saw that very clearly, standing before her fireplace in her bare feet and her beautiful dress. Josh might be intelligent and successful and rich. But God valued her every bit as much as He valued Josh. Her worth, just like Josh's worth, was found in Him alone. Without consciously knowing it, she'd let doubts creep in and distort her vision.

If she cleared her mind, she could see how Josh's return

to Martinsburg might even be considered somewhat . . . ordained. Amanda and Ben could have married in any number of fabulous destinations. Instead, they'd decided to marry here, which had brought Josh back into her life.

It was as if God was saying, *Do you trust me, Holly? Do you believe my timing is best? You've been asking me to prepare you for someone and someone for you, and I've been busy doing exactly that. You and Josh were too young the first time. You both had a lot of maturing and growing to do. But now I've brought him back because he's ready and you're ready and he's the one. I've brought him back to you, Holly. I am, after all, a God of grace and second chances.*

She dearly wanted a do-over of that moment on the patio when fog had encircled them like a blessing and Josh had been on the verge of kissing her. She might not get a do-over. But if she did, she'd draw on God's strength and use it to kick her fears to the curb.

Then she'd risk all.

"Chao ban," Sam greeted Holly the next day.

It was lunchtime and they'd decided to meet at restaurant number ninety-five in their Year of Restaurants. Martinsburg's only Vietnamese food place centered mostly around the take-out side of their business. They offered a mere two tables, both pushed up against a wall.

"Can you repeat that?" Holly took the seat opposite Sam. The restaurant's interior had been painted in clean, bright shades of orange and pale green and white. The smells were promising.

"*Chao ban*. It's Vietnamese for hello, friend." Sam held up her phone. "I googled it."

"In that case, *chao ban*."

"Your appearance here leads me to believe that you were able to sneak away from the preparations for the wedding of the century."

"Yes, but I have to hurry back. There are dozens of

people at Trinity right now doing all sorts of decorating. It's taking every bit of my energy to defend the church's dignity."

"Has Amanda's professional wedding coordinator gone on a rampage?"

"On the contrary. Mitzi's remained firmly in control of herself and everyone else. Especially me. I think she views me as her handy and inexpensive personal assistant."

Sam sipped her ice water. "If I were you, I'd tell her to stick that assumption where the sun don't shine."

"But you see, unlike you, I'm a nice person." Holly winked.

"Niceness isn't all it's cracked up to be."

"No. Mitzi's already informed me that she needs me to wrangle the seven flower girls and one ring bearer from the time they arrive up until the start of the ceremony."

"Dare I ask the ages of these children?"

"Two through six."

Sam rolled her eyes. "I recommend giving them all Benadryl. I've heard a rumor that it calms kids down."

"Sam!"

"You disapprove? Fine, then give yourself some Benadryl. I have nieces and nephews that age. Trust me when I say you're going to need an emergency stash of non-messy candy to pacify the kids. I suggest gummi bears."

A server arrived and patiently explained the menu choices to the two Vietnamese food rookies.

"So?" Sam asked, after the server moved off. Her expression communicated expectancy.

"So?"

"Tell me about the rehearsal dinner."

A memory of how Josh had looked last night, sitting beside her at dinner, turning his head to watch her with affection, filled her mind. She relayed all the critical information to Sam. Everything but the almost-kiss.

"Holly, are you totally in love with your high school love turned billionaire? Or are you merely halfway in love?"

"I've never admitted to any degree of love for my high school love turned billionaire."

"You didn't have to. It's written on your face. Now fess up. If you asked me a pointed question about my husband, you know I'd give you a straight answer."

"I don't want to ask you a pointed question about Mr. Perfect. The answer would just depress me."

Sam's smile glinted with self-satisfaction as she flicked her long sable hair over her shoulder. "After he finished vacuuming this morning, he encouraged me to get a pedicure and do some shopping. He's going to be busy all day building me a backyard water feature and planning next week's menu."

"See? Depressing."

"Rob's into you, Holly, lest you've forgotten."

"I haven't forgotten. I like him. He just doesn't make my knees go weak."

"And the billionaire makes your knees go weak. I understand why. I saw him at Das Lokal with my own eyes, remember. He has this really sexy, brainy, intense thing working for him. It's not possible for mortal women to resist that kind of thing for long."

"No," Holly agreed. "It isn't."

Sam considered her, lips pushed to the side. "Have you been taking my advice? Remember the first part? Nothing ventured nothing gained?"

"I'm working on it."

"What about the second part? Have you been viewing yourself as superior to him?"

"Funny you should mention that. I spent a lot of time thinking on that topic last night."

"And?"

"I'm working on that part too."

Sam released a long-suffering sigh. "Your time with him is almost done, Holly. I'll be honest with you. At this point, there may only be one hope left for you and Josh."

"Which is?"

"Divine intervention."

Four forty-five p.m. Fifteen minutes until the wedding ceremony.

Fifteen minutes had never before seemed like such an impossibly long stretch of time. Holly had been corralling the flower girls and the ring bearer for an hour already. At first, she'd trailed the photographer around as the intrepid woman attempted to capture pictures of the little tykes. That hadn't been too terrible, because most of their moms had been in the mix. But then the moms had deposited the kids in this boring anteroom that was beginning to resemble a prison and deserted Holly to go find seats in the jam-packed sanctuary.

The church was *so* jam-packed for Amanda and Ben's wedding, in fact, that Holly had said a prayer asking God to keep the choir loft from buckling under the extraordinary weight. *Here's hoping the ceremony doesn't include architectural collapse and death-by-crushing.*

"I'm hungry," one little flower girl stated.

"I'm thirsty."

"I need to use the potty."

The ring bearer! He'd climbed on top of the bureau with the help of a chair. Holly dashed over, scooped him up, and deposited him safely on the floor.

Each of the children were gorgeously dressed. The ring bearer in a mini-tux. The seven flower girls in dove gray gowns with satin bodices and full tulle skirts. Every hair had been combed into place by the moms. Every black ballet slipper tugged into position. Their angelic appearance had so far proved deceiving.

One of the flower girls screeched and pushed her sister, also a flower girl.

"Girls." Holly placed herself in between the fighting siblings. "Let's be sweet to each other."

They both released a string of tattling aimed at the other.

Oh, no. The ring bearer and the tiniest flower girl were on their way back up the bureau. Determinedly, Holly intercepted the climbers. "Would anyone like some gummi bears?"

"Me!" they all chorused.

She went to her purse for the big package of gummi bears she'd purchased on her way back to the church after lunch. The itty-bitty set followed her as if she were the Pied Piper. God bless Sam.

"Sit down nicely in a circle, everyone, and I'll come around and give you each gummi bears." With child number two, she learned the importance of making sure she gave them each the same number of gummi bears in the exact same variety of colors.

After she'd dropped gummi bears into the final child's hands, the door creaked open and Josh leaned in.

Joy suffused Holly at the sight of him, as if it had been months since she'd seen him instead of hours.

Josh's face seemed to ease at the sight of her. He stepped fully into the room. He was wearing—*Have mercy on me, Lord*—a tuxedo that looked as if it had been made for him. Which it probably had been. It fit him the way James Bond's tuxedos fit.

The children peered up at Josh while chewing loudly.

Holly skirted the circle of kids and approached him, slightly mortified at the thought of what she must look like. She'd dressed in jeans and a long-sleeved mint green cotton shirt this morning because she'd planned not only to oversee the wedding setup, but also to offer a helping hand if needed. She'd intended to return home before the wedding to change and fix herself up. The second part of her plan hadn't materialized. Mitzi had kept her flat-out busy. A while ago, she'd gathered her hair into a low side ponytail, but even that felt bumpy and askew at this point.

"Hi." She stopped near him, wishing she could blurt out how sorry she was about her kiss-fail.

"So this is where you've been," he said, his voice pitched low.

"Yep. I've been hanging out here with the flower girls—"

"—and the ring bear," the lone boy added. "Grr. I'm a bear."

That set off a round of giggling and loud talking. The sisters began to fight again, so Holly plopped a curly red-headed flower girl in between them.

"Can we have more gummi bears?" one of them asked.

"I still need to go to the bathroom!"

"Keeping care of this group seems like a fun job," Josh remarked.

"Oh, it is. My heart is full of thankfulness."

Just then, one of the girls made an awful choking sound. The best behaved of all the flower girls, a dark-haired five-year-old girl with her hair in two side buns, was half-coughing, half gagging.

Holly knelt beside her. "Are you okay, Olivia?"

Olivia couldn't answer. She was hunched over, wheezing too much to speak. Fear spiked deeply into Holly. *What should she do?*

Josh lowered onto his knee on Olivia's other side, his hand on her back.

Should they give Olivia the Heimlich? she wondered, panicking. *Get water? Thump her back?* Holly wasn't a mom and didn't know—

Olivia hacked and threw up a wad of chewed-up gummi bears right into the lap of her tulle skirt. After a few deep breaths, she straightened and looked up at Holly, eyes round.

"Are you all right?" Holly asked.

She nodded.

Thank God! Holly smiled tremulously and patted her shoulder. Thank God she was fine.

What wasn't fine?

Olivia's dress.

"New rule, everyone." Holly went to the cupboard and found napkins inside. "You may only eat one gummi bear at a time. Chew it very, very carefully before swallowing. All right?"

They chorused assent.

Josh calmed Olivia and the other kids by asking them questions like *Are any of you married yet?* and *Who did you have to pay to get the gig of flower girl in this wedding?*

With Olivia's attention diverted, Holly did her best to keep her bile down while using the napkins to scoop the . . . *mass* from Olivia's lap. Though she wiped the area as best she could, a stubborn round stain the color of red gummi bears remained.

Holly caught Josh's eye and gestured toward Olivia's skirt, asking him with a somewhat wild-eyed expression, *What in the world should I do about this?*

Mitzi would have her head. She'd been the one pumping the kids full of hard-to-chew gummi bears.

"Any scissors around?" Josh asked.

"I'll check." Was he thinking to cut the stain out? How? Inside a bureau drawer, she found a pair of scissors that looked like they were circa 1952. She handed them to him.

"How many layers of fabric do your dresses have, girls?" he asked the group. "A hundred?"

"Mine has forty thirty."

"I think mine has a million!"

"I'm two," the youngest flower girl offered.

"I think whoever said a million is probably right," Josh said. "Your dress has so many layers, Olivia, that I don't think it'll miss the top few. What do you think?"

She just blinked.

He escorted her to an empty patch of floor and went to work cutting off the top-most layers of tulle.

When Olivia shot her an uncertain expression, Holly responded with a big smile and a thumbs-up. That dress had probably cost a bundle. If Holly had been the one with the scissors, she'd have hesitated and debated with herself. Josh didn't.

When he finished, Olivia's dress looked slightly less puffy and slightly more sheer, but otherwise as good as new. Olivia scampered to one of her friends. Josh hooked the ring bearer (who'd ascended halfway up the face of the bureau again) under his arm and walked over to Holly.

"I suspected that you were a superhero yesterday," Holly said. "Now your secret identity is definitely busted."

"And here I'd worked so hard to protect it."

Mitzi tossed open the door. "Josh! The wedding is starting in two minutes. I need you to take your position at point D." Mitzi's method of assigning letters to ceremony positions would have baffled a field general.

"I'm on it." He met Holly's gaze, ruffled the ring bearer's hair, and disappeared.

Mitzi's huge earrings pulled at her lobes as she aimed her laser-beam focus on Holly. "It's time for the children to assemble at point B."

Holly passed the flower girls their petal-filled baskets. She handed the ring bearer his pillow, which didn't actually cushion any rings since Mitzi would never have trusted a child with something so critical.

Out in the hallway, Holly worked to keep peace among the squabbling sisters. She pulled a gummi bear from where it had been hiding, stuck near the hem of the redhead's dress. And she kept reminding the girls to keep the petals *inside* the baskets until the right moment.

Amanda's mom passed by Holly's group with an I'm-thoroughly-charmed-by-you "Mmm." High praise.

Mitzi arranged everyone in the order of the procession, then the enormous group slowly made their way into the church's foyer. The first piece of music gusted through the organ's pipes, all but causing the church to vibrate with majesty.

The flower girls and ring bearer gradually edged closer to the front of the queue.

A dash of white caught Holly's eye and she turned in time to see Amanda and her father enter the foyer. *Oh*, Holly thought, awe settling over her at the sight of Amanda as a bride. Amanda had always been stunning. But today, in her beaded ivory gown, so full of delight and excitement, she looked prettier than Holly had ever seen her look. The kind of pretty that could put a single girl in a mint green V-neck shirt into a trance of fascination.

Amanda had parted her blonde hair on the side and swept it into an intricate style at the base of her neck. Her veil had been positioned at the top of her updo. Its sheer fabric cascaded downward into a train. Her bouquet burst with fall colors of russet, apple green, pale orange, and trailing vines of autumn berries.

Holly earnestly wished Amanda and Ben the very, very best. She caught Amanda's eye. "You look beautiful," she whispered.

Amanda beamed. "Thank you," she mouthed back.

When the flower girls and the ring bearer reached point A, Mitzi sent them down the aisle. The guests responded with a collective "Aww." Then the grand notes of the wedding march began and Amanda and her father swept into the sanctuary.

Holly found a spot in the far corner of the foyer where she could listen and watch the ceremony unobtrusively through a window. If the choir loft came crashing down she'd be squashed like a bug.

Ah, weddings. She loved them. She really loved them. Weddings were magnificent declarations of all that was good in this life. Loyalty. Honor. Love. Esteeming another above yourself. Weddings never failed to stir her or arouse in her a bittersweet wistfulness born of her own hope of marrying one day.

When Amanda and Ben exchanged vows, Holly sighed and went a little teary-eyed. Or maybe she was going teary-eyed over Josh, standing so solidly next to Ben. The best man. Indeed.

One of the candles in the unity candle set was slow to light. And the maid of honor almost bobbled Amanda's bouquet at one point. But those were the little things that made weddings charming and real. Everything else went perfectly.

When the ceremony concluded, Holly dashed around like a runner on a steeplechase course, making sure that the flower girls and ring bearer were all returned to their rightful owners. Then Mitzi trapped her and fired a dozen staccato questions at her regarding parking issues and when the decor could be taken down.

After Mitzi departed, Holly looked around and saw that the entire church had emptied faster than a glass bottle of Dr Pepper. She hadn't caught even a glimpse of Josh since he'd walked down the aisle during the recessional with the maid of honor on his arm.

She let herself into the sanctuary and trailed her fingers along the long swags of ribbon, the glass hurricanes confining candles that had already been blown out, the sprays of flowers mounted on the inside ends of the pews. She took a seat on the very first row.

She needed to rally herself, go home, get cleaned up, then make an appearance at the reception. She'd sent in a response card saying she'd attend. Far more critically, the reception would be her last chance to see Josh.

She'd rally. She would. But the day had drained her physically and emotionally, and she needed a minute to sit and take in the hushed calm of her surroundings.

One of the decorators had brought in a towering wrought iron arch that stood on the dais in front of the altar. A garland of large waxy leaves, twigs, and the same flowers that had graced Amanda's bouquet covered the entire arch and even rippled a few feet onto the dais on either side. Lovely.

During the ceremony, the arch had served as a picturesque frame for Ben and Amanda. But it hadn't framed only them. On its far side, it also framed the altar. As Holly studied the altar, light gleamed and slid along one plane of the cross.

When she'd parted from Josh eight years ago, God had remained. He'd been at her side through her hardest moments, her saddest moments, her loneliest.

Whatever comes, I trust you, God. If your plans for me don't include Josh or don't include marriage, then I'll keep on trusting you. The silence of her aloneness settled over her like pixie dust. She couldn't stop herself from adding a short p.s. to her prayer. *If Josh does happen to . . . perhaps, maybe, please . . . be the one for me, then I pray that you'll give me just one more opportunity with him.*

The side exit door whooshed open and Holly snapped her head to the side to see Josh standing in the opening, backlit by a late November sky. His dark gaze cut across the space and locked onto her.

Her pulse leapt then began to pound. What could he be doing here? He was the best man. He was needed at the reception.

He walked toward her. "I was looking for you. Out in the parking lot, and then on the road to the winery. I couldn't find you."

"I'm not," she motioned to her clothing as she pressed to her feet, "dressed for the reception yet."

His brows drew down. He appeared both determined and unsettled, standing there, sleek in his gorgeous tuxedo. "I've been looking for you a lot lately, Holly. All day today. Last night at the rehearsal dinner. Just now. I . . ."

His hair was slightly mussed. His eyes bright with fervency. "I realized that I've been looking for you for years. I've been looking for you ever since I left Martinsburg."

Hope rose within her painfully. What? Had he . . . had he really just said that?

He continued, recklessly honest. "I don't want to spend the rest of my life looking for you."

"You don't?" Her voice emerged as fragile as a skein of silk.

"No. I don't want to make a fool of myself in front of you, either." He raked a hand through his hair. "I've been telling myself to keep my mouth shut around you until I leave Texas. But I'm not going to make it." His lips settled into a hard, resolute line. "I'd rather make a fool of myself than remain silent."

She gaped at him in patent astonishment.

"I can't not tell you that I love you," he said. "I . . . I desperately love you."

Holly inhaled a jagged gasp. His words were almost too marvelous to process. He'd handed her dearest dream to her without warning. He loved her? Joy began to unfurl inside her.

She walked to him, stopping so close that she was able to rest her palms on his chest. She hadn't touched him in a girlfriend-like manner in ages. To do so now felt like pure, heady bliss. She smoothed his lapels, feeling the tremor in her hands.

He stared down at her as if he was afraid to believe that the news might be good.

The news was very good. For them both. She was still a

little afraid, but God was faithful. He countered her fears by filling her with an undeniable sense of rightness. She looked directly into Josh's eyes. "I love you too."

He gave her the exact same crooked smile he'd given her the day he'd first told her that he loved her. "You love me?"

"I do. I love you."

"I've loved you since high school," he said. His arms came up to support her back. "I tried to stop but I couldn't. Seeing you again has only made me positively sure that you're the one for me."

"I've loved you since high school too." She interlaced her hands around his neck. Laughing breathlessly, she quoted his words back to him. "I tried to stop but I couldn't. Seeing you again has only made me positively sure that you're the one for me."

He kissed her. And she kissed him back. And he kissed her more for good measure. There, with the altar's cross watching over them and the day's last sun rays pouring through the stained glass like a benediction.

Holly's heart soared with amazement and gratitude and love. Josh! Josh loved her.

He pulled back a few inches. "I lied about needing your help to find a rehearsal dinner location. My assistant booked the olive oil farm months ago. I misled you because it was the only way I could think of to spend time with you."

"Your assistant booked the olive oil farm?" she asked, like one of those parrots that repeats things. It was hard to think straight at this particular moment. He'd just incinerated her with his kisses and sent her whole world spinning with the declaration that *he loved her.*

"Yes."

"Months ago? Your assistant had the very same idea that I had and booked the farm months ago?"

He nodded and swept a section of her hair away from her cheek. "I'm sorry for deceiving you."

"You're forgiven. And also, by the way, you have a *very* good assistant. Has she considered turning her attention to brokering peace in the Middle East?"

His expression warmed with amusement. "I love you."

"I love you."

"I'll stay in Martinsburg," he said. "I can work from anywhere."

"So can I, Josh. I'm a writer." Her hands were still intertwined behind his neck. Oh, the happiness of this! "Relocating to Paris for a while doesn't actually sound too shabby to me."

"It doesn't?"

"If this is Paris, France, home of the Eiffel Tower and the Louvre and croissants that we're talking about, then no. It doesn't."

"You'd move to France?"

"Yes," she answered, growing more sure of it. "I would." He'd given her an irresistible motivation to grab hold of her very own real-life adventure.

"I love you, Holly."

"I love you, Josh. Now kiss me some more." She was grinning and crying at the same time. "But be quick about it. You're the best man and we have a wedding reception to attend."

Miracle of miracles, God had brought Josh back to her. And this time, she wouldn't let him go. This time, Josh wouldn't leave her behind.

This time, the timing was perfect.

Holly,

Today is our wedding day. In just a few hours I'll get to see you in your wedding dress, you'll walk down the aisle to me, and before God we'll promise ourselves to each other for the rest of our lives.

Thank you for agreeing to be my wife. For loving me. For showing me what matters in this life.

Neither the years we spent apart nor the distance between us had the power to change my love for you. My heart was, and is, and always will be yours.

Je t'aime, Holly. I love you. Till death do us part, my love.

—Josh

I'm grateful to Becky Philpott, my editor at Zondervan, for inviting me to participate in this wonderful collection of wedding-themed novellas. Thank you, Becky! You're kind, outgoing, and a pleasure to work with. I truly appreciate the opportunity you extended to me.

Many, many thanks to my agent and *Love in the Details'* very first reader, Linda Kruger. Your feedback on this novella was extraordinarily helpful, Linda. Oh, how I value your insight and friendship.

My husband has staunchly believed in my writing since the very first time I ever mentioned to him that I might like to attempt a novel of my own. His hands-on help (making dinners, watching the kids, doing the dishes, and giving me pep talks) made this novella possible. I love you!

And lastly, to my kids, who (almost) never complain about the hours I spend working. I'm so glad that I get to be your mom. Thank you very, very much for supporting my writing.

1. Holly and Josh were one another's first love. Did anyone here marry their first love? Name one thing that you still remember clearly about your first love.
2. At its heart, *Love in the Details* is about the perfect nature of God's timing. When in your life did you face a disappointment, only to later realize that God's timing was ultimately best?
3. Near the end of the story, Holly realizes that her almost subconscious belief that she's not enough for Josh is holding her back. We all struggle from time to time with deceptive self-talk that assures us that we're "not good enough" or "not worthy enough." When has this most been a stumbling block for you? Share a story of how God has helped you have victory in this area.
4. How would you characterize Becky Wade's writing style? How was it different and/or similar to the style of other writers included in this collection of wedding novellas?
5. How is Holly and Josh's love story a picture of God's love for us?

About the Author

Becky Wade makes her home in Dallas, Texas, with her husband and three children. She's the Carol Award and Inspirational Reader's Choice Award-winning author of contemporary Christian romances *My Stubborn Heart*, *Undeniably Yours*, *Meant to Be Mine*, and *A Love Like Ours*.

The next chapter in
A Year of Weddings begins anew . . .

THEY'VE HELPED ORCHESTRATE THE PERFECT day for countless couples. Now twelve new couples will find themselves in the wedding spotlight in the second Year of Weddings novella collection.

www.tnzfiction.com/weddings

9780310392187-A